MURDER, SHE WROTE

CARRY MY SECRET TO YOUR GRAVE

More small-town murders.
More big-time thrills.
Read them all!

MURDER, SHE WROTE

CARRY MY SECRET TO YOUR GRAVE

AN ORIGINAL NOVEL BY

STEPHANIE KUEHN

SCHOLASTIC PRESS

NEW YORK

Murder, She Wrote © 2023 Universal City Studios LLC. All rights reserved.
Photos © Shutterstock.com.

ISBN 978-1-338-76458-1

10 9 8 7 6 5 4 3 2 1   23 24 25 26 27

Printed in the U.S.A.   40

First printing 2023

Book design by Keirsten Geise and Cassy Price

For those with good intentions.

TRUEMAINE.COM
Unpublished Draft

"Help Wanted"

I've always believed that mystery serves a purpose. In fact, three weeks ago, if you'd asked me what I believed that purpose was, I would have answered that a mystery is meant to be solved.

Only now I'm not sure.

Last month, with your assistance, I was able to solve the cold case surrounding Chrissy Lambert's long-ago death. It turned out Chrissy, a beloved Cabot Cove teenager whom everyone believed had been murdered decades earlier, had tragically died by suicide after suffering at the hands of her controlling father. In a final silencing of Chrissy's agency, her father had colluded with others to cover up her true cause of death, staged a gruesome murder scene, and spread panic through the town that a bloodthirsty child killer was on the loose.

Along the way to learning the truth about Chrissy, however, I stumbled across another mystery, a more personal one, as I searched for my friend Jackson, who'd disappeared under unsettling circumstances. I soon learned Jackson wasn't the only teen reported missing from Cabot Cove over the past year. Four others had as well. One, a boarding school student from out of state, was eventually found dead—it turned out she'd drowned on a school hiking trip—but the other three remained missing. All were local students that attended my own school, Cabot Cove High, and all came from the gated community of Seacrest, a place whose residents shared the same values as Chrissy Lambert's father—appearances, above all else.

Diving deeper into my investigation, I started to unearth a conspiracy that members of the Seacrest Homeowners Association had cooked up. Fed-up parents were paying to offload their own rebellious teens by having them abducted and sent to a coercive and physically violent "troubled teens" program in Utah while claiming they'd run away. The program has since been shut down, and though I can't reveal their current whereabouts, I can say with confidence that all the Cabot Cove Four are now safe and protected from their abusive families.

But I've encountered a new mystery, dear readers, and now I need your help. Because in all honesty, I'm terrified to even tell you about it.

I'm terrified about what could happen.

Mere days after I published my last column—a celebratory one in which I'd finally revealed my real name—a package was delivered to the TrueMaine offices in Portland.

Addressed to me.

The website's cofounders, brothers and Bitcoin enthusiasts Aaron and Vince Kanofsky, then graciously forwarded the package to my home, along with a handful of other letters they'd received. "Here's your fan mail!" their accompanying message exclaimed.

Well, I was as surprised as anyone at the notion that I might have fans or people who care about the words I write. But when I opened the package in the living room of the house I share with my dad and my sweet elderly cat Lemon, I found something else entirely.

Inside was a wilted bouquet of flowers, the blooms rotted and putrid in their decay. I'd stared, confused, because the flowers appeared to be calla lilies, my mom's favorite, and that's when I saw what was beneath the flowers—a large glossy photograph of my mother's gravestone, a mere four miles away, tucked in a spot of shade beneath a towering red maple. Written in Sharpie across the photo were the ominous words:

YOU'RE NEXT

1

GRIPPING THE OVERSIZED RED ENVELOPE, I wait as the trio of well-dressed Broadmoor Academy students, Leif, Leisl, and Carlos, huddle close around me. Our friendship, our connection to one another is still new. Still tentative. There's no denying I'm the rough-edged townie girl to their boarding school shine, that fresh-faced glow that comes from living in brick and ivy-draped dorms on a secluded campus in the hills overlooking Cabot Cove's working class streets and glittering blue bay.

Even so, I welcome their presence. More so than usual, seeing as being alone isn't something I'm able to enjoy much these days. Standing shoulder to shoulder in the dense woods, all four of us shielded from the worst of Maine's dreary November chill, I not only feel a surge of purpose.

I feel *safe*.

Mostly.

I turn and glance back at the trees, the dark shadows, before returning my attention to the group.

"Do it." Leisl arches a dark blond eyebrow and offers me the wryest of smiles. The faintest twitch of her pink glossed lips.

My cheeks warm, but I do as she says, prying open the red envelope containing the next clue in the century-old game they're playing. It's called *tenace* and apparently, it's a Broadmoor tradition, one best described as high-stakes and highly secretive. Warned to trust no one and nothing, players set out in search of red-coded clues rumored to lead to some wondrous—yet unknown—prize. From what I've gleaned, this game's built on a foundation of illusion and mystery and is only played once every four years. I'd never heard of it before—not a hint—despite having grown up in Cabot Cove.

But this is how it is with Broadmoor. Our town's boarding school has always had its own secrets. Its own circles. In fact, my current involvement with tenace was only made possible by my childhood friend Jackson who recently plotted to escape his family's cruelty. In the process, he not only managed to connect with his biological father—a Broadmoor alum who was also my psychiatrist at the time—but in his wake, Jackson left a mystery so compelling it basically ensured I'd join forces with these three in order to solve it.

In other words, I'm playing the game, too.

Holding back the torn glued flap, I peer directly into the envelope, which is stuffed full and straining at the seams. "It's papers. Like, a whole bunch of them. They're all folded up."

"Here." Beside me, sixteen-year-old Carlos, who's got shy good looks, short dark hair, and brown skin that's just a touch lighter than my own, extends his hands, palms cupped tight together. "I can hold them."

"Thanks." I pull out the contents, careful not to tear or damage what I now realize are long-form news articles, each paper-clipped separately. Some are on newsprint—the pages, thin, yellowed, and smeared with ink—which contrast starkly with the articles printed on magazine stock, thick and glossy, alongside color photos. There are four in total, all originals that hail from the following publications: *Miami Herald*, the *Daily Mail*, *Underwater!*, and *Occupational Health and Safety*.

"Is that it?" Leif's sharp-eyed gaze meets mine, and though he possesses the same lean, cherubic beauty as his twin sister, Leisl, their personalities couldn't be more different. Both have proved craven in pursuit of the game's glory, but in the brief time I've known them, Leisl's shown me genuine mirth and boundless invitation. Leif, on the other hand, is hard edges and bolted doors. Toward me, at least.

"That's it." I dutifully tip the envelope upside down and give it a shake.

"Well, what do they say?" Hands on his hips, Leif turns to Carlos, who's already working with Leisl to smooth the creases out and ensure everything's readable.

"We don't know yet," Carlos says.

Leif sneers. "How can you not *know*?"

"Could you give us a moment?" Leisl holds a finger in her brother's face as she scans the articles, one by one. "You know, I think I need glasses."

"I was just thinking the same thing!" Carlos exclaims. "But I mean me. I think I need glasses, too. I keep getting these headaches from the computer. They make me—"

Leif groans, loudly. "Can we please diagnose your insecurities later? Some of us have finite lives."

"Rude." Leisl sniffs. "Anyway, these articles are weird."

"How so?" I ask.

"They're just random stories about accidents. But they take place in all different parts of the world. Different time periods. Plus, the writing style ranges from clickbait to academic and almost unreadable."

"That's not *weird*," Leif says. "The word you're looking for is *varied*."

Leisl ignores him. "How about I read the headlines? Then you can decide for yourself."

"Go for it," I say.

I spot that lip twitch hint of a smile again as Leisl clears her throat. "First off is 'Famed Fort Lauderdale Aquarium Suffers Mass Die-off. Over 1,000 Organisms Feared Lost in Unexplained Tragedy.'"

"Organisms?" Carlos echoes.

"I assume they mean fish and plants. And maybe snails?"

"Keep going," Leif says.

"Fine. Up next is 'South of the Border Horror: Two American Teens Found Dead in Cabo Resort Pool. Vacationers Report Hearing Mum's Screams for Hours.'"

"That's the *Daily Mail*, isn't it?" I ask.

"Did 'mum' give it away? Oh, here's my favorite: 'In the Ocean, No One Can Hear You Scream: An Exploration of Three Commercial Diving Fatalities and Recommendations for Improved Safety Planning.' Finally, we end with the dry but informative: 'Lawsuit Filed against Maldivian Dive Shop That Allegedly Filled Tanks With a Toxic Mix, Leading To Four Deaths.'"

"These are *grim*," Carlos says. "*Alien* reference notwith-standing."

Leisl nods and looks up. "What do you all think?"

An idea pops into my head. "Could this be related to—"

"To what?" Leif asks.

But then the fear surfaces and I bite back my words. Shake my head vigorously. "Never mind. Anyone else?"

"I got nothing." Carlos sighs. "I usually need a day or two to sit with this kind of stuff. It's not natural."

"He lacks a conspiratorial mind," Leisl says.

"Is that supposed to be a bad thing?" he asks.

She shrugs. "Generally, no. In this context, yes."

"This conversation's pointless," I snap. "Who cares how our minds work? We don't know anything about these stories."

Carlos's eyes widen. "We know people died."

"So these clues are always about death then?" My voice rings with petulance. "It's kind of getting old."

Leif cocks his head at me. "How could that possibly be a problem? Isn't *death* the reason you're here? You write a whole column about unsolved murders. Or you used to."

"I still do," I say quickly, but the flutter of nerves roosting in my stomach awaken at the mention of my true crime column. The one I've been avoiding since that package arrived. That threatening note. All I've got to show for the last month is a handful of unpublished drafts. Words I'm too scared to make public. In fact, I haven't even told my friends about the note I received. "And yes, I like murder mysteries. It's just . . ."

"It's just what?" Leisl asks.

"I don't know."

She reaches to squeeze my arm, a gesture that makes me die a little inside. "That's okay. Why don't you take the rest of the weekend to look over the articles and see what comes to mind? We can meet up again in a couple days."

"You want *me* to take them?" I squeak.

She pauses. "I thought you'd want to. This being your first clue and all. Well, first official clue. Plus, I kind of have to get back to campus now. I've got midterms next week."

"Don't tell me you plan on studying," Leif sniffs. "That would be a first."

"I'm also doing set design for the winter play," she says. "Turns out it's a lot of work."

"I'd better go, too." Carlos is looking at his phone. "I've got to get back for auditions."

"For the play?" Leif asks.

He nods. "I'm behind on performing arts credits. I thought I'd give auditioning a try. Can't hurt, huh?"

"Oh wow." Leisl puts a hand to her mouth. "I cannot picture you acting."

"I appreciate the confidence," Carlos tells her.

"What's the show called?" I ask, and the thing is, I *can* picture him acting. Carlos is quiet, but he's got a presence to him that's grounding. Like someone born to lead. A little like my father, actually.

"*The Visit,*" he says, "It's Swiss. And very dark."

"I don't know that one."

"Thank God," Leif groans. "There's something you don't know."

"I'm sorry about my brother." Leisl bounds over to give me a hug, all good manners and boisterous energy, like an overgrown Irish setter pup, and I don't want her to let me go. I don't want her to leave. "He's been in such a mood lately. You want to meet up on Monday? Can you get up to Broadmoor after classes are out? I'll have time then."

"Works for me."

She shoves the articles at me. "These should probably stay in the envelope. But just keep them somewhere safe."

"I will."

"I'll try and make Monday, too," Carlos says. "I'll even tell you more about the play, if you want. Or if I manage to humiliate myself in the process."

I smile. "That'd be great."

Then it's over in a crush of hugs and waves and murmured good wishes, and I'm buoyed by the warmth emanating off Carlos and Leisl, my new partners in adventure. Their patter and friendship are a welcome antidote to the abject loneliness that has filled my days of late. Along with the dizzying fear and near certainty that I've set something into motion that I can't stop.

But what?

I suck in air, forcing myself to breathe, *in then out*, to not lose my mind or my body in some soul-crushing wave of dread. It works. I stay grounded, but before I know it, they're gone, the two of them hiking side by side while they continue talking and joking and enjoying themselves. I watch, near bursting with envy—maybe a little jealousy, too—as they depart, following the steep coastal trail leading back to their boarding school, their forms fading and shrinking into the cool mountainside mist.

"So what do you think?" Leif appears beside me like a ghost. "Is there something going on there with those two?"

This startles me more than I want to admit. "You'd know better than me."

"Could be an interesting development."

"You should probably stick to your own love life," I say.

He shrugs. "What do you want to do now?"

"Oh, so it's our turn for a date?" I start laughing until I see the chilly look on his face. "Wait, you're serious? You don't have plans or anything?"

"It's noon on a *Saturday*. What plans could I possibly have?"

"I didn't realize—"

"I didn't mention anything about a date, though," he says.

I roll my eyes. "I wouldn't go on one with you if you did."

"Glad that's cleared up." Leif gestures at the envelope I'm still carrying. "Look, I came out here to work on that. So why don't we do it together?"

"Uhhh," I say slowly because this is unexpected. In the short time we've known each other, Leif's shown zero interest in me—and that's a generous interpretation. He's mostly been outwardly hostile to my presence. According to my own conspiratorial mind that means he must be pretty eager to get a look at these articles. More eager than he wants Leisl and Carlos to know.

Or maybe he just *wants* me to think he's eager. It's hard to get a footing on reality when you're playing a game whose primary rule is "bad faith." But as I turn once again to peer over my shoulder into the forest gloom, my breath hitches and my stomach knots, and I realize how vulnerable I am. How vulnerable I always am because how do you prepare for a threat when you don't even know who made it?

When you don't know who it is who wants you dead.

So I lift my chin and gaze up at Leif while pressing my lips into what I hope resembles an earnest smile. "Yeah, sure. We could do that."

In return, Leif doesn't smile back, but his cool brown eyes light up with what could easily be mistaken as charm as he reaches to hook one arm through mine so that we're joined at the elbow.

So that I can't get away.

"My dear," he purrs, guiding me firmly toward the stone steps leading back into town. "You don't happen to know any place we can go that's, like, comfortable?"

2

"Hey, Dad," I call out as Leif and I walk through my front door. After ducking out to return the spare key to its hiding spot under a potted plant on our cluttered porch, I come back in, pull the door shut, and lock the deadbolt behind me. Leif watches in amusement.

"I've got someone with me," I call again. "His name's Leif Schoenholz. He's from Broadmoor Academy."

"Welcome, Leif!" My father's voice booms down the hall from his office near the back of the house where he's taken to working of late. I know he's making an effort to spend more time here, in light of the threat I've received, but the at-home setup turned out to be a trap. He's working way more hours than if he'd just stayed at the office to get stuff done.

I make a game attempt to herd Leif up the stairs since I'm well aware other people's parents are the worst. Not to mention my dad only knows of Leif as someone who helped me search for Jackson and investigate Chrissy Lambert's long-ago death. What he doesn't know is that after all that's happened since, I'm still chasing mysteries. I'm still seeking answers.

Against all better judgment.

Unfortunately, Leif's got prep school manners as well as an innate instinct for how to get under my skin. He thwarts my efforts at containment by smugly ducking around me and marching straight through the entire house—down the hallway, through the kitchen, the dining room—to shake hands with my father and call him *sir*. Thankfully that's *all* he says, and I guess faux formality's a thing with a certain breed of boy, but it's beyond obnoxious. Like, they know how others see them—handsome, educated, and most importantly, someone to be trusted—and they think it's all a joke.

"No one likes a kiss-ass," I hiss as we finally head upstairs.

"You sure about that?" Leif shoots back.

"I'm starting to regret bringing you here."

"That's what all the ladies say."

I groan. Once in my room, I hastily gather up my strewn-about clothing, assorted dishes, and other messes while Leif pokes around through my belongings in a way I don't like. Not that he's a pervert or anything, but it's the exaggerated way he's walking around like he's in a museum that gets me. It's so performative, how he's got his arms clasped tight behind his back and the way he leans forward, every now and then, to inspect with mock fascination such items as (a) a terrible self-portrait I drew in art class and framed as a joke because even my teacher's response to it had been "Burn it. For your own sake. Please." (b) an ancient half-eaten container of chocolate frosting that has managed to grow a near two-inch layer of green mold on the top and which I'm loath to throw out because it might grow more, and finally,

(c) my personal collection of mass market paperbacks titled *Brain Child*. I currently have six, each penned by a different author.

"You can sit down, you know." I wave at my desk chair, an old rolling thing with a wooden frame that I rescued from the curb of my grandparents' home when they downsized for their move to Manhattan a few years back. "You don't have to be Sherlock Holmes."

"I was thinking more Howard Carter," he says.

"Who?"

"He discovered King Tut's tomb."

"Oh boy." I chuck an armful of clothes into the laundry hamper before shoving the whole thing in my closet.

"So were you dating this kid or what?" Looking up, I see Leif's pointing at a photo of Jackson that's pinned above my desk. It's a recent one, from this past summer, and Jackson's holding up a piece of driftwood from the beach, his face warm and awash with golden-hour light.

"Nope." I bite back a swell of loss. Jackson's alive, but he's not here anymore, in Cabot Cove. There's a whole new life he's building, which I'm wildly proud of, but since he's gone, all I'm left with is the letter he wrote me, the one I found this morning, tucked in with the hidden tenace clue.

By the time you read this, I'll be gone . . .

"Well, why not?" Leif asks. "He's a good-looking guy. Probably out of your league, to be honest, but stranger things have happened."

"Do you flatter all the ladies whose homes you visit this much?" I ask. "However are you single?"

There's that prep school smirk again. "I try."

"Well, we're just friends if you insist on being nosy. Jax and I've known each other for years. It'd be weird to change that. Like dating my brother if I had one. Or you dating your sister."

Leif lifts a skeptical eyebrow. "That's the best you've got?"

"Not even close," I say.

"And who's this?" He points at my oversized buff-colored cat, who's curled at the foot of my bed and is currently pretending we aren't here.

"This is Lemon." I settle beside her and scratch her chin. "She's ancient and soft and I love her. Now sit down already. Stop touching my things."

He obliges, although he sits on the floor, on my oval rag rug, with his long legs sprawled out in front of him.

"You're like the physical manifestation of passive aggression," I tell him.

Leif brushes his blond bangs back. "Shall we?"

I reach into my backpack to retrieve the red clue envelope and begin removing the news articles.

"Careful," he says.

I nod because of his tone but also from the sudden stillness in the air. The stillness inside of me. It's as if the whole world's paused in anticipation of me holding these articles. Of mining them for their secrets.

"You want to help?" I ask Leif.

"Sure."

I slide from bed to rug, onto my hands and knees, and together we work on smoothing the papers and laying all four articles out on the floor so that we can look at them at once.

"What're your initial thoughts?" I ask when we're done.

"You first," he urges.

I sit back on my haunches. "Well, there's the obvious. We've already talked about it. These stories are all tragedies, and they all involve death."

"Organism death," Leif clarifies bluntly. "Not necessarily human."

"True. And they also involve water. Or bodies of water. Both natural and man-made. Saltwater and fresh."

"Okay . . ."

A hunch pops into my head right then. It's the same one I stopped myself from voicing earlier when we were all back in the woods. I glance up at Leif, at his dimpled chin and furrowed brow, and remain unsure of how to broach the topic.

"You can say it," he says softly, and it's almost as if he can read my mind.

Or at least my hesitation.

I clear my throat, place my palms on my thighs. "Back at the Hollow, what I was going to say . . . or what I *wanted* to say was that these articles make me think of Eden Vicente."

Leif says nothing.

"Is that weird? I'm sorry if it is."

He still says nothing.

I fumble to explain my reasoning. "It makes sense, don't you think? Tenace is a Broadmoor game, and Eden was from your school. Plus, she died last year in a body of water under mysterious circumstances. And well . . ."

"Well, what?" Leif asks, and I'm conscious suddenly of how physically close we are. I can see the veins in his neck, his forearms. The sweat starting to bead on his temple.

I push forward. "It's just, *I've* heard rumors about her death. Even before the Jackson stuff. First there was the search party. I was there for that. Then I heard she had a weird toxin in her blood and her parents had her cremated before an autopsy could be performed. I also heard she had salt water in her lungs even though she was found in a fresh-water lake. I mean, I don't have any evidence of that, so for now it's just gossip. But also," I squirm a little bit, "the other connection is Carlos."

"Carlos?" Leif echoes.

"Eden was his girlfriend, right? I'm not saying he had any connection to what happened," I say quickly. "I'd never think that, and I know he wasn't there when she went missing. But *that's* why my mind went there when I saw these articles. Because that's how the game works, right? You look for patterns? And well, Leisl has a connection to her, too. Since she was Eden's roommate at the time."

Leif's eyes widen. "I see."

"What about you?" I feel *embarrassed*, I realize, which doesn't make sense. I'm only repeating what I've heard, the things I know. Then again, none of this can be new for Leif. He actually *attends* Broadmoor, and who am I to tell him anything about his twin sister and best friend? Surely, he knows all about what happened to fifteen-year-old Eden Vicente last spring better than I do. "Look, I have no frame of reference for how this is supposed to go. I'm sorry if I'm making you uncomfortable."

"You're not," he says. "Eden's as good a guess as any, I suppose. Her death . . . well, there are a lot of unanswered questions. And honestly, you're right to be looking at connections not just with the articles, but to us. That *is* how tenace works. Why did *we* get *this* clue? It's good thinking."

"Yeah?" I can't help but grin. "Thanks."

His gaze meets mine. "Do you remember when Leisl mentioned Carlos not having a conspiratorial mind?"

"Sure."

"Well, that's significant. Something like that's a real disadvantage in a game where you need to assume nothing's coincidental. You can't ever hold back because you're afraid of hurting feelings. Not if you want to win."

"But conspiracies are based on lies," I say. "How can believing in them be an effective strategy?"

Leif shakes his head. "I'm not talking about *believing* in conspiracies. They're garbage. What I'm talking about is a way of approaching information. A whole cosmology. In order to play a game like tenace, one must assume, fundamentally, that everything that happens, happens by design."

"Is that what *you* believe?" I ask.

He shrugs. "Not really. I tend to think life's pretty random. Looking for answers that aren't there is just a way of avoiding responsibility for the ones that are. Not to mention, I'm a good Jewish boy. Conspiracies haven't been kind to us, so I prefer a little healthy skepticism with my worldview."

"I get that." I glance back at the articles spread out on the floor. "Look, maybe we should just try and figure out how these people and organisms actually died. There has to be info online."

Leif brightens. "Awesome. Why don't you do that?"

I stare at him. *"Me?"*

There's a knock on my bedroom door right then. I look up to see my dad peeking his head in, glancing around.

"Hi, Mr. Fletcher." Leif sits up straight.

"I'm sorry to interrupt. Are you two studying?"

"Sort of," Leif says cheerily. "Beatrice is a hard worker, sir. I wouldn't mind having some of her ambition rub off on me."

"Gross," I tell him.

"Ambition?" my father echoes.

"Forget it," I say. "What's up?"

"I need to talk to you when you have a minute. Can you come find me?"

"Yeah, sure."

"You can talk now." Leif waves a hand in the air as he crawls to his feet, his knees cracking in the process. "I should be going anyway. Got tons of homework this weekend. Junior year is no joke. It was nice meeting you, sir. And Beatrice—let

17

me know when you figure some of this stuff out. I'll, uh, look into some of your suggestions, too."

"Bye," I say.

"He seems nice," my father says when he's gone.

"What did you want to talk about?" I try and shove aside my irritation at Leif, since he apparently expects me to do all the work.

My dad nods and slips into the room, sitting on my bed next to the cat, which is how I know it's bad news. I brace myself.

"I was hoping it wouldn't come to this," he starts. "But I'm going to need to leave town for work tomorrow. Probably only for a week. Ten days at most. It's an emergency."

My jaw drops. "You're *leaving*?"

"It's not an ideal time. I realize this, and if I could get out of it, I would. I tried. Believe me."

"But where are you going?"

"Atlanta. Then Tucson. Possibly Philadelphia."

"Oh," I say.

"You could come," he offers. "I don't want to leave you here alone. Not after . . ."

I nod. I know what he means and why he's worried. Immediately after it happened, we'd reported the package and threat I received to the Cabot Cove Sheriff's Office, along with some of the nastier messages I'd gotten via my TrueMaine email. There were promises it'd be taken seriously, but nothing's happened since then. The responding deputy did tell us that the fact the package was sent to the TrueMaine offices in

Portland meant the sender didn't know where I lived. Plus, the originating scan on the package was from South Carolina, so it was likely the sender had gotten the photo of my mother's headstone off the internet somewhere.

Only I'm not convinced of this. I know my dad isn't either.

I look him in the eye. "I don't want to go. I can't. You'll be in meetings all day. Plus, I have school. There're two tests this week."

"We'll make it work."

"I'm not running away," I say firmly. "And I'll be fine. I've stayed home by myself before. It's not a big deal."

He shakes his head. "You can't stay here by yourself. That's not something I'll compromise on. Uncle Abe has said you can stay with him. I've already talked with him about it. He's excited to have you. Aunt Callum is, too."

"*Uncle Abe?*" I groan. It's not that I don't like my dad's younger brother, it's just that he seriously lives in the middle of nowhere. Also, he's kind of depressing. He's either got too much going on inside him or nothing at all. "How will I get to school? How will I get anywhere?"

"Callum can drop you off on her way to work. She can bring you home, too. And you can do your homework in the office. They'd really love to see you." Like my dad, my aunt also works at Bio-Mar—she's head of the marine division—and while I adore *her*, I'm not pleased with the idea of spending my afternoons in the office of the company that's sending my dad away in my time of need.

I sulk. "What about Lemon?"

"You can bring her. I asked. Callum says it's fine."

"She's allergic."

"They've renovated the basement into a separate in-law unit. You and Lemon can stay there. You'll have tons of privacy."

"Fine." I wrap my arms around my knees. I don't like any of this, but I'm smart enough to realize there aren't any other options. Not good ones, at least. It's not like I can stay in the dorms at Broadmoor with my cat, and my great-grand-aunt Jess doesn't need houseguests at her age. My only other local relative is my grandmother's niece, and she had surgery last month to remove a tumor from her brain. She'll be fine, apparently, but is understandably not up for visitors. Also, she's mean.

"What's the emergency?" I ask.

My dad looks up. "Huh?"

"You said it was an emergency. Having to go on a trip with such short notice."

"Oh, right. Well, these meetings are essential to staying on schedule with data collection, and Mel had planned on going." That's his boss, the vice president of market research. "But now he's flying to Lisbon last minute. I didn't get the details, but Andi called this morning and begged me to fill in. So I'm going."

"When's your flight?"

"Tomorrow morning. Nine a.m.," he says. "Callum says she can pick you up at noon."

"Great."

He leans to kiss me on the cheek. "Thanks for being understanding."

"I'm really not."

He smiles. "I know that. It's why I love you."

TRUEMAINE.COM
Unpublished Draft

"Family Tradition"

Hey, TrueMainers, just a quick check-in as we get closer to the holiday season, which is the perfect time to hunker down and reopen some mysteries of yore. I was hoping to take a poll, to see if there were stories or cases that you've been interested in. Or maybe you'd like to vote? I've been digging around and looking into our news archives and there are a lot of unsolved Maine-ish happenings to choose from.

For instance, back in December 1957, a forty-eight-year-old man named Park Sargent vanished on his way to work at the Cabot Cove Public Library. Bunny Winslow, owner and founder of Bunny's Bakery, reported seeing Park that morning when he stopped in for his usual coffee and cheese roll. They talked about an impending blizzard and how rough flu season had been on the children that year. The library was only a block farther past the bakery, but Park never arrived.

Later that month, another library worker failed to show up for her shift. Eighteen-year-old Dorothy Carson rode with her mother, who dropped her off in the library parking lot at approximately 10:45 a.m. on a Thursday morning. Coworkers reported seeing Miss Carson's footprints in the snow, heading toward the entrance, when they abruptly vanished, almost as if she'd been plucked from the ground by a giant predatory bird. On that same day, a fight broke out at a closed-door city hall discussion over downtown expansion . . .

3

WITH A DEFEATED SIGH, I lean forward, reach for the keyboard, and in one fell swoop I delete the whole column. What is wrong with me? That was *terrible* writing, and I'm embarrassed I even entertained publishing something so ludicrous.

It's me. There's something wrong with me. Old Bea would never wax poetic and imply a grown woman might've been snatched from the snowy streets in broad daylight by an actual bird. Not to mention it's not a good mystery. Not the way I'm painting it, at least. Park Sargent and Dorothy Carson *did* disappear, obviously, but there's been a long-running theory that Dorothy was inadvertently knocked—or perhaps fell—from the library parking deck into an open construction pit next door only to be buried by an earthmover without anyone knowing. Park, for his part, was rumored to have a troubled marriage and had been looking for a way to leave.

Why can't I find a real mystery to write about?

You know why, my mind whispers.

You can't find what you don't want to have.

With a shudder, I grab my phone. Before I know it, I'm texting someone and asking if they've got time to meet with me.

It takes a moment, but when they respond in the affirmative, I get ready to go. Quickly changing into winter clothes that will accommodate the near freezing temps and frigid wind, I tiptoe down the staircase and slip into the night without telling my father, who's still holed up in his office. The blinking light on the coffee maker indicates he's in for a long night.

Normally, this would frustrate me. I love my father and I know he loves his work, but he's been giving so much lately. It's wearing him down. Physically. Emotionally. But tonight I'm thankful for whatever research complication or biopharmaceutical dilemma he's wrestling with because it means he won't be up to check on me.

It means he'll never know I'm gone.

× × ×

I walk around to the side of our detached garage to retrieve my bike. Standing in shadows as I pull on my helmet and zip my jacket, I gaze up at our house. It's a little on the shaggy side—the shutters need painting, the porch has a noticeable lean to one side, and the slate walkway is chipped and worn—but it's undeniably *home*. This century-old farmhouse is the place my parents bought impulsively when they were first weighing the choice to move to Cabot Cove from Ann Arbor. My microbiologist father, with his brand-new doctorate, had just been offered a job in his childhood hometown at a biotech start-up called Bio-Mar, and the three of us had traveled out here to visit and look at potential properties to rent.

This house was the third one we looked at, and my parents fell in love with it instantly. Maybe it was the neighborhood—lined with tall trees and wide streets that were full of children during the day, but quiet enough at night that with the windows open you can just barely hear the roar of the ocean. Maybe it was the wide plate glass windows and built-in window seats, perfect for cozy reading while a storm wails outside.

I don't know what magic charmed them exactly, but I do know that they forgot about renting and put in an offer to buy that day. A month later, the house was ours, and I guess what I've always loved about it is that this is the place they picked to raise me. And ever since Mom died, it's been the place where I've felt her presence the most. Where I've always felt safe.

Until now.

4

THE BIKE RIDE'S A LONG one—maybe four miles south on the coastal highway—but I finally reach my destination, which is a Dunkin' Donuts parking lot that sits across the road from a Cumberland Farms gas station. Local ordinances don't allow chain eateries within Cabot Cove's city limits, so technically this is an unincorporated part of the county.

Even so, the place is packed on a Saturday night. Most orders are to-go obviously—travelers coming through, people heading out for the night or coming home—and when I arrive, the line's out the door. They close at midnight, so everything smells stale, and seated in the back corner booth is the person I've come for: a young, uniformed sheriff's deputy with sleepy eyes, a bad case of hat hair, and a creepy handlebar mustache. He's also got a large coffee and a powdered jelly sitting in front of him.

I walk over, my sneakers squeaking on the sticky linoleum floor. "I don't know, Deputy. This feels uncomfortably close to a stereotype."

Deputy Williams rolls his eyes while brushing powdered sugar from his mustache. "Did you know that twenty percent of law enforcement officers refuse to eat donuts in public because they don't want to conform to negative stereotypes?"

"Sounds like you're the conformist," I tell him.

Deputy Williams shrugs. "I'm just comfortable with who I am. And I don't care about labels."

"How brave," I say.

"You want anything?"

"Nah, I'm good."

"Then sit down, already." He cranes his neck and looks around. "You're making me nervous."

"Thanks for meeting me on such short notice," I say. "I really appreciate it. It's a weird time for me right now. I can't sleep. I can't write. I can't do anything."

"Sit down," he repeats. "I want to hear all about it."

So I sit, sliding into the tan-and-brown vinyl seat on the other side of the booth and setting my bike helmet beside me. And look, Maine's the whitest state in the nation, so it's not like I don't know that everyone in the Dunkin' Donuts line is staring at us, just doing a little racial profiling of their own and wondering why on earth a biracial teen's hanging out with a white cop who basically looks like the embodiment of the Blue Lives Matter movement.

But neither of us is here by accident. Last month, Deputy Williams and I both schemed to use each other in what were ultimately mutually beneficial ways. We were also both outsiders, newly introduced to the game of tenace. And not just the mere existence of the game but the way in which the mysteries involved are often connected to the past. My old psychiatrist, Dr. Wingate, pretty much confirmed to me that Deputy Williams's much older brother had once been the late Chrissy Lambert's boyfriend—a poor scholarship kid who'd gone to Broadmoor Academy and fallen in love with the wrong rich man's daughter.

"What's up, kid?" He taps his finger on the table and looks at me with heavy-lidded eyes.

"Hear anything new about the library fire?" I ask. It's been over a month since the school library up at Broadmoor Academy burned to the ground under highly suspicious circumstances. The fire almost took Leisl with it, and though it's hard not to believe she was targeted on purpose, there's been no suspect identified. No motive, either. Meaning she, like me, could still be at risk.

"Not really." Deputy Williams says.

"Would you tell me if you had?"

"I'd tell you if I knew anything definite," he replies. "Is this what you wanted to talk to me about? An unsolved fire?"

"Not really. No. I don't know."

"Then what?" he asks.

I lick my lips, gather my courage. "How did Eden Vicente die?"

An odd smile creeps across Deputy Williams's face as he leans back in the Naugahyde booth, really settling in, and sort of strokes his blond mustache in approval. "My goodness, Beatrice Fletcher," he says. "Now *that's* the question I thought you'd never get around to asking me."

× × ×

Stunned, I stare across the table, trying to take in the implication of his words.

"I finally remembered where we know each other from," I say slowly because that was what he'd said the first time we'd met in private, when he'd urged me to write publicly about the Sheriff Office's failure to find Cabot Cove's missing teens. *You don't remember me, do you?* he'd asked. "I figured it out a while ago. You were there when I joined the search party for Eden last spring. Leisl was there, too. I remember her. Also Carlos. Maybe Leif."

"*No.*" Deputy Williams sits up straight. Sets his coffee down with a splash. "Uh-uh. Not him. Not that boy twin. He wasn't there for the searching."

I blink. "Okay. Well, why did you want me to ask about it?"

He leans forward, his blue eyes bright with interest. "What do you remember about the search party? How did you get involved in the first place? You didn't even know the Broadmoor kids back then. So tell me everything."

5

TELL ME EVERYTHING.

Only it's not my story to tell, is it?

Even clouded with apprehension, a growing tempest of uncertainty, my mind does what a mind is wont to do, which is flutter back to last spring when the whole thing with Eden happened. It was late April. I remember that. The air wasn't warm, but it also wasn't frozen, and by then the ground had thawed and softened and green buds were just starting to sprout in the hills, on the trees. New life. New vigor.

The rain had come, and local creeks and waterways ran fast and full, spilling down the hillside to soak yards and flood streets. Mudding season was here, and flowers had begun popping up in planters and other places where forward-thinking homeowners had buried bulbs long before the frost. Such showy beauty. Riding around town, you'd see technicolor tulips, irises, daffodils, lilies just starting their bloom, filling the air with their sweetness.

Thinking back, it was probably on TrueMaine that I first heard rumors about a missing girl. I hadn't written anything for them at that point, but Jackson mentioned they were looking for local writers to bring a new angle to crime reporting from their specific Maine communities, and I'd signed up for the discussion boards. Under the forum "Incidents and Updates" someone had started a discussion thread titled "What's Going On at Lake Paloma?"

Opening it, the first thing I saw were user-contributed photographs of the Lake Paloma parking lot, crowded with vehicles from local law enforcement, as well as the Department of Inland Fisheries and Wildlife, which was who my uncle Abe worked for. The rumors in the thread already ran wild, speculative, and yes, conspiratorial. A *child* had gone missing, and it was undoubtedly foul play. Murder, most likely. Or maybe drugs. Gang members. Sex trafficking. Cannibals, even. But it wasn't until Uncle Abe and Aunt Callum stopped by that I got a real understanding of the situation.

As a game warden, my uncle lives close to Lake Paloma, in an inland region known as the Fire Mountain Wildlife Management Preserve. Although wildlife conservation and ecological health are his primary focus, my uncle's job falls under state law enforcement, and his jurisdiction covers all the preserve as well as the lake, its campground, and a large section of the popular Skyline-to-the-Sea public hiking trail. So it made sense he was one of the first people to respond to reports of Eden's disappearance.

"A hiker went missing this afternoon," he told my father that evening when he and Aunt Callum stopped by for a late dinner. The strain in his voice was evident. "She's young, too. Fifteen. Sixteen, maybe."

"They'll find her, babe." Aunt Callum had rubbed his tense shoulders, then pressed her cheek against his back. "She's probably not even in the park. All this worry for some high school prank."

"You're not expected to find her, are you?" Standing in our kitchen, my father shot me a worried look. One I understood instantly because my dad's always worried about his younger brother. According to him, Uncle Abe's got a history of being impulsive in ways that defy logic. Some of this is a matter of personality. My dad's always been the high achiever, excelling in school, in work, even in love until he was widowed, while Abe's been the wanderer. He took years to finish college, picking up credits here and there, while he moved around the country and worked in communities recovering from natural disasters. California wildfires. Oklahoma twisters. Flooding in Houston and across the South. When I was young I pictured his life as wildly romantic—the nomad riding in to save the day by rescuing people trapped on roofs or cornered by flames. But my dad always corrected me, describing his brother's efforts as far more despairing. He counted bodies, I was told, and sifted through the remains of people's homes, and later, he'd try and help communities better prepare for the next disaster. Or the one after that.

A critical incident postmortem, Uncle Abe called this process, because natural disasters were also human disasters, and we needed to learn what we could. *Hell on earth* were the words my father used to describe this sort of work because in his mind, it was something you only did when you didn't have the fortitude to put down roots in any one place. But Abe returned to Maine once my mom fell ill, and that's when he got serious about becoming a warden and living in the woods. He's done a good job, too. He's got senior standing at his post, and he even got married a couple years back, which surprised everyone. But the way my dad looks at him, the way he looks after him, it's like he's always waiting for his little brother to disappear again. Like he knows one day he'll be gone.

"Of course, I'm expected to find her." Abe scratched at his beard, a telltale sign of impatience. "She's a child. Regardless of what my job is, I care enough to try."

"So what'd you do today, Aunt Callum?" I did my best to draw my aunt away from the conversation, away from the kitchen, that felt wrought with rising tension. In contrast to my uncle's stoicism, Callum's bubbly, extroverted, and prone to making corny jokes. I'd once asked her how they got along so well seeing as my uncle is a man of so few words and she loves talking, and Callum informed me that I'd already answered my own question.

But on that Saturday evening in April, I remember her smiling at me and tucking her black hair behind her ears, which are just a smidge oversized for her face. "Want to go outside?" she asked.

"Yes," I said eagerly, because Aunt Callum's always felt less like an aunt and more like an older cousin to me. But a really impressive cousin. Not only does she have a doctorate and an amazing career where she's one of few women, and also the boss, but she's easy to talk to. Aunt Callum won't grill you with questions about Your Future or offer lectures on Important Matters Kids These Days Don't Understand.

"I hope I didn't sound flippant earlier," she whispered, once we'd snuck out onto the back deck to huddle under a flannel blanket and gaze up at the stars. "Talking about that missing girl. I just . . . it's really bothering Abe, and it's not like there's anything he can do about it. He's already done everything he's supposed to, but he didn't even want to come out here tonight. It's like he's taking this missing girl thing so *personally*. But he had search teams, dive teams, all ready to go in a matter of hours. Total overkill, but like, you couldn't ask for a more thorough response. Then when the staties turned up, they took over and dismissed him without so much as a thank-you. They didn't even send the teams into the water, said they were focusing their efforts elsewhere. Abe was furious, but that's how I finally got him in the car, to keep him from decking somebody. Well, that and the search moved to an area out of his jurisdiction. But if they don't find her soon, he'll be out there at daybreak, coordinating more resources, keeping the scene secure. He's even got a pilot ready for the morning if it's necessary."

"A pilot?"

"To search the mountains in case she's out there. Hurt or whatever. They can do heat imaging. They'll send drones out, too. Cover as much terrain as possible."

"But you don't think she's lost," I said.

Aunt Callum shrugged and tipped her wineglass back. "I don't know what to think. I just know that because of who she is and where she's from, all the stops are being rolled out. More than they would for you or me, that's for sure. So they'll find her. She's either lost or just snuck off to do her own thing. Or else she's back at campus fooling around with whomever she's dating and has no clue anyone's even looking for her in the first place."

"Campus?" I echo. "So she's not from the campground?"

Aunt Callum shook her head. "Broadmoor Academy."

"Oh. *Oh.*"

"See what I mean about resources? Little Rich Girl Lost. Her dad's a bigwig CEO from Kentucky, and she was part of some hiking club or something. They were doing the Skyline-to-the-Sea Trail. In and out on the same route by the swimming hole, so they know where to look. And currently they're focusing out by the school. But as of yet, no one's found her."

"That's a long hike, though. It's steep, too."

"Wouldn't know," she said. "My terrain's strictly aquatic. I'm not into sweat or heatstroke. There's a reason I left Arizona. Well, more than one." And that was that. My dad came out on the deck and announced it was time to eat.

But the whole rest of the night Uncle Abe still looked so distressed that he barely touched his food or said a word, and I didn't dare broach the subject again. Still, the next morning, I was the first one up, and sure enough, when I went online, the home page article on our local *Cabot Cove Gazette* was near breathless:

BROADMOOR STUDENT VANISHES!

"SHE WAS JUST GONE," LAMENTS MISSING GIRL'S TEARFUL CLASSMATE

The rest of the article was equally dramatic while also being short on details:

>An unnamed freshman girl from Broadmoor Academy was reported missing yesterday afternoon at approximately 5:08 p.m., according to the Maine State Police spokesperson, Trooper Monteverde. The missing student was reportedly part of the boarding school's Outdoor Adventure Club, which regularly partakes in hiking and backpacking trips across the Northeast. Yesterday, one of the club's faculty leaders, Miriam Diamond, says that she and coleader Ryan Jameson took a group of eight students on a round-trip hike from Broadmoor Castle to Lake Paloma, located in the 7,500-acre Fire Mountain Wildlife Management Preserve.
>
>Sources close to law enforcement, who have not been authorized to speak publicly, tell the Gazette that the group stopped for lunch at the lakeshore's south side for approximately an hour before turning around and hiking back along

the same section of the Skyline-to-the-Sea Trail that they had come in on. This trail, which opened five years ago, runs all the way from the western side of Fire Mountain to Cabot Cove Harbor and includes more than 6,000 feet in elevation gain. The girl's disappearance is especially puzzling as the missing freshman was accounted for as the group departed the lake. However, she did not return to the Broadmoor Academy campus that afternoon. "She was just gone," one of the other students told this reporter with tears streaming down her face. "No one saw anything or heard anything. It was just, like, she vanished."

"What do you think's going to happen?" I asked my father when I walked into the corner bedroom he once shared with my mother. Crawling beside him, seeking warmth, I curled my legs beneath the thick down duvet and showed him the article on my phone. "People who are lost are usually found, right?"

"I'm sure she'll turn up soon," he told me after he'd gotten his glasses. "There's only so many places she could be given that it was a school outing and they stayed on the main trail. But she could've fallen and been injured. I'll bet they find her today. That's what I told Abe. Only . . ."

"Only what?" I asked.

His lean face was grim. "Only they should fire those two teachers who didn't notice they'd lost one of their students. *They're* responsible for this."

I nodded because that seemed reasonable. How *do* you

lose a student on a hiking trip? The article said there'd been eight other people around. And these were high schoolers. It wasn't like when we used to visit the commercial fisheries back in second grade and you'd have sixty schoolkids running up and down the dock and hanging over the edge of the boat. Back then it always seemed like sheer luck that no one fell in or got themselves tangled up in the netting.

"What if someone hurt her?" I asked. "What if she didn't get herself lost? I saw something online about feral predators who hide out in national parks and wait to kidnap children. Sometimes they *eat* them."

"You've been reading too many of Aunt Jess's books," my dad said sternly. "Not everything's a plot."

Yeah, well, *that* was even scarier—how a random accident or situation could make a person simply disappear. Whether it was my young mother dying from a cancer she'd battled once and believed was in remission or a world filled with pandemics and wars and multiple slow-motion catastrophes, it was the randomness of fate that lurked behind my anxiety, my fear of death. My fear of *everything*.

The night before, after Uncle Abe and Aunt Callum had left, I'd gotten out my laptop and started documenting everything I knew about the missing girl. Every detail they'd told me. Now, once Dad got up to make breakfast, I returned to that document and proceeded to add to it, along with my rambling thoughts and Dad's own commentary. It felt good to do this. Like I was creating a routine, a real journalistic practice I could carry forward with me if I were lucky enough to get the chance to work for TrueMaine.

But by Monday, Patriot's Day, it didn't feel like enough. The girl remained missing, and so I went online and verified that volunteers from the public were welcome to help in the search efforts. People were meeting up near Broadmoor, where the hiking group had started out on the Skyline-to-the-Sea Trail, and I asked my father if I could go. He said yes and I set off in search of a stranger.

A girl I'd never met.

6

"THAT WAS THE DAY I first saw you," I tell Deputy Williams. "You were organizing the search groups and handing out maps."

He nods. "That was the third day and the whole mood changed for some reason."

"Did you learn something new?"

"I didn't, but someone must've. Don't know what, though. But the messaging shifted, too. They finally put the girl's name out to the public along with photos of her. National news outlets started broadcasting pleas from the parents that were focused on the girl having asthma and needing her medication. Like *that* was the big concern. A possible medical emergency."

"Is that kind of messaging normal?" I asked.

"It can be. It can also be a way of containing the family if they have reason to suspect their loved one's disappearance wasn't taken seriously at first."

"But it was taken seriously."

"I know. But we aren't parents who sent our kid away to an out-of-state school only to have them lose her. That changes things a little. Plus, it turned out the mom was a

Kentucky state rep. Dad was a CEO of some big pharmaceutical company. The story was bound to blow up. These people had influence."

"Who found her?" I ask.

"You don't remember?"

I shake my head. The most vivid memory I have is of Eden's family. When I got to the trailhead staging area, her parents and two younger sisters were there. I knew who they were by their shell-shocked expressions, as if they'd woken up and found themselves on a different planet, a place hostile and cruel and wholly unknowable. I also recognized them by the matching T-shirts they wore: bright yellow and bearing the message BRING EDEN HOME printed over a blown-up photo of a smiling girl with crooked teeth.

"It took five days to find her," Deputy Williams says. "The clearest info we had was that the girl was physically accounted for when the group left Lake Paloma. You see, one of the students had taken a photo on their phone and in it you could clearly spot Eden about a half mile from where they'd had lunch. The lake is still visible, but the group is on the move, heading back out onto the trail they'd hiked in on.

"With that evidence in hand, we scoured every inch of the nearly four-mile stretch between the school and the lake. You walked it. You know it's rugged out there. Our working theory was that maybe she'd wandered off the trail and gotten lost, then headed over to the other side of the mountain range. State troopers brought in dogs, helicopters, all of it.

Plus, the weather was clear, so that wasn't a problem. But Eden wasn't anywhere."

"What'd you think?" I ask.

He looks up at me with those tired eyes of his. "What would *you* think?"

I take a deep breath. "That maybe someone else had found her before any of the searchers could."

He lifts an eyebrow.

"Or that she wanted to be lost," I offer. "Like Jackson. But I remember thinking how outrageous it was that those faculty members who were on the hiking trip with Eden could lose a student in broad daylight. My dad said they deserved to be fired."

"Sounds reasonable to me."

"So if I were in charge of the investigation, at some point, I'd want to look into those people. The teachers. Maybe even the other students who were on the hike, as well. And anyone else who was on the trail that day."

"Good." Deputy Williams nods approvingly. "That's what we were trying to do. Expanding our scope from the simplest solutions to the more complex ones. That second time you came back to help search, when was it? Wednesday?"

"Yeah," I say. "Day five. We had a half day at school that day and Dad drove me all the way out to Lake Paloma on his lunch hour."

"That's right. We'd come back to the lake because nothing else was panning out. So that was the day we were trying to cover the area around those lakefront homes. Kind of a long-shot effort. The houses are on the northwest end of Lake Paloma, and according to the report, they hadn't walked that way. They'd come in from the east, had lunch on the south side, by the swimming hole, and then hiked out the same way. Still, talking to the homeowners and searching the properties felt like due diligence. A formality to cross off so that we could delve into some of the other possibilities. And I specifically remember being told we'd gotten clearance from all the homeowners. Only when we got there, we were allowed onto every property, except one."

"The old cabin," I say slowly. It was hard to forget. When the wildlife management preserve had been established fifteen years earlier, the whole lake was designated as public land. But because a dozen or so private lakeside residences had already been built, a deal was made with the home-owners. They retained their homes and property borders, no other development would be built on Lake Paloma, and the only catch was that the owners would have to allow state access whenever necessary for maintenance or other projects—with advance notice, of course. In return, the state paid them an easement.

The number of search volunteers had dwindled by Wednesday. No more Broadmoor students or kids from my school, but a dedicated group still showed up, including me. They were older folks, mostly—people with free time who enjoyed feeling involved. And who genuinely cared, even if their way of talking about the Vicentes felt overly familiar. I caught snips of conversations with comments like: "Eden's a smart girl with a sensible brain. She knows not to panic." "I can't stop thinking about her asthma. I couldn't sleep all night. I keep picturing her struggling to breathe." "You can tell she cares about fitness and taking care of her body. Not in a trashy way, though, like other teens. There's resilience in that girl."

Although intended as complimentary, their words left a bad taste in my mouth. I struggled to imagine Eden's real family hearing any of this. It felt like a horror movie, like the real Eden, whoever she was, was slowly being replaced by a vision of her strangers had chosen to conjure up. Like a tulpa. Or an urban legend.

We marched together toward the homes on the far side of the lake, only splintering into smaller groups as we approached the individual properties. Roughly ten of us followed Deputy Williams, who was assigned to the very last home that sat on the western end of Lake Paloma, which is shaped like a pear and fed by ice melt off the surrounding mountains.

Personally, I didn't expect we'd find much; the place we were searching wasn't one of the flashy hunting lodges decked out with multi-car garages, warming huts, and dirt bike tracks. This cabin looked abandoned. Compared to its stately peers, this was a boxy two-story structure that sat hidden in shade, mostly concealed by overgrown foliage. The cabin's yellow paint was peeling, and it had a huge screened-in porch to keep bugs out, which was its most defining feature other than a sagging private dock with a couple of tired-looking canoes tied to it.

The property behind the home, however, was fenced and padlocked, and extended far into the marshy woods, up toward Fire Mountain where the lakeside trail reconnected with the western edge of the Skyline-to-the-Sea Trail. When we arrived, however, a handwritten sign was posted on the main gate and front door denying law enforcement access without a warrant. NO TRESPASSING, it read. NO SEARCHING THIS PROPERTY WITHOUT A LEGAL WARRANT OUTLINING CAUSE. BY ORDER OF THE OWNER.

"Were they allowed to do that?" I ask. "Could they just say no when someone's missing?"

Deputy Williams shrugs. "Constitutionally, sure. It's within their rights. Doesn't mean it's not suspicious. I don't know what you remember about the rest of the day, but I wanted to force the issue. I mean, who doesn't let people search for a missing child?"

"Cops don't have a lot of goodwill in some places," I say.

He sniffs. "This isn't Seattle."

"Neither was Ruby Ridge."

"Fine," he acknowledges. "Well, we planned on getting a court order from a judge in Portland to deal with our Gadsden flag friends, but before that could happen, she was found the next morning."

"In the lake," I say.

"That's right. And not out near the houses. Where they found her wasn't far from the sunny spot where her friends had eaten their lunch."

My nose wrinkles. "How does that make sense? You said another student took a photo of her *after* the group had left the lake."

"I know what I said."

"Then how do you explain it?"

"I can't," he says. "All I know is that on Thursday morning, a dive team went into the water for a third time and brought her back. She might've been trapped beneath a branch the whole time or maybe the current moved her from elsewhere. Who knows? The medical examiner ruled drowning as the cause of death, with a time of death estimated right around when she went missing. This quieted down some of the more extreme theories, but if you ask me, there are questions that remain unanswered to this day. Officially, the case is closed. Her death was ruled an accident."

"But you don't believe that," I say.

"I don't know what to believe. But I know Eden's family has filed a lawsuit against the school, and those two teachers were put on administrative leave. They've probably been fired by now unless new information has come to light. Poor girl sounded like the perfect daughter. No drugs or trouble-making. She was a talented musician, a gifted student, and ultimately wanted to follow in her father's footsteps and make scientific discoveries that would help improve people's lives."

"Is it true Eden's lungs had salt water in them?" I ask.

He frowns. "Where'd you hear that?"

"The internet."

"Strong source."

"It can be. So what should I do if I want to learn more about what happened to her?"

"Isn't that what we're doing right now?" he asks. "Isn't that the point of this whole meeting?"

"I guess," I say slowly.

Deputy Williams downs the last of his coffee. "I see wheels spinning in that weird head of yours."

I press my fingers to my temple. "Well, I can't help but notice that you haven't given me any actual answers. I feel like you've just unloaded all the questions about Eden that *you* still want answered."

"I haven't given you *all* my questions," he says. "Not even close."

"But you are using me."

"How so?"

"To gain access to what you can't. Broadmoor. People who might've known Eden."

"You know you're using me all the same, Miss Fletcher." The deputy's tone grows more pointed. "I don't get what's so hard about this. Why can't this be a relationship of give-and-take?"

I lift my chin. "Quid pro quo?"

"Whatever you want to call it."

"I don't want to call it anything."

"Fine." He crumples his donut paper and stuffs it into the empty coffee cup. "It can stay a mystery."

He follows me outside where I've locked my bike up across the road by the gas station's air pump.

"I can give you a ride," he says. "Roads aren't safe this late. Too many cars. Too many people drinking on a Saturday night."

"I'm fine," I say, although it's so cold, I can barely pry the lock open.

He watches me, then gives an exasperated sigh. "We're still keeping an eye on your place, by the way. But it won't last forever. You get any more hate mail? Either online or the real deal?"

"Yeah." My cheeks warm at the mention, but I've finally got the lock off.

"Which one?" he asks.

"Online. Emails mostly." I glance up, embarrassed by a sudden rush of neediness. By how much I long for reassurance that the future ahead of me will be a safe one. "It's not anything like that package. Just general nastiness. People are angry about everything these days. And it's always easier to be angry at a teenage girl than someone with actual power, you know?"

"I *do* know." He grips my bike's handlebars. "That's why you need to take any kind of harassment seriously. Document everything. Better yet, have me document it."

"I will."

"Good."

"Do you think Eden's the reason I got that package?" I

ask before adding hastily, "I know that sounds weird, but whoever sent it is upset about something I wrote, right? And we solved the mystery of the missing teens. And Chrissy Lambert. Eden Vicente is the only other person I wrote about whose mystery I haven't solved."

"Maybe they just hate your writing," Deputy Williams says.

"I'm serious. I want to know what happened to Eden as much as you do. But . . ."

"But what?"

"I'm scared."

He softens. "I don't want you to feel that way. If you're worried, lay low. Take care of yourself, Bea. Don't do anything with Eden. I'll still be keeping an eye on your place like I have been. Everything will be fine."

I pull my helmet on. "You don't have to do that. My dad and I won't be around for a while. Maybe a week or more."

"Where are you going?"

"Dad's traveling for work. I'm staying with my aunt and uncle. They're the ones who live out by Fire Mountain. Weird coincidence, huh?"

"You still believe in those?"

"I don't know what to believe."

"Wait, you're staying at Abe Fletcher's place?" he asks. "I know Abe. I just didn't put him together with you until now."

"Not a lot of family resemblance," I say.

"Does he ever talk about Eden? Or about the search?"

"Not with me. Why?"

"No reason." Deputy Williams glances at his phone.

"Come on. I'm giving you a ride. It's not optional. The roads are freezing."

"They're not freezing."

"Black ice warning. Just came through." He holds up his screen.

"Fine." I groan.

He stares at me. "Why does it sound like you're the one doing me a favor?"

"You know we're supposed to be having a heat wave next week," I tell him. "Just in time for Thanksgiving. How's that for bad news?"

"You really can't help it, can you?" He shakes his head.

"Caring about climate change?" I snap.

"Resisting help at all costs."

7

THE NEXT MORNING, I WATCH my dad double-check his suitcase while he waits for the airport shuttle that will drive him to Bangor. Traveling out of Maine is no easy feat, and to get to Atlanta he'll have to fly to Boston first, where there's a three-hour layover.

"You want me to look in the dryer for anything?" I ask. Neither of us are great about putting clothes away after we wash them.

"I think I'm good." He stands and peers into his hard-shell carry-on. My dad's one of those immaculate packers who uses special cubes and luggage dividers and has to make sure everything matches. It's exhausting to witness but is probably his way of managing his flight anxiety.

"You could drive," I tell him.

"It'll be fine," he says, snapping his suitcase shut.

"What're you going to be doing?" I ask.

"First stop is Emory. We're coordinating with their epidemiology and biomedical departments on data collection, and I need to meet with all our active teams to provide training on our updated research protocol and critical values. I'm the national coordinator on this, and the entire project is bigger than just Bio-Mar. When I'm in Arizona, we'll actually be out in the field doing some real-time surveillance monitoring."

"This is that prion thing you mentioned?" Lately, he's been working on an early detection system for high-risk environmental contagions.

"That's what it started as, yes. But the scope of the project, well, it's . . . evolved. A lot."

"The prions evolved?" I ask.

"I really hope not. No, I'm referring to our technology and the potential applications. But I'm not at liberty to talk about it yet."

"Fine." I sulk. "Be like that."

He smiles. "When I can tell you, you'll be the first to know. For the moment I'm bound by a plethora of NDAs. You want to come downstairs with me? I have to get my work bag together."

"Sure." I grab for his suitcase. "When's the shuttle getting here?"

He checks the clock by his bedstand. "Fifteen minutes?"

We head out of the master bedroom and walk down the hallway to the back staircase. Our funky farmhouse has a layout that consists of two wings built off what was the original structure. As a result, there are twin wooden staircases leading up from both the front entryway and a small hallway behind the kitchen and dining area, which opens into the south-facing space my father's carved out as his office.

With tall ceilings and tall windows overlooking the garden, this is by far my favorite room in the house. I flop down on the sunlit velvet love seat my mom bought when they first moved here, and I run my palms against the rich purple fabric. Sometimes, I imagine I can still smell her in here, in this dusty and perfect space, although I know it's not possible. Not when she's been gone for so long.

I watch as my father packs up his laptop and cords and backup batteries and also a locked HIPAA-compliant document bag that I know for a fact contains his work files. All those corporate secrets he can't tell me about yet.

"Can I ask you a question?"

"What's that?" he replies.

"Do you have any idea how a person who drowned in fresh water would end up with salt water in their lungs?"

My dad turns sharply to look at me, his brown hair flopping over his eyes. "Wait, what? What are you talking about? When did this happen?"

"It's a hypothetical. I'm just asking a question."

"Oh. Well, no, I don't know how that would happen unless this person had spent time in both fresh and salt water prior to drowning and managed to inhale some of both. Not a great swimmer, I guess. But it could happen, depending on the location. Like if someone were at an oceanfront resort and went for a swim in the ocean before later drowning in a pool. Or maybe it was a case of secondary drowning?"

"What's that?"

"It's when someone inhales water into their lungs, only

to die hours later when fluid buildup causes the lungs to stop functioning."

I groan. "Something new to worry about."

"It's rare, though. There are usually warning signs."

"Still scary. Any other ideas?"

My father's phone chirps, and he grabs it. "That's my ride. I'm sorry, sweetie. You should ask Aunt Callum about this. Marine biology is her wheelhouse. She doesn't have a medical background, but she knows way more than I do about water chemistry, okay? She'll be here in a few hours. Ask her all the questions you'd like. She'll love it. I mean, you know how she is. And how my brother is."

"Strong and silent," I say.

My father smiles in a way that feels wistful. "You got the last part right."

I stare at him. What an odd thing to say.

"I'm going to miss you." He leans down to kiss my cheek, slight stubble pressed against soft skin. I inhale the faint scent of mouthwash and sleep, desperate to hold it tight in my lungs. Then I help him grab the last of his chargers and adapters, and earbuds for the plane. Once he's done a final check of his desk, we hurry outside, hustling down the front steps, his wheeled bag clomping with each drop, and out to the white conversion van that sits idling in the street. It appears there's a grand total of two other passengers. At the sight of us, the driver jumps out and opens the trunk before plucking the suitcase from my hands.

"My glasses," my father says in a panicked voice.

"They're on your face," I tell him.

He laughs and looks bashful, then kisses me again before disappearing into the van as the driver slides the door shut with a bang. Once seated my father turns and waves to me.

I wave back.

I don't want him to go.

✕ ✕ ✕

The van drives off as my mind balloons with newfound worries and fears. Mostly on my father's behalf. He has strong aversions to planes, large cities, and public speaking—pretty much anything where he feels subjected to the judgment of strangers—and it's not hard to figure out where my own anxieties come from.

With a quavering sigh, I stand shivering in the cold, squeezing my frigid hands into fists, while waiting to watch the van vanish around a corner. This feels important somehow. Out of sight, out of mind. And when the vehicle's made its turn, I whip around and sprint back up our front porch steps only to stop abruptly and shriek in horror.

Someone's standing there.

"It's just me," my neighbor Evie Ranier says scornfully. "You're so dramatic."

"You *scared* me." I have to crane my neck to look up at her, seeing as Evie's not only standing two steps above me, she's also built like a redwood tree. And yes, I am dramatic, but my heart's currently beating triple time thanks to Evie's sneaking around. "Where'd you come from? What are you doing here?"

She cocks her head, shiny blond hair spilling past her shoulder. "Where do you think I came from? I walked over here on my own two legs like I've done a million times before."

"Yeah, okay, fine," I say. "Well, what's up?"

Evie sort of purses her lips at me, like she's tasted something sour, and I hate seeing the flicker of contempt that flashes across her face. She and I have been good friends for years. Well, *she's* been the good one, really, the sporty, popular girl who extended kindness to me during a time when she didn't have to. Recently, though, things have cooled between us. I wasn't honest with Evie about my friendship with Jackson, and well, I wasn't honest about a lot of things, and so although she lives a mere two doors down from me, I haven't seen a lot of her lately.

I also haven't apologized.

"You know, Evie, I'm sorry about everything," I manage to say in a stumbling rush. "I'm sorry for lying to you about Jax and not being very cool about it all."

Evie melts a little, even going so far as to give me a quick hug. "You know I don't care that you lied to me."

"You don't?"

"Well, I *did* care," she says. "But I'm over it. I read what you wrote about Jackson and his parents and everything that was going on. Those were good secrets to keep. You were a good friend to do that for him."

I try smiling. "Thank you."

"Stop looking so miserable, Fletcher. *I'm* the one whose feelings were hurt."

"I know."

"And you could've come and talked to me earlier. It's been *weeks*."

"I know. I'm sorry about that, too."

"That's not why I'm here, though," she says. "I need to show you something. It's important."

"What is it?"

"Come on." Evie beckons me to follow her before pausing. "Well, actually . . ."

"What?"

She gestures. "You should probably close your front door."

× × ×

Good advice. Not only do I close the front door and lock it, but while I'm at it, I also shed my bathrobe and trade it for a jacket from the hall closet. It's cold out.

Back outside. Evie leads me down the street toward her house, which sits at the very end of the block. The Raniers, as a collective, are the walking definition of chaos, which is kind of what I love about them. Evie's the oldest of four children and their front yard is perpetually littered with bikes, scooters, racquets, bats, balls, and other sports equipment. There's even a volleyball net set up in the side yard for Evie to practice on, and in the back, they've got their own zip line that Evie's dad installed a few summers back. It runs from the back porch over the pool then down a steep ravine to the creek running behind the house.

As we approach, I hear the not-quite-rhythmic pounding of a bass and snare drum pouring from the Raniers' detached garage. I glance at Evie who rolls her eyes.

"That's Colton," she says. "He's in a band."

"It's Sunday morning."

"Please see my previous answer."

"Are they any good?"

"God, I hope not. They're looking for a bass player, though. So if any of your fancy Broadmoor friends are into death metal, let him know. I doubt he's choosy."

"They're not fancy," I say. "They're just . . . nice."

Evie snorts. "Yeah, right."

"What'd you want to show me?" I ask.

"It's in the backyard." Evie reaches up to unlatch the gate and we both squeeze through. Their pool's covered for winter, the patio furniture's been put away, and the trees have gone bare. Past the paved pool area, the yard slopes downward until it hits the property line, which is marked by a dirt path that winds behind the houses on our block. Beyond is the burbling creek where our younger selves spent summers luring frogs and crawdads with tiny pieces of food.

"You see these?" Once we've reached the path at the back of the property line, Evie points to a pair of overhead floodlights installed by her parents. They're motion sensitive and timed to work at night.

"What about them?" I ask.

"Look at this." She pulls up an app on her phone and holds it in front of me.

I squint, unsure of what I'm watching, until I realize it's grainy footage of the exact location where we're standing. The floodlights must have cameras attached to them. At first, I can't make anything out. Just a lot of shadows, and everything's in black and white. Then I spot what looks like a large raccoon waddling out of the ravine.

"Keep watching," Evie urges.

I do. Soon the footage skips ahead, and I spot a figure crawling from the ravine not far from where the raccoon emerged. But this isn't a wild animal. It's a person, no doubt about it, although it's impossible to make out any defining features. They're dressed in black, including a ski mask and gloves.

A chill goes through me. I stare at Evie, but she points back at the screen. The footage shifts to the second camera, and I watch, horrified, as the figure steps from the shadows, looks around, then turns and scurries down the dirt path out of view.

"Who was that?" I ask. "Where are they going?"

Evie points in the direction of my house and starts walking again. "Come on. There's more."

I jog after her. "When was that video taken?"

"Last night."

"What time was it?"

"Around two-ish. And before you ask, no, I didn't hear anything. I just happened to check the footage because I know Colton's been sneaking out recently, that little jerk. I want to know what he's doing."

"Was it him?" I ask weakly, already knowing the answer. Evie's fifteen-year-old death-metal brother is built like a linebacker.

"No way," she says.

"Okay." I'm starting to feel sick. Like mouth-sweats-and-migraine sick. How am I supposed to deal with prowlers in ski masks? I'm so not equipped for this. Within minutes we reach the back border of our property, which is lined with evergreen hedges. Our lot size is narrower than the Raniers' but stretches back just as far, and we don't have a pool. As a result, our yard gives the illusion of vastness.

Evie pulls ahead of me. Her legs are long, and she knows what she's looking for. I watch as she bends at the waist to peer at the foliage.

"Right there!" she exclaims.

I have to crouch to get a look at what she's pointing at. But when I do, my legs nearly buckle. First, I spot footprints in the dirt, then pressed up against the roots of a large hedge, I see what looks like an oversized playing card. It's facing away from me and the illustration on the back is an intricate black-and-gold design I don't recognize. My mind swirls with thoughts of tenace and its connection to bridge, but as I pick up the card I recognize it's from a tarot deck. Not a regular set of cards. And in a haze of either premonition or paranoia, I know exactly what the card will be even before I turn it over and see the intricate drawing of a grinning skeleton riding a white horse.

Death.

8

"Did someone put this here on purpose?" I force myself to act normal. Like I'm not utterly terrified and that seeing this card doesn't have greater implications for me or my personal safety.

In other words, I'm lying again.

Evie's eyes go wide. "You think someone dressed in a ski mask just happened to drop a super creepy tarot card by your yard in the middle of the night?"

"I guess not." I sigh. "Is there anything else on the video?"

"Nope." She peers at the illustration. "Do you think it could be, like, satanic?"

"Now you're being dramatic."

"Your hands are shaking."

"Well, it is odd," I acknowledge.

"You should be careful," Evie says. "What if someone's stalking you?"

"Like who?"

"I don't know! Someone who's read your writing and now they're obsessed with you. Like a crazed admirer. Maybe now they're leaving clues because they want you to star in your own cold case—"

"Can you stop?" I say sharply. "You're letting your imagination run wild."

Evie makes a sound of frustration. "Bea, I saw your dad leave just now. You're all alone. That's *scary*."

I grit my teeth. "Have you told anyone else about this?"

She frowns. "I wanted to tell *you*."

"I appreciate that," I say. "But you don't need to worry about me. I mean, yeah, it's creepy someone's sneaking around at night. But it's not like they *did* anything. Besides, I'm staying somewhere else while Dad's gone. I'll be fine."

"Where?" she asks. "You can stay with us. You know that, right?"

"I'm staying with family. Look, I'll tell my dad about this when he gets back. I swear. Okay?"

Evie looks doubtful. "Okay."

"Do you think you could keep quiet about it?" I ask. "I don't want weird rumors about me spreading around town or whatever."

"What about my parents?" she asks.

"Please, Evie?" Even I can hear the panic in my voice. "Just until my dad gets back. He's doing something important for his work. It's a really big deal, but he'd fly back in a second if he thought something was wrong. I don't want to worry him."

She smiles, then nods. "Okay, sure. That makes sense. I won't tell, Bea. I promise."

× × ×

Back inside my house. I lock the door behind me as my whole body starts to shake, and then I sort of crumple to the floor.

Tears well in my eyes and I struggle to catch my breath, to stay whole. Reaching wildly for the staircase banister, I manage to grab it with one hand, and hold on, as tight as I can.

A ragged sob escapes me, a release of pressure building up in my chest. It *hurts*, being this scared. This alone. A part of me longs to call my dad, to beg him to turn around and come back to me. But I know I can't. What I told Evie is one hundred percent true; I'd never forgive myself if my anxiety and inability to deal ruined this opportunity for him.

Plus, I *can* do this. I just need to find my own path forward and take control of the situation. I've worked on this in therapy, and I know what to do.

There is no immediate danger.

I will be safe at my aunt and uncle's house.

I am capable of handling my emotions.

As my breathing slows, I take action. I quickly photograph the tarot card and text it to Deputy Williams, along with a message:

Not an emergency, but neighbor's night vision camera caught a prowler behind our houses last night. This was left at our property line. What do you think? Could it be the same person from before?

There's no answer, but when I'm able to, I go upstairs to swallow my Paxil and pack my clothes and feed the cat. There's still a whole ninety minutes until my aunt arrives.

In need of a deeper distraction, I bury myself in yet another mystery.

Or maybe it's the same one.

Settling in front of my laptop with a notebook and pen, I pull out the four news articles that comprise the tenace clue. My chest swells with resentment recalling how Leif told me to research them on my own. I cannot overstate how much I loathe the way he swings from belittling me for knowing nothing to making fun of me for being a true crime nerd. Maybe it's time I prove my real value.

Then again, maybe that's what he wants me to think.

Ugh. Regardless of Leif's intentions, I turn my focus to the first news article, which is the one about the aquarium die-off in Florida. The headline and accompanying story seem straightforward; approximately two years prior, at the Fort Lauderdale Aquarium, a massive tank containing an elaborate display of rare coral and other reef aquaria experienced a catastrophic event in which approximately 96 percent of the tank's occupants were killed overnight.

The initial investigation targeted the aquarium's state-of-the-art water maintenance system. Completely automated, the system was programmed to maintain optimal water chemistry for all the aquarium's tanks, each of which had individualized needs and requirements.

However, maintenance records for the reef tank indicated that the automated system had inexplicably dumped a lethal amount of potassium nitrate into the water overnight, something that shouldn't have been possible. It wasn't until more than six months later that a follow-up story featured in the *Miami Herald*'s Sunday Science section finally pinpointed the cause of this fatal malfunction.

When Fail-Safes Fail

Six months ago, the unthinkable happened. On a nondescript Tuesday morning in early July, Lynne Robinson, director of the Fort Lauderdale Aquarium and Preservation Center, received a panicked phone call: something had gone horribly wrong overnight in the reef tank. Nearly all its occupants (more than 200 species of endangered plant and animal life had been housed in the 850,000-gallon tank) were dead.

When investigators tested the deadly tank's water, they found devastating levels of potassium nitrate, which is an additive nutrient used to bring out color in the coral. "It's not a compound that's associated with much risk," marine specialist Harvey Elkhund said. "That's what was so strange. Levels get a little high, it's no problem." However, according to necropsy results, the tank's occupants were exposed to potassium nitrate levels so high the creatures went into shock and died before the automated maintenance system had a chance to register any irregularity.

Initially, Robinson believed human error had led to the tragedy. Perhaps the wrong titration of nitrates had been added into the computer system. Or someone erroneously put the compound into the wrong dispenser. However, neither of these hypotheses could explain why only one tank was impacted. Intentional sabotage was considered, but there were no obvious suspects.

Four months later, a new theory arose. Multiple inspections of the coral tank and its maintenance system revealed calcium buildup in the tubing and filtration system. "This was normal," Robinson stated. "We adjust for water hardness, but calcium buildup can occur over time and it doesn't harm the animals. But then a clue appeared. We went back and looked at the nitrate readings prior to the incident and discovered that the potassium nitrate level was nonexistent in that specific tank for at least two months. Now this hadn't set off any alerts as there's no health risk for low nitrate readings. Still, the automated system should have kicked in to supplement the nutrient to the level we'd set as optimal. Only it hadn't."

Investigators then hypothesized that calcium buildup coating the nutrient delivery system had caused a blockage in the potassium nitrate tubing. This would have led to a scenario in which blocked nitrates inside the clogged tubing would've continued to accumulate every night as the system attempted to correct the zero-nitrate reading coming from the tank. The failure would've occurred when the now-clogged nitrates backed up all the way to the top of the dispensing system and held the release valve open. At this point, due to the downward force of gravity, as well as the combined weight of accumulated nitrate, the clogged calcium was shoved out of the tubing, releasing everything behind it into the tank.

According to renowned failure analyst Dr. Veronique Emerson: "Once this action had been set in motion, the end result was inevitable. A lethal dose was administered in a matter of seconds."

I take furious notes while reading through this detailed account. It's hard to know what's important, but I try and hit the big themes. When I've finished going over the entire story, I reread what I've jotted down and then use a highlighter to bold the words that jump out at me:

Clogged tube + Weight of nitrate buildup + Gravity = Accident

Fail-Safe: System designed to do least amount of harm in the event of failure

Renowned failure analyst Dr. Veronique Emerson

Okay, well, that last note is less about the incident itself and more about my curiosity regarding a potential future field of study or work. Failure analysis sounds a little like true crime, in a way, except trying to understand the motives of things instead of people. Also, when I search Dr. Emerson's name, I find out that she's a professor at Rice University. Not to mention the only Black woman in their chemical and bio-molecular engineering department.

On to the *Daily Mail* article, which is about two teen-agers who drowned in a resort pool in Mexico. There's no mention of salt water, but some of the details remind me of my dad's hypothetical dry drowning scenario. Eight years ago, a French American family of four living in Seattle flew to Puerto Vallarta for spring break. The family's children—Laurent, seventeen, and Millie, fifteen—were described as notably strong swimmers. Millie was on her high school swim team and Laurent worked as a lifeguard during the summer. On their first full morning at the resort, while their parents were with the concierge making snorkeling reserva-tions, the kids entered the small plunge pool outside their suite.

Witnesses described hearing the mother's blood-curdling scream the moment she found her children at the bottom of the pool. A young couple walking by watched as the parents and hotel staff attempted to rescue them. A mal-function in the pool meant the power had to be cut, and by the time they were pulled from the water, Laurent and Millie were gone. Apparently, they'd been trapped underwater by a missing drain grate, which is not a thing I knew could hap-pen, but sounds absolutely terrifying.

The questions I scrawl down are:

Why was the grate missing?

Why was the power turned off?

There's no obvious connection to the aquarium story, however. Other than some kind of general malfunction or equipment failure. The failing fail-safe. But that's about it. I jot down a couple more notes, then reach for the third article, only my phone vibrates at the exact same moment. When I pick it up, I see a text from my aunt Callum.

You ready? I'm outside.

Rising from my chair, I peek out my bedroom window. Sure enough, Aunt Callum's waiting down there in her battered green Subaru, the one that's crowded with Greenpeace and SAVE THE OCEAN stickers on it, along with her favorite nineties bands: Nine Inch Nails, Garbage, The Pixies, Love and Rockets, Ministry. Trust me, as a scientist and researcher, Aunt Callum makes a very different impression than my dad does when he pulls up in his boring old factory-white pickup. The most flare he's got is a University of Michigan license plate holder that reads GO WOLVERINES!

This reflects their personalities, sure, but also their professional interests. At least that's a working theory of mine. My dad, who heads up Bio-Mar's epidemiology and technology division, is focused on disease surveillance and transmission prevention. Over on the marine side, however, Aunt Callum's got all these ambitious ideas about sustainability and aquatic health. Also, she really loves fish. Originally from Tempe, Arizona, she moved to Maine for college and she's never left.

Well, that's all nice enough, but short story long, the stickers on her car definitely don't endear my aunt to Cabot Cove's long-established community of trappers and lobstermen. The ocean is their livelihood and their families' livelihood, going back generation after generation. They know the ways of the sea and are wary of people like my aunt, who, in their mind, care more about securing patents and saving crustaceans than the well-being of the town's residents. Callum would say she cares about all of those things, but she's an outsider. Not a lot of people are going to trust her on that. But whatever. That's for her to deal with.

I text her back:

Coming.

9

ONCE I'VE GOT ALL MY stuff in the car—myself included—Aunt Callum hands me a latte and a bag of warm raspberry muffins from Cabot Cove's Main Street Café. She's wearing a black baby doll dress, black tights, and black boots. This look, along with a preheated car seat and industrial music playing over the speakers go a long way to soothing my nerves and getting me to look forward to the coming week, to spending time with her, even if where I really want to be is home.

"Thanks for coming to get me." I slam the car door shut. "It'll be good to not be alone while Dad's gone."

She grins, shifting the Subaru into gear as she peels away from the curb and navigates her way through the residential streets out to the coastal highway. Oh, and that's another thing about Aunt Callum. She drives fast. Too fast, probably, but I'm not complaining. "Your dad told you to say that, didn't he?"

"Not exactly."

"Of course, he did. Frankie's all about manners. About being *respectable*. I love that about him."

"You do?"

"Absolutely. You should see him at work. He's always making these gorgeous PowerPoint presentations so that he can highlight his salient points and then ask for feedback so that everyone feels invested." She mimics his deep voice before laughing. "He'd make a great professor."

"He's just stressed these days."

"No, no, I'm serious. He's great. I should be taking notes or whatever 'cause that's how to do it. I can't even be bothered to send an email when I've got a new idea. I just dive right in and expect everyone else to catch up. It's how my mind works, but it's gotten me in trouble before."

"He's had a lot of practice," I say. "Public speaking doesn't come naturally to him. He calls it a necessary evil."

"Amen." Aunt Callum glances back at Lemon who's mewling incessantly from the middle seat. "By the way, I've cleared out a whole section of the house for you two. You'll have your privacy, and Miss Kitty here will have plenty of room to run around."

"Is that the basement?" I ask.

"It is indeed and let me not embellish that fact. But you'll love it, Bea. I promise. Abe and I had it finished over the summer and there's heat and everything down there. Even a good view. I'd move our bed down in a second if Abe weren't so attached to his observatory. God. Let me tell you, that man's heart belongs to the heavens."

"Dad mentioned you'd had a lot of work done," I say.

"Did we ever! But it was *such* a pain getting approval

from the state. You could make a Netflix series about the bureaucracy I've dealt with. Like a real whodunnit. But in the end, they came through, and the house is gorgeous. Top to bottom. Wait until you see the kitchen, Bea. You'll die. It's perfect. You haven't even been out since . . . well, I don't remember when."

I think back. "Was it my dad's birthday?"

"Maybe." Aunt Callum kind of bops her head, and suddenly I feel awful because that was all the way back in May. Nearly six months ago. And I mean, yes, it's a thirty-minute drive into the mountains to get to their place, and yes, it's far from absolutely anything and Aunt Callum works in Cabot Cove anyway, so it's not like we don't get to see her. But I'm fairly certain she knows these aren't the reasons keeping us away. She's not the reason, either, and I'm sure she knows that, too.

Once we're out of Cabot Cove, Aunt Callum turns inland, heading over the coastal hills and dipping down into the tree- and boulder-lined valleys. It's colder away from the water, and I spot what looks like frost on the ground in a few places where the sun won't reach. For a while we drive through this sort of liminal space between coast and countryside, where craggy volcanic remnants rear and twist from the ground like spokes on a dragon's back.

Soon we're heading into the mountains again. Higher, this time. Fire Mountain, where we're going, is one of the tallest peaks in Maine, with views to the ocean and all the way down to Massachusetts on a clear day. Lake Paloma sits two-thirds of the way up, and was once glacier fed, although now snowpack feeds it. The wildlife reserve has done its job, and on any given day out here you're apt to spot bears, moose, wildcats, beavers, and more. Only bow hunting and fishing are allowed, both by permit only.

We haven't passed any vehicles for at least five miles by the time Aunt Callum slows the Subaru and turns onto a fire road marked PERMITTED VEHICLES ONLY. This is a private entrance to the reserve; the public entrance, which takes visitors to the lake and campground, is another mile or so up the road. There's also a small village of cabins up there that are occupied by seasonal hires. It's also a spot where visitors can purchase parking permits, firewood, gas, and other supplies.

As senior warden, however, Uncle Abe has the luxury of living in separate housing, and before long that house comes into view. Owned by the state, it's a spectacular piece of property—a large lodge-style structure with two stories' worth of balconies and a unique geodesic dome on the top. Built right on the edge of a canyon, the views from the dome—especially the sunsets—are stunning. Like something out of a photography book.

"Home sweet home," Aunt Callum says.

I turn to look at her. "You're hosting Thanksgiving this year, right? Everyone will be over to see the new renovations then."

Callum loves holidays, which has always surprised me. One part of her is all rebel and punk rock, but then she's got a whole bag of decorations that she drags out for *Groundhog's*

Day, of all days. And hosting Thanksgiving is kind of a big deal. But when I mention it, her jaw tightens and her brow furrows ever so slightly, as she guides the car over a suspension-rattling pothole and up their home's unpaved driveway.

"Are you not looking forward to it?" I ask as she stops and sets the parking brake.

"That's not it." Aunt Callum unclips her seat belt and opens the driver's side door. Mountain air rushes in, cold and raucous. "I just wish my parents could come out for once. It'd mean a lot to me."

"Why can't they?"

"Arizona is far," she says.

"But you've gone to them."

She shrugs. "Well, my sister is there with her family, and my folks have this thing about needing to be home every holiday, and they're super inflexible with it. I'm not sure if it's about wanting me to come back or disapproving of my having left in the first place. Either way, the end result is that I don't get to see them unless we go there."

"I'm sorry," I say. "That stinks."

"Stubborn runs in the family, I guess."

"Maybe they just like warm weather?" I offer.

"That they do," she agrees, turning around to look as Lemon starts up with the mewling again. "Oh boy. We'd better get her inside."

✕ ✕ ✕

Crossing the threshold into their mountainside home, I feel a twinge of guilt as it dawns on me that I've just consoled my aunt about her family not visiting right after blowing off the fact that Dad and I haven't been around either.

Did she do that on purpose?

"Oh, it's *beautiful*!" I stop suddenly, cat carrier pressed tight against my chest, and take in the newly remodeled space. Everything is so bright now. Stepping past the entryway I can see that the fresh paint and restored wood detailing fill the house with natural light and warmth. To the right, three steps lead down to a large wood-paneled room with a high vaulted ceiling and cathedral windows that illuminate what would otherwise be a dark and dreary space. Known as Thoreau Hall, this room is essentially its own wing of the house. It's often used for formal Department of Inland Fisheries and Wildlife events, so my aunt and uncle have limited say in how it's decorated.

What's here is sort of a stately marvel, a space filled with large antique rugs, sun-faded leather couches, and a massive stone fireplace. The hearth is at least twelve feet wide and whenever it's roaring, my morbid mind envisions a child or two tumbling in. In the more predictable category, various hunting trophies and stuffed wildlife are staged around the room—a moose head, a couple of stuffed foxes, a red-tailed hawk, and most alarmingly, a looming brown bear posed at full stature with its paws raised not unlike an advancing mummy or the lurching walk of Frankenstein's monster.

After a thorough inspection, I follow Aunt Callum through a quaint sitting room and into the kitchen. This part of the house looks completely different. I kind of can't believe it's the same place. Old linoleum floors, rotting cabinetry, and Formica counters have been replaced with earthy ceramic tiles, warm cherry and glass cabinets, and glittering stone countertops that feel as if the materials were mined straight from the surrounding environment.

"Where's Uncle Abe?" I ask.

Aunt Callum's at the fridge, pouring two glasses of water from the in-door dispenser. She hands me one, which I gulp down gratefully.

"Working," she says.

"On a Sunday?"

She arches a brow. "Have you ever known him to take a break?"

"I guess not."

"He and Fritz are working on the bike trails out in the west end. Trying to get everything finished before the snow comes, hence the Sunday work hours. Apparently people out here actually mountain bike in the winter? It's, like, a *thing*."

I grin. "Anything you can do in summer, people in Maine will do in the winter."

"I suppose." Aunt Callum glances around. "I should show you where you're staying. That cat probably wants to get out, huh?"

"Probably. You're not sneezing yet, though. That's good."

"I took a pill earlier. Otherwise my eyes would be swollen shut."

"Oh," I say.

"Come on." She sets her glass down and leads me through

the kitchen to a second hallway that's got a combination boot and laundry room. Past that is a door with a staircase leading down into the basement.

It's a steep walk and I grip the banister as I go. When we reach the bottom and turn the corner, my aunt flips on an overhead light and announces: "Ta-da!"

I gaze around in awe. This is the best surprise of all. Last time I was down here the basement was filled with spiders and piles of rotting wood. But fresh drywall, thick carpet, new windows, and modern furniture have turned it into a spacious in-law unit. There's a compact living room area outfitted with a television and desk, plus a separate bedroom and full bath. The walls have been painted a soft aquatic blue and they're adorned with framed prints of Callum's beloved fish and other sea life.

"I had no idea it would look like this. It's incredible." I lean down to let the cat out and she promptly darts under the bed. Aunt Callum gives her a nervous look but says nothing.

"I'll let you unpack," she says. "Your uncle should be back in a couple hours. Sunset at the latest. Or you can go out and meet him if you want. It's maybe a ten-minute walk at most. He'd love to see you."

"You sure?" I ask.

"Of course, silly. Are you kidding? He's thrilled that you're here."

"Thrilled?"

"For him, anyway. Come back up when you're ready. I'll show you where to find him on the map. It's not far."

10

DARKNESS COMES EARLY THESE DAYS, ever since we set the clocks back, so I don't linger. After getting Lemon settled, figuring out how to connect to the Wi-Fi, and changing into real clothes that aren't slobby sweats, I head out on the trails—Aunt Callum's detailed map in hand—to meet up with my uncle.

Following the Granger Trail, which moves away from Lake Paloma and into higher elevation, the water soon comes into view beneath me. The lake's maybe a quarter mile away, and as I stare down at its cool green water, those vast fathoms ringed by trees and craggy sections of beach and sparkling with late-day sunlight, it's hard not to wonder if Eden walked this same path.

It's likely that she did, although I haven't mapped the exact route taken by the Broadmoor group. I do know that they came in and out of the lower trail leading into Lake Paloma, which would intersect here at some point. There's also a steeper route at the far end of the lake that connects back up to the same trail at a higher elevation point; however, that's not the one they took.

I try and picture what that day might've looked like. We're not in the Rockies or anything, but Fire Mountain tops out at close to five thousand feet. In April, its ridge trail would've been a blustery hike. Challenging, too. I'm not close to the peak, but coming from sea level, I feel the difference in my lung capacity, in how quickly I work up a sweat.

But how do you lose someone? Did the group stay close together or did they fan out? I've seen plenty of photos of Eden. They were all over the internet after she vanished. She was a small girl, slightly built, with olive skin, deep-set eyes, and stringy dark hair that she wore parted in the middle. Usually dressed in oversized T-shirts and pleated skirts, Eden had the plain looks and presence of a girl who'd easily fade into the background of any photo, the one who could maybe convince you she hadn't been there in the first place. Eden appeared destined to be described as a "friend of a friend," or "that girl in math class." Never the protagonist, never the lead even in her own story. Not until her disappearance.

Until her death.

Last month, I'd been surprised when Leisl painted an entirely different picture of Eden than the one I'd crafted based on statements from her family and friends. Leisl and Eden had been roommates, a reality I still have a hard time envisioning. In my mind, Leisl resides in a whole different universe; she's all classic beauty and old money and good New England breeding—her father's a famous constitutional law professor at Yale, and her mother's a renowned photo-journalist. But Leisl was fond of Eden, and rather than the shy, owl-eyed asthmatic of the news stories, she described to me a vibrant girl who was both passionate and intensely driven. Eden, she told me, had a hunger for knowledge and art and love, even. She'd relished her blossoming romance with Carlos, and in addition to being the girl driven by music and art and science, she also enjoyed serenading her new boyfriend by flute in the grassy meadow behind their boarding school.

What else didn't I know about her, this girl who'd made every effort to live her life so fully? Who put my own life to shame. *Had* she been athletic? Was she drawn to physical challenge and adventure? Hiking at this elevation would've been a far cry from playing flute in a field of wildflowers—especially given her lung issues—but perhaps she'd come on the trip for other reasons. I know Carlos hadn't been there that day, but maybe Eden had come on the hike with other friends. Other people who cared for her. Or inspired her.

But then how did she vanish?

And how did no one notice that she was gone for the entire trip back to Broadmoor? Surely, the group must've stopped for water along the way. Or snacks. Or to take in the view. *Something.*

The more I think about it, the less sense it all makes. I pull my phone out, eager to search for the names of the two suspended teachers, to see if they'd ever given any further explanation for the oversight. Only there's no cell service out here in the reserve, which is frustrating.

As instructed, I follow along a narrow stream, a trickling

offshoot of the main river, as the trail I'm on dips and rises before intersecting with a paved bike trail that runs parallel to a remote parking lot that's for day use only. Peering through the brush and trees, I spy maybe three cars parked in the shade. In the summer it would be packed, but we're in that dead zone of activity that falls between the end of leaf-peeping season and the full brunt of winter. Once the snowpack builds up, us Mainers will be back out here with our snowshoes, cross-country skis, and yes, even our mountain bikes.

Just as I've passed the parking lot, a raspy whisper of wind crests the hillside from behind me, whipping up and through the bare trees before stirring up the fallen leaves that litter the ground. With a shiver, I look over my shoulder, craning my neck and peering down the fire trail, but there's nothing. There's no one.

Facing forward once again, I push my legs to move faster. I know I'm alone, but once a thought enters my mind, it's easy to spiral with it, to surrender to the death grip of possibility of *what-if, what-if, what-if.* But at least I'm self-aware enough to know it's my own mind that's freaking me out. That no one else is doing that for me.

Except, my mind whispers, *whoever mailed that package referencing your mother's death.*

And left that foreboding card.

That someone knows where you live.

And whomever they are, they want you to know . . .

You're next.

"Uncle Abe!"

Relief courses through me as my uncle appears. I come over a rise in the trail, surrounded by dappled shadows and mossy ferns, and as I step into sunlight, he's suddenly right there, just a few yards away in the shade. I'd know my uncle's silhouette anywhere; he's built like my father. Uncle Abe's a shade taller than he is, with broader shoulders, but he's still rangy through the hips and legs. And despite his physicality and strength—much of his job involves manual labor—there's an almost cautious languor to his movements. As if he's always anticipating the worst. But for now, he straightens up, sets down the pickaxe he's holding, and waves to me.

I bound forward, buoyed by the sudden restoration of safety. For as odd as my uncle can be, I'm no longer alone. Uncle Abe's black truck with the blue-and-red department seal painted on its side is parked about twenty yards up the road from where he's standing, and just past that, I spot Fritz Romero, a junior warden who moved up here last winter. Fritz is originally from Mississippi, and he hates the snow, but he also hates the heat, so he's perpetually unsatisfied. I like him, though. He's only a few years out of college, and, like me, he's multiracial—a mix of Black, Italian, and Thai, he says—giving us a shared reference point of understanding.

When I reach him, my uncle gives me a hug, wrapping me in his long arms and lifting me into the air. I hug him back, feeling muscles and sweat through his long-sleeved shirt. But there's also a weariness to him, and guilt surges through me for not visiting more, for not wanting to be around what my father calls *his moods*. Why do we judge people by their worst moments? Gazing up at my uncle, with his gaunt cheeks, bearded chin, and deep-set dark eyes, I resolve to make the most of my time out here in the mountains. Family is everything to me.

It's all I have.

"How ya doing, darling?" Uncle Abe deposits me gently on the ground. I turn and wave wildly at Fritz who grins and waves back.

"Good to see you, kid!" he calls out. "You bring your mountain bike with you?"

"Absolutely not," I say.

"You gotta borrow one then. We'll take you out one of these days. Something easy. We've been working on these trails for months."

"We'll see."

"How's Frankie doing?" Uncle Abe asks, and if my dad feels his brother is prone to nomadic bouts of avoidance, both emotionally and physically, then my uncle's critique of my father is that he's work obsessed because it's the only thing in his life that makes him feel in control.

"He's good," I say. "He's in charge of some new project at the office. He's probably told you about it."

Uncle Abe gives a noncommittal grunt.

"How's it going out here?" I ask. "Aunt Callum says you're building single track."

He nods and swipes an arm across his forehead. "We're

about four weeks behind schedule. Unfortunately, the rocks didn't come in until this week and I still need to order more."

"Rocks?" I echo.

He points to a mound of bowling ball–sized rocks that are heaped on the far side of the truck. "For erosion control."

"Cool," I say.

"If you want to ride on the completed portion, I'm sure Cal's got a bike you can borrow. We'll find you something."

"I'm terrible on a bike," I tell him.

"I thought you rode one to school."

"But that's on the street," I say. "No jumps or rocks. I'm not ready to die."

"Glad to hear it." He sighs and looks around. "You know, we're just about done for the day. You mind riding along with me? I need to take Fritz back to the village, then I'm heading home."

"Sure thing." I help them load the tools into the back of the work truck before crawling into the middle of the bench seat.

The drive through the woods is jiggly and slow, the truck inching its way over soft loam. The view's beautiful. Everything's shaded and lined with ferns. It's an odd contrast, though, to the inside of the truck where I'm wedged between my uncle's stoic silence and Fritz's jaunty banter.

"See that? Over there? We put it in over the summer." Fritz points toward the passenger side window and I lean and see a narrow suspension bridge spanning a steep ravine, landing on the opposite side where the single-track bike trail picks up again.

"Can you really ride across it?" I ask.

"I personally wouldn't, but yeah, people do. Wild, huh?"

Once we're out of the woods, Uncle Abe guides us from the fire road and onto the intrastate. It's another mile or so until we reach the turnoff for the campground entrance and the small warden village, and on the way, Fritz recounts a story about some guys who came out to ride in August with their brand-new gear and eight-thousand-dollar bikes. They didn't want to stay on the groomed trails and went up into the mountains where the talus slopes and slate rock faces are notoriously unstable. Two crashed coming down the back-side of Fire Mountain and the third left them behind when the terrain got too challenging.

"Your uncle had to locate them by drone and send a helicopter in to rescue them. Guess how much it cost?"

"The helicopter?" I ask.

Fritz grins. "Yeah."

"Five thousand dollars?"

"Try forty-five."

"For the rescue?"

He nods. "They got billed for every dollar. That should teach them some respect for Mother Nature."

"Would you ever want to do that?" I ask. "Search and rescue training? Kind of sounds more exciting than building bike trails."

Fritz looks bashful. "Nah. That's for the adrenaline junkies. I just want to be outside, working with my hands, keeping the world—or at least a small part of it—beautiful and accessible."

"I like that," I say.

"Me too. Abe'll never tell you this, but we've actually had a good season out here. Me, especially. I met this great girl—"

"Here we are," my uncle interjects gruffly as the truck rumbles to a stop. I look up and realize we've reached the warden village, with its small general store, gas station, and horseshoe cluster of rustic cabins.

After sliding out, Fritz waves and promises he'll come by for dinner later in the week. Then he slams the door shut. When he's gone, I turn to my uncle and ask, "Do you miss living out here? Like you used to?"

"Not at all," he says. "Why do you think I got married?"

I tilt my head. Is that a joke?

He looks over at me, his expression unreadable. "Would you want to take a walk around the lake? Not many people'll be out right now and it's something I like to do. It keeps me . . ."

"Keeps you what?"

"Here," he says.

11

WE PARK BY THE BOAT launch. The public campground is in the opposite direction, in a flat stretch of meadow to the east of the lake. But it's closed for the season and the only people around are two men on the pier who've got poles in the water. Dusk and dawn are the best times for fishing. Even I know that.

Gravel crunches underfoot as we walk from the truck toward the shoreline. In the distance, I spot a small Sunfish drifting in the breeze. With an almost three-mile perimeter, Lake Paloma's a good-sized body of water. Nestled in the crook of the Fire Mountain ascent, its core is ringed by giant boulders and thick groves of spruce and pine trees. The lake's also dammed at the far end, where spillover watershed feeds into the Paloma River and flows out to the valley. At its deepest, coldest point, Lake Paloma's close to sixty feet down. I know this because Aunt Callum told me. And she would know. She studies and cares for the lake, completing yearly counts on the algae levels, as well as the freshwater mussels, trout, turtles, and other creatures.

Uncle Abe and I keep walking. The swimming area and snack shack sit silent. The platform raft's been pulled off the water, and signs are posted everywhere that warn: SWIM AT YOUR OWN RISK. NO LIFEGUARD ON DUTY.

There's zero chance of me getting into this lake, but I'm drawn to it, nonetheless. Walking close to the waterline, small waves churning against the rocks, my heart pounds in unison, knock-knock-knocking against my ribs. I inhale the rich evergreen scent of mud and decay, and is it irony or fate that's brought me here? To the same toenail sliver of a beach where Eden had eaten lunch on the day she disappeared?

Even I'm hard-pressed to believe it's a coincidence. How could it be? I was already obsessing over Eden and her potential connection to the tenace clue even before I learned my father was leaving town, that I'd be coming here.

Wasn't I?

I strain to remember, but details elude me. There's something in the thin mountain air that dulls my clarity. My ability to form answers from a multitude of questions. What do I really know other than the fact that Eden's dead and there are multiple people around me, all around me, who've been damaged by her passing? Who continue to feel the rippling effects of anguish and sorrow and grief in the wake of a young girl's life being snuffed out. But maybe there's nothing rare or profound in this.

Maybe it's just what tragedy is.

Closing my eyes, I breathe deeply and try to re-create the scene, the way it must've been for Eden on that day. April would've also been too cold for swimming, all that snowpack runoff, but that time of year, the shallows would've been filled with birds just back for the spring and ready for nesting. Egrets, herons, little black-billed ducks, all pecking and diving and digging for worms and minnows amid the lazy buzz of the dragonflies. It would've been paradise—green leaves unfurling on the trees, the earth and water both ripe with growth and abundance.

I let my eyes flutter open. Other than the lapping of the waves, everything's so *quiet,* but in a way that feels more like absence than tranquility. As if I'm standing in negative space. Then and now. Here and there. Mingled with the way the pinky late-day light's coloring the lake's surface, I can almost imagine I've slipped between universes, tumbling past some event horizon where I can almost see her. Hear her.

Know her truth.

"Over there." From beside me, Uncle Abe's sudden presence and hushed tone knocks me from my reverie, putting me on alert. I follow his outstretched arm, pointing to a rocky spot on the shore just ahead of us, maybe fifty yards away. I squint and through the shadowy marshland reeds, I'm able to make out the dark shape of a bushy-haired creature as it pads to the water's edge and dips its muzzle for a drink.

"A coyote?" I whisper.

"Gray fox," he replies. "See those red highlights she's got on her chin and tail?"

I nod.

"That's how you tell the difference. Also, the gray ones climb trees. They're almost more cat than dog. Here. Take these." He hands me a small pair of high-end digital binoculars he must've fished from his jacket pocket.

I zoom in on the fox. She doesn't notice us and stands calm, still, with her tongue out, her tail down, just taking in the view.

My heart soars.

Right then an explosive *crack!* rings out from across the lake, ricocheting wildly off the rock walls and bouncing through the canyon. The gray fox bolts and I leap back in surprise as my uncle grabs for the binoculars, fumbling, pulling them from my grasp.

"What is it?" I ask breathlessly. "Was that a gun?"

"No." After a moment of inspection, Uncle Abe stands up and waves both arms over his head to someone on the other side of the lake. "It's fine. Everything's fine. There's nothing to worry about."

I scowl. "How can you know that?"

"Here." He hands the binoculars back. "See that house across the way? The one on stilts that's partly over the water?"

It takes a moment, but I finally see what he's talking about. "Okay."

"Guy on the side there's working on his truck and just blew a tire. He's lucky he's okay, but he gave me a thumbs-up. Should be all right."

I gape. "You mean he could've *died*?"

"Absolutely. That's a lot of force."

I hold the binoculars up again, giving the homes on the opposite side of the lake one last sweep. It takes me a second, but I finally land on the last house on the far north end— the old cabin I'd approached with the search party, led by

Deputy Williams. From what I'm able to make out, the place is more overgrown than ever, brush and trees leaning right up against the structure, the drive completely covered with weeds.

"Hey, who owns that one?" I ask "The very last house. The old cabin with the screened-in porch?"

Uncle Abe clears his throat. "You talking about the old Vaughn place? Why do you want to know about that?"

"Does someone live there?"

"Not really. No. Doesn't exactly belong to anyone anymore."

"How does that work?"

"Well, the last heir of Sigurd Vaughn passed a while ago. He built the cabin but ownership's been wrapped up in litigation for years now. House sits in a trust, and to the best of my knowledge, it's been managed by some national company. They rent it out in the spring and summer months to make a little money to pay for upkeep. Which never happens. But essentially, no one person owns that house at the moment. It's in limbo."

"You seem to know a lot about it." Handing the binoculars back, I feel a little stunned. This is probably the most I've ever heard my uncle say at one time.

He frowns. "I know about all these houses. But you still haven't told me why you're interested in this particular one."

He's right, of course. "You remember that Broadmoor girl last year? The one who drowned?"

"Eden Vicente," he says somberly. "How could I forget?"

"Well, when I came out here to help with the search party, our group was supposed to search that property. The Vaughn one. We were with a sheriff's deputy, and he said we had permission from the owner. But when we got there, we weren't allowed on the property. We weren't allowed to look for a missing *girl*!"

My uncle blinks. Very quickly. "How strange."

"I'd call it suspicious."

"That, too." He gives a long sigh. "What happened with her—that girl—it's one of my biggest regrets."

I stare at him. "How so?"

"I wish . . ." He stops himself. "It wouldn't have changed the outcome, but I wish I'd done some things differently at the outset."

"What are your other regrets?" I ask.

Uncle Abe offers me a flash of a smile, one that shows his teeth and fails to reach his eyes and whose message is glaringly clear.

Back off.

"You ready to head back?" he asks me.

"Sure thing," I say.

✕ ✕ ✕

He's silent for most of the ride back. I stare out the truck window, head craned east, watching as dusk rides in, leaving the sky purple and pink and thick with haze. It's my least favorite time of day, sundown. It's too claustrophobic. Too final.

"How's your column?" my uncle asks abruptly. "You haven't written anything in a while."

I whip my head up. "You've read it?"

"Sure."

"Well, that's good to know. Dad says he reads it, but I know he doesn't. He's too busy."

"I'm sure he wants to."

"I don't think it's his thing."

"Frankie's never been the sort to read for pleasure," Uncle Abe says. "Not even as a kid."

"Really?"

"He used to check out engineering books from the library, just to figure out how things worked."

"Pretty sure that is pleasure for him," I say.

"I was the bookworm," Uncle Abe says. "I loved science fiction and fantasy. And I read everything Aunt Jess wrote. I still do. I'll read everything you write, too."

"Thanks," I say. "But you're not obligated to do that."

"I know I'm not obligated."

I bite my lip. "I want to write more. But I've been stuck, lately. Not knowing what to write about. It's kind of gotten into my head."

"I see."

"You got any suggestions?" I ask. "A good mystery from the past that I could dig into?"

I don't expect an answer, and for a moment, Uncle Abe is silent. It's a silence that stretches on and on until I rest my head against the window and let my eyelids droop. I can only assume he's checked out of our conversation and is currently daydreaming about dropping me off, then driving to the ends of the earth. Chasing catastrophes. Finding solace in ruin.

"I might know of something," he says finally.

"Oh yeah?"

He tightens his grip on the steering wheel. "I'll tell you about it, if you want. I'll tell you everything I know. But I don't want my name mentioned when you write about it. Is that okay? People who know will know it's me, but . . . still."

"Of course." I lift my head. "That's not a problem."

"You promise?"

"My journalistic integrity depends on it," I say. But when I see he's still concerned. "Yes, you've got my word."

Uncle Abe sort of rubs his chin and moves his jaw, like he's chewing air and what he's just agreed to is the last thing he actually wants to do. The turn onto the private road is up ahead, and he brakes gently, easing the truck off the highway and bouncing onto dirt. But rather than continuing on toward home, he pulls over in a cloud of dust and turns the engine off.

We sit in the cab's darkness.

"It's not a nice thing." He reaches up to flip on the cab's overhead light.

"What's not nice?" I ask.

"The story I'm going to tell you."

"You're going to tell me right *now*?"

He frowns. "Callum wouldn't want to hear it. She knows, of course, but it's ugly stuff."

I fumble for my phone, my voice recorder. "Can I turn this on? Is that okay?"

"Sure."

"Whenever you're ready." I hit record and Uncle Abe grimaces at the flashing red light but then turns to stare out the front windshield. The headlights are still on and bugs are swarming in an orangey glow.

"I didn't realize this would be so hard," he says. "I don't know where to start."

"Start at the beginning," I suggest.

"I'm not sure I know what that is."

"Is this a story you heard from someone else?" I venture.

"No," he says. "I was there. Not when it happened, but when they came for him. I was actually there. I saw it."

"But what happened? What is this about?"

Uncle Abe sort of shudders, then shuts his eyes.

"We don't have to do this now," I tell him.

"It's the Sousa murders," he says. "I was there when they arrested him."

TRUEMAINE.COM
Home Page for the State of Maine . . . and Murder . . .

"Of Rabbits and Men"

I read *Watership Down* two years after my mother died. Maybe if that hadn't already happened, I would have been more upset by Richard Adams's story of life as a prey animal. The message that there's more death than living when you're a rabbit. Survival is brutal and rare and desperate, which is the reason rabbits have so many babies. There's more death than living because everyone and everything is out to get you.

I knew what death was when I read the book. I understood it was final and inevitable and the way that all life will end. And I also knew the ways in which grief can wield its own power. How it can damage our capacity to love and hold joy.

What I didn't know then was that in a world of cancer and accidents and illnesses, there are humans who prey on their own.

Not for survival or for resources.

For sport.

I know this now, as someone who's drawn to write about the horrors people inflict on one another. Yet every once in a while, I come across an event so heinous and dark that it's difficult to process. What follows is an account of one such event, as well as my own struggle to understand it. Fair warning: Please read with care.

The Sousa Murders

In the late nineties, an ambitious and accomplished woman named Dr. Alexia Trenta-Sousa was hired as the new dean of students at Broadmoor Academy. At the time, the decision was revolutionary in ways that might feel less significant today. With a PhD from Berkeley, Dr. Trenta-Sousa was brought in to revitalize the culture of an uninspired prep school that had become bogged down by mediocrity.

Right from the start, Dr. Trenta-Sousa worked to update the school's nondiscrimination clause to include sexual orientation, to hire more diverse staff, and to expand the literary curriculum beyond the great books of Western civilization. Unsurprisingly, Dr. Trenta-Sousa's presence caused pushback from some older alumni and parents. But she was also hailed as a visionary—someone who could lead the ailing school into the next millennium.

Dr. Trenta-Sousa also had the charisma to sell her vision. The daughter of Portuguese immigrants, she was worldly, well educated, charming, and she was also family oriented. When she moved into campus housing, Dr. Trenta-Sousa was joined by her devoted husband, Daniel, and their three young children: Eva, Dan Jr., and baby Roberto. Daniel took on a lot of the childcare responsibilities, but as someone who enjoyed working with his hands, he was also hired as the Broadmoor facilities manager. During the summer, this meant he oversaw a small group of student workers who repaired and moved furniture, painted dorm rooms, and completed other odd jobs around campus.

After completing their first school year at Broadmoor, the young family took a vacation over Fourth of July weekend to the Trenta family cabin in northern California, near Lake Tahoe. After the holiday, Daniel Sousa returned to Maine alone and told his work crew that his family would be continuing their vacation for another week.

No one reported anything out of the ordinary, and things seemed normal for Daniel until the cops showed up six days later to arrest him. It turned out Dr. Trenta-Sousa's parents had arrived at their cabin that day only to discover the decomposing bodies of their daughter and three young grandchildren. It wasn't much of a whodunnit; all four victims had been brutally bludgeoned in the cabin's living room, and a sledgehammer tossed in the bushes outside had Daniel's fingerprints all over it.

× × ×

From the outside this seems like an open-and-shut case: Daniel quickly confessed and was extradited back to California, where he pled guilty to four counts of murder. The only question was whether he would receive the death sentence or life in prison. Daniel did not testify on his own behalf. However, at the sentencing hearing, his defense attorney attempted to enter a letter into the evidence. Signed anonymously, this letter insisted that Daniel had been targeted by an unknown group prior to the murders. This group was not named or identified but was described in the letter as a "secret organization dedicated to restoring honor to the greater Broadmoor community."

With no way of verifying the contents, the letter was rejected by the court, and the judge sentenced Daniel Sousa to death. To this day, he remains housed in San Quentin's death row. He has never appealed his conviction and to my knowledge, he's never spoken to anyone about what happened.

However, someone else is now speaking about the events of that summer. Someone with firsthand knowledge of Daniel Sousa's actions in the weeks leading up to the murders and the days immediately after. This individual, who spoke with TrueMaine on the condition of anonymity, reports that Daniel had been growing increasingly paranoid and distraught. He told multiple people that he was being followed and that he'd been "formally targeted and marked" for harassment by a group he called the "Honor Guard." He also stated that his wife couldn't be trusted, and that he feared dangerous messages were being sent to him via radio and television waves.

My source also told me they assumed Daniel Sousa was either having a psychotic break, which led him to murder his family, or he was setting the groundwork for an insanity plea. However, after learning of Sousa's confession and knowing he'd be locked up with no chance for parole, the distinction ceased to matter. There was no reason for them to come forward with any of this information.

Until now.

My source says that after reading my article on the Seacrest HOA and learning how that group had worked in secret to influence Cabot Cove's political landscape, they got to wondering if Sousa's "Honor Guard" might be a real thing that exists within our community. Maybe a real thing whose intentions were distorted and misunderstood by a sick man's mind, but real nonetheless.

So here's my question: Has anyone heard of such an organization? And what do you think of the letter to the lawyer and the behavior our source claims to have witnessed? Is there more to Daniel Sousa's story? Or is he simply a monster?

Or both?

Until next time, stay safe and be kind. And watch out for each other.

—Bea

12

DEPUTY WILLIAMS IS WAITING FOR me when I arrive at school the next morning. Aunt Callum drops me off at the end of the block, and as I walk toward campus, I see him standing at the main gate, arms folded, dressed in full uniform.

"You're a brave kid, Bea," he says as I approach. In the morning chill, he's got his shearling jacket on and his nose is pink, and his eyes are, too. He's not that much taller than I am, I realize, and I'm not tall at all.

"Late night?" I ask, but he just cocks his head in confusion. "Never mind. What am I brave about?"

"What do you think?" He holds up his phone with his web browser open to the column I posted last night on TrueMaine and lets out a low whistle. "Have you looked at the comments? You're getting roasted."

"I am?" A knot forms in the pit of my stomach. "What are they saying?"

"Um, well, the ones without four letter words say things like 'The devil doesn't need an advocate' and 'Why are you apologizing for a man who killed babies in cold blood?' Those are the nicer sentiments." He puts the phone down and tries meeting my gaze. "This post is not what I meant about keeping a low profile. Oh, and I got your text, you know. About what went down at your house."

"Oh, right. That." I shiver but can't help but look around. We're standing in the middle of first-period traffic flow. Waves of students are streaming by, and it feels like everyone's going out of their way to shoot me looks of unconcealed disdain.

"Tell me what happened," he says. "With the tarot card."

I tug at my backpack straps. It feels so long ago. "My neighbor Evie Ranier saw it on her security camera. It was Sunday morning."

"Does she still have the footage?"

"I don't know. You can ask her. But you can't even see anything. Whoever it was wore a ski mask."

"Did you notice anything else?"

I shake my head.

"What did your father say?"

"Nothing. He doesn't know."

The deputy's eyes bulge. "You haven't told him?"

"I don't want to bother him. He's traveling."

"It's not optional. You need to tell him or I will. Today. Have him call me to update the police report."

I groan. "Fine. *God*. I wouldn't have told you in the first place if I knew you'd be so uptight about it."

His face clouds with frustration. "You should be *thanking* me, Bea. My being uptight means I'm making sure this is taken seriously. Which is how you should take it. Someone's trying to scare you. For reasons we don't know yet."

"Well, you're getting info in return for your efforts, so don't act like this is charity."

"Are you kidding right now?" he asks. "Are you really this dense?"

"And just so we're even, you should know I learned some new information about the lake cabin. The one we couldn't search." I quickly recount my uncle's description of the cabin's ownership, the fact that it's in limbo, and that a national firm is responsible for overseeing rental contracts and maintenance.

"What was the name of the family?" he asks.

"Vaughn."

"Interesting," he says. "Okay, I'll look into it again. This might help."

"I can help look, too."

"That's not necessary."

"Oh, so you're still pretending you're actually worried for my well-being?"

"I *am* worried," he insists. "Not just about whoever's leaving this stuff, but about *you*. You act like you're so anxious and doom and gloom all the time, when really it's a story you're telling yourself to excuse your own recklessness. That's the worst kind of self-destruction there is. The kind you're in denial about."

"What would you know about self-destruction?" I snap.

"A lot," he says.

I bite my cheek and look over at a group of senior girls. One flips me off. "Yeah, well, you've managed to ruin my high school reputation in all of five minutes."

"Pretty sure *you* did that," he says. "Look, I'd better go."

"Lot of crime to chase in Cabot Cove?"

"Why do you think I'm here?" he asks.

"I thought *I* was why."

"Unfortunately, that's not the case. Someone vandalized your school last night. But seeing as you've got an alibi, I'll assume you had nothing to do with it."

"Vandalized?" I ask.

He nods. "Hose got put into one of the computer labs. Ruined thousands of dollars' worth of equipment. Plus, whoever did it took off with some nice new iPads. Oh, and a bunch of stuff from the theater department was set on fire in the parking lot. Teachers are pretty upset. It's not a good look."

I gape. "That happened *here*?"

"Don't look so shocked. It can happen anywhere. There's nothing special about Cabot Cove. Heck, you just got finished writing about a quadruple murderer living up at fancy-pants Broadmoor. So watch your back, okay?"

I open my mouth to ask more questions, but the first-period bell rings before I get the words out.

"Go on." Deputy Williams makes a scooting motion at me, like I'm a kitten he needs to corral. "You don't want to get caught up in the tardy sweep. Principal told me they're doing them all this week."

"They are?"

He nods.

I turn and run.

× × ×

I reach my US history class right as the second bell rings. Sliding into my desk near the back of the room, I'm sweating, breathing hard, but I've made it.

The boy who sits one seat over, Ivan Sussman, stares at me with his mouth kind of open.

"What?" I hiss. Class isn't close to starting; Ms. Haskins is up front fumbling around with the projector again. Technology is not her strong suit. "Yes, I was talking to a cop earlier. And no, it's none of your business."

Ivan keeps staring, and I know him obviously, because I'm friends with his sister Roo. Or *Evie's* friends with her, really, so we're friends by association. But anyway, Ivan and Roo, along with their sister, Marin, make up our school's only set of triplets.

"You're being rude," I snap. "I can see you looking at me."

Ivan leans closer, filling the space between our desks. He's a tall boy, with a soft build and a full head of thick brown curls. "My grandpa says you don't know what you're talking about. Like, at all."

I turn my head. "What do you mean?"

"That article you wrote. He says you got it all wrong."

"Because he thinks I'm making excuses for a killer? That wasn't my intent."

Ivan arches an eyebrow. "Kind of sounded like it was."

"Great. Thank you."

"But that's not what Grandpa was saying."

I sigh. "So what did he say?"

"He said that that woman, the one who died, she was a real—" Ivan catches himself, licks his lips. "He didn't use a nice word to describe her."

"You mean Dr. Trenta-Sousa? The woman who was *murdered*?"

"I guess. Grandpa says he knew of a lot of people who would've wanted to bash her head in if they'd had the chance. Probably applied to the husband, too."

My jaw drops. "He actually said that?"

"All right, let's bring our attention to the front of the class," Ms. Haskins calls out as she claps her hands. The projector's finally working and her slideshow on the Gilded Age is up. "Who can tell me what one of the four primary conflicts were in this period of American history? Beatrice?"

I groan. Teachers have a real sixth sense for when you haven't done the reading. I rack my brain for anything I can remember, but all that comes to mind is *The Great Gatsby,* only not the book, the movie version with Leonardo DiCaprio that had Jay-Z on the soundtrack. Panicked, I glance over at Ivan from the corner of my eye. He's scribbling what looks like a light bulb in his notebook then points vigorously at it.

"Thomas Edison!" I exclaim.

Ms. Haskins shakes her head. "I asked for conflicts."

Ivan's hand shoots up. "Wealth inequality?"

"Very good, Mr. Sussman. Anyone else? Elise?" Ms. Haskins moves on, but I turn and glare at Ivan for giving me the wrong answer. Although now I see that he's written the word *industrialization* below the light bulb, so that's on me.

"Thanks for trying," I whisper.

Ivan doesn't answer, but I take his cue and scrawl a message in my own notebook, then sort of angle it in his direction.

You think I could talk with your grandfather?
About what you mentioned?

Ivan responds once Ms. Haskins switches to the next slide.

I'LL SEE WHAT I CAN DO.

Then:

DON'T TELL ROO.

I frown at this, and Ivan writes:

HE'S GOT DEMENTIA.
EARLY STAGE BUT SHE GETS PROTECTIVE.

Oh dear. That's unfortunate, but I mouth *thank-you* to Ivan just as the school's alarm system goes off, sending a whooping alert blaring from the loudspeaker and causing everyone to jump up at once.

"That's the fire alarm," Ms. Haskins yells. "Everyone outside! Remember to line up by room number."

"Are you sure it's for fires?" someone calls out. "What if it's a shooter?"

Ms. Haskins, who's barely five feet tall, hesitates before shaking her permed head. "No. That's not right. Intruder alarm is different. That's the fire alarm. It definitely is."

Bright lights begin flashing inside the classroom, illuminating the exits we're meant to move toward. We gather our belongings as Ms. Haskins continues to shout instructions: "Stay calm! Meet in the practice field and await further instructions! No running or pushing!"

Sarah Steinmeyer, who's closest, pulls open the classroom door to reveal pure chaos in the hallway. People are running everywhere, in all directions.

"I don't smell anything," she says.

"Go!" Somebody pushes Sarah over the threshold and the rush is on; we're spilling into the hall with a momentum that would be impossible to stop even if we wanted to. Out here the siren's even louder, and it's an effective strategy—emitting a noise so piercing and irritating any hearing-capable person would instinctively flee the building to escape it.

"Ivan," I squeak, eager to continue our conversation, but my voice and my body are swallowed up by the crush. I'm carried along with the human current, rushing down the echoey stairwell and flowing out into a strangely warm November day.

"Line up! Line up!" Our vice principal is screaming into a megaphone and waving people toward the practice field at the back of the main classroom building. I continue moving with the crowd, although once I'm on the field, there are no lines at all. Everyone's clustered by the fence watching the fire engines roll onto campus.

"Their lights aren't even on," a voice behind me says. "It's a false alarm. They're just obligated to check."

I whirl around and see Dane, who is Roo Sussman's on-and-off girlfriend, and another friend of Evie's. Technically, yes, I'm friends with all of them, but Dane's the one I spend the least time with. Which isn't for lack of trying. She's wildly smart and has a dry sense of humor, but she holds her cards close. She's one of those people who treats their whole lives like a secret.

"I heard there was a break-in over the weekend," I say. "Maybe it has to do with that?"

"You're talking about in the theater?" She brushes back her bangs.

"And a computer room."

"It's all going to be extra work for me. I was supposed to lend some of our theater pieces out to Broadmoor for their play, and that's part of what was ruined. Not looking forward to explaining that scenario."

"I'm sorry," I say. "I actually know someone who's working on the set design up there. She'll be understanding."

"I don't need them to be understanding. I just need them to pay me to make new ones." Dane shrugs. "They should be good for it. Still, it's kind of a cursed day, though, huh?"

"Doesn't bode well."

She turns around, leaning her full weight back against the cyclone fence. "That's not all. Did you hear the news from the harbor?"

"What news?"

"I'm like the harbinger of doom today. Whole coastline's been shut down indefinitely as of eight a.m. this morning. No more shellfish for the rest of the season. No traps. Nothing."

My stomach drops. This is bad on a whole different level. "What happened?"

"Red tide," Dane says. "Pretty much unheard of this late in the year, which has the rumor mill going. Needless to say, both my uncles are going to be a barrel of fun at Thanksgiving next week. It's already been a bad season, so this is a real kicker. They can't afford this."

"Red tide," I echo and even I know how big a deal this is. November's the last month of the lobster season, and it's usually a big one with a food-centered holiday. Losing out on your last bit of income before a long winter and months off the water is beyond devastating. It's people's livelihoods. How they feed their families. How they stay warm in frigid Maine.

But the conspiratorial side of my mind notes both the color red and the mention of rumors. Because while toxic shellfish can't be conjured up for the purposes of a game, misinformation can. In both good faith.

And bad.

"I don't like this," I tell Dane. "Any of it."

She nods in agreement. "Like I said, this day is seriously cursed."

13

Riding the shuttle up to Broadmoor after classes get out feels lonely for reasons I can't explain. I am alone, as the sole passenger on a shuttle that's twisting its way through the bare trees and winding up the mountain. But I'm also going to see friends.

So why am I like this?

To pass the time, I pull my phone out, finally braving the comment section on my column. Ouch. Deputy Williams was not wrong when he said people hated it. I scroll through comment after comment, all expressing the same outraged sentiment of *How dare you?* And *You don't know what you're talking about.* Even *Only the devil would speak such evil into existence,* which feels a little silly since none of my words were spoken. But that's a technicality.

Oddly, though, a wave of relief comes over me as I read through the comments, negative as they are. They kind of run together and honestly, what are they going to do to me other than hurt my feelings? None are overtly threatening or personal, which is what I dread seeing the most. And I don't know. It's hard to explain, how much it consumes your world, the way you see *everything,* when someone tells you they want you dead. But by picking a completely new topic to write about, and a provocative one at that, it appears I haven't provoked my hater's wrath any further.

Thank goodness.

One comment does stand out, however. Rather than expressing outrage or righteousness, it simply reads: *You don't want to be doing this. Trust me. Ask Daniel. He would know.*

It's cryptic. But in a way that's less threat than warning. Like maybe the writer is referencing their own personal experience.

The frequency of the commenting trails off around mid-morning and this must be when the red-tide announcement got into wide circulation. News cycles and their attention spans. For once, though, I'm thankful for a distraction, even as I remain perplexed by the public's response to what I wrote.

Was it really that bad?

I shove my phone away as the shuttle rumbles through the Broadmoor gates and over a series of rattling speed bumps. Peering through the windows, the first thing I see is the spot where the boarding school's famous slate-roofed library once stood before it burned last month. My memories of the fire are vivid, wild. I can recall racing up here on my bike to meet with Leisl, only to find the building in ruins and her suffering from smoke inhalation. Leif had rescued her just in time.

He'd been furious with me. I remember that, too. He hated that I'd asked Leisl to help find Chrissy Lambert's boyfriend. And he hated that she'd said yes.

After, there was talk of a stranger in the library. Leisl said she'd seen him right before the fire broke out and then she ended up locked in a stairwell. Arson seemed likely, but after four weeks, nothing's been confirmed. At least according to Deputy Williams. I have to trust he's been honest.

What choice do I have?

The shuttle drops me off at a roundabout in the main parking lot, right in front of the admissions building. Thanking the driver, I step out onto the flagstone walkway and look around. The campus is vast and decentralized, with walking paths that fan in all directions, toward dorms, the athletic facilities, the dining hall, and more. But I'm not sure where I'm going.

"Boo!"

I whirl around to see Leisl grinning at me like a Cheshire cat, and I resist the urge to throw myself into her arms. It's not that I think she'd mind, but it's not in me to be bold, and so I stand and smile back awkwardly. And by the way, never let it be said that Leisl doesn't know how to make an entrance. It's Monday afternoon, and she's got her hair done up in girlish pigtails and she's wearing what looks like a suede-trimmed barn coat and gleaming black riding boots over leggings.

"Were you actually on a horse?" I ask.

Leisl's Cheshire grin grows wider. "There are no horses here, silly. Just wishes. You ready to get started on those clues?"

"Absolutely," I tell her.

She reaches for my hand, her skin warm and dry. "Let's go."

× × ×

We end up in the common room of Leisl's dorm—Hobson House—which is less than glamorous. Furniture consists of two coffee-stained couches and an unstable floor lamp. There's also a flat screen mounted to the wall, but someone's covered it with a silk curtain panel.

"What's that for?" I point to the curtain.

"Television's so uncivilized," she says. "This is our way of encouraging the girls not to turn the darn thing on."

"Are you kidding?" I ask. "You know the internet exists, right?"

Leisl purses her lips. "Some of the freshmen were inviting boys over to watch *The Masked Singer*. It had to be stopped."

"Oh my," I say. "Sometimes I think we live in different dimensions."

"How so?"

"I like reality shows. Not the singing ones, but I don't know. I find people interesting. I like watching what they do."

"I'd rather watch you," she says. "You're interesting and you can tell me about the shows. I hate them all."

"Where are the boys?" I try changing the subject.

"Carlos'll be by as soon as he can. He's in play rehearsal. He got a part, a big one. Oh, and for set stuff, I've arranged to borrow some pieces from your school. You have some good artists in your town."

"About that," I say. "You should probably give them a call."

She smiles and pulls me down next to her on one of the couches. "Leif, I'm not sure about. He'll probably stop by, but he's been unreliable lately."

"Lately?"

She rolls her eyes. "Always. Do you have the clues?"

"Yeah." I unclip the top pocket of my bag and reach inside for the manila folder now holding the news articles. "I haven't been able to do a deep dive on all four, but my initial impression is that all, except one, are variations on a similar theme."

She glances over the headlines. "What theme is that?"

"System failure of some kind." I start pointing to the relevant articles as I talk. "See, the situations are all different—an aquarium water-balancing system, a swimming pool with its drain cover missing, and then these industrial diving accidents. Something went wrong in each case that should've been accounted for ahead of time."

Leisl wrinkles her dimpled nose. "That seems—broad. Can you think of an accident where better planning *wouldn't* have stopped it?"

"I don't know. Well, there's acts-of-God-type stuff."

"Force majeur," a voice says, and we both look up to see Leif swaggering into the room with Carlos trailing behind him.

"We're talking about accidents," I say.

"I know. *Force majeur* is the legal term for when a contract's voided in the case of a natural disaster or other act of God."

"Oh."

Leif sneers. "You could probably apply it to that column you wrote. Talk about a disaster."

"I liked it," Carlos pipes up. "The column, I mean. It was disturbing, but I can't believe you got someone to tell you that story. I'd never heard anything about it. Not something Broadmoor likes to advertise, that's for sure."

"It was my uncle," I say. "Who that happened to. I guess he worked up here one summer. He's a pretty intense guy, but this helps me understand him. Being close to something like that has to mess with you."

Carlos nods. "I bet."

"Is that your script?" Leisl gestures at a bundle of paper Carlos is grasping.

"The one and only." He holds it up proudly, and I see *The Visit* typed on the first page.

"I hear you got a good part," I say. "Congrats."

Leif smirks. "He's playing a rapist."

Carlos gives a weary sigh. "I'm playing the mayor. It's one of the leads. And yes, the character is a terrible person. He doesn't know that yet, though, which makes him interesting."

"How's the actual game stuff going?" Leif looks around. "Hey, no one's listening to us, right? You know someone in my dorm found a hidden camera in their room."

"Then I hope you apologized," Leisl says tartly. "But we don't have to worry in here seeing as I'm in charge of the common room."

"What are you in charge of?" I ask.

"Keeping it tidy. Everyone's got a house chore. This is mine and I'd notice any hidden cameras." She looks at her brother. "To answer your question, we haven't gotten anywhere with the game. Other than a theme of system failure. Design failure, maybe. I don't know."

"I did have another idea." I glance over at Leif, gauging his reaction since he's the one who's already heard my suggestion. "I thought the articles might be pointing us to Eden Vicente. She *was* found in water. And she's connected to . . . most of the people in this group."

The room goes silent. My instinct is to apologize, to back off what I know to be a sensitive topic, but Carlos—who was once Eden's boyfriend—is the first to respond.

"It's crossed my mind, too," he admits. "It's not really something I want to revisit, but yeah, that could make sense."

"I understand," I tell him.

"Well, I don't like it." Leisl frowns. "What mystery is there? She drowned. It was an accident. A real live accident. Not to mention, Eden didn't live a mysterious life. She was boring."

"Leis," Carlos sounds pained.

"I'm sorry, but she was. She was my roommate! I knew her best."

"But we don't know everything that happened," I insist. "Like, what were the two teachers doing who were there? How did they lose a fifteen-year-old girl? And how did they leave without her? Or if they didn't, why would she go back? Plus, *you* told me that there was salt water in her lungs. In a freshwater lake."

Leisl's spine stiffens. "I never said that."

"But you did!"

"I'm not listening to this anymore. It's ghoulish. She's dead and she's buried and that's it! That's the end!" Scowling, her eyes flashing with anger, Leisl snatches up her own backpack and flees the common room, her own dorm, before storming outside.

"Sorry, folks. I'd better take this one." Leif gives us a quick nod before chasing after his sister.

I turn and stare at Carlos. "What just happened?"

He sighs, running a hand through his short-cropped hair. "I'm sorry, too. I think you just found the one topic our little group has a hard time talking about. Especially in the context of this." He gestures at the coffee table.

"I didn't mean to make light of her death," I say.

"I know."

"I feel awful about what happened to her. I really do. But I didn't know her. It's not the same."

Carlos gives me a shy smile. "Sometimes I think I didn't know her either. We were only together for a couple months, which can be a lot in boarding school terms because—well, because everything's more intense when you live together. It's like summer camp. But things weren't even that serious between us. I wanted to get to know her but we both had a lot of other commitments at the time, and that's what's been hardest for me, you know?"

I nod.

"She was fifteen," he says. "After she died, I got shoved into the role of the grieving boyfriend, which had to look a certain way so that I could comfort her family. They wanted to know everything. How she spent her days and what made her happy. It meant so much to them, the little details, and I tried to comfort them as best I could, but there was so much I didn't know. In a normal situation, I probably would've been the boyfriend she'd forgotten about in a year. In five, she wouldn't have been able to pick me out of the yearbook. Instead, the worst thing ever happens, and I'm all she ever knew and that's the real tragedy. No one should die young. It's not fair."

"No," I say.

His eyelids flutter, as if he's working to pull himself back from the depths of the past and the never-will-bes. It's a grief response I recognize—that desire to disappear from the present, from what's always been the cruelest timeline.

"You want to see something?" he asks. "Let's get out of here."

I gather up the articles, sliding them back into the envelope, and clipping them into my bag. "Where're we going?"

Carlos shoves his rolled-up script into the back pocket of his jeans as he heads for the door. "Outside."

We walk out together, ambling side by side down the steps. We get a few stares from students I don't recognize. Presumably this is because I don't go to Broadmoor and Carlos doesn't live in a girls' dorm, and honestly, I'd stare, too, if I were in their shoes.

Carlos leads me deeper into the boarding school's campus, snaking past the performing arts center, what appears to be an actual archery range, and a quaint clapboard chapel. Finally, after cresting a small, meadowy hill, we reach a fenced-off clearing that's accessible only by a waist-high wrought-iron gate.

"I haven't been out here in a while." Carlos speaks in a hushed tone as he pushes the gate open and waves me through. He's really quite different than Leif, who's all swagger and smirk. But from the moment we met, I've admired Carlos for his quiet confidence and his willingness to slow down and resist impulse. He's not unlike my father in this way—the careful heart of a scientist who's ready to test all theories before committing to what he knows to be true.

I enter what appears to be an untended garden. It's not a large space, and it's dotted with a few oddly spaced benches and ornamental trees. One corner boasts a large vine-covered pergola, another an intricate stone labyrinth, and a shallow reflecting pool shimmers near the back fence line.

"What is this place?" I ask.

"The Broadmoor Memorial Garden." Carlos walks to a patch of what look like tea roses that are begging to be cut back for the season. At the base of the roses sits a thick slab of cream-streaked white marble, rearing out of the earth a good two feet. Engraved metal plaques have been fixed across the top of the stone.

Bending over, Carlos searches the plaques until he finds what he's looking for. He points.

EDEN MARIE VICENTE.

"That's what's left of her out here," he says gruffly. "Eight months of her life spent at this school, and this is all that remains. Her family took everything else. As they should have. They really came to hate this place, and I don't blame them. It took their child."

"How'd you and Eden meet?" I ask. "Through Leisl?"

"No. We were both big science nerds. It was the reason we both came here, to this school, so we kind of bonded over that."

"That's *right*," I say. "You told me you wanted to make weather in a lab. With my dad or something."

He smiles. "Not with your dad, but at his company."

A gust of wind rumbles through, sending the iron gate slamming back and forth. Again and again.

"I should probably get back to the shuttle," I say.

"Hold on." Carlos reaches for my arm. "There's something else I thought you'd be interested in."

I'm stilled by his touch. "What is it?"

"It has to do with the column you wrote. About that family." He walks farther into the memorial garden, nudging me along with him. "Was it hard for your uncle to talk about it?"

I nod. "He's sort of a haunted person anyway. My dad told me once that something had happened to him in high school, with some Broadmoor kids. This was it, I guess. Trauma like that's forever."

Carlos shrugs. "It can be. But your past isn't destiny. Or, it doesn't have to be. Unless you actively try and forget it. Like *some* people."

"Some people who?"

"Leif, for one." And when he sees my surprised expression. "You don't know that story?"

"Should I?"

"*He* wouldn't tell you, but Leisl might. I'm kind of surprised she hasn't. I think she tells people an abbreviated version when she's afraid they'll judge Leif for being a snob. Which he is. But also he isn't. He's got problems."

"She's hinted at something before. What's the story?"

Carlos looks around. "I feel bad talking about it, but I'm the one who brought it up. So here's the quick version. When Leif was twelve, he saved a little girl's life. She was in a fire at a hardware store and would've died if he hadn't gone in there and gotten her out. Leif was hailed a hero and got some valor award from the mayor. Even had his picture in the paper. Only if you look online, you'll never find any mention of it. You won't even find his name. Do you know why that is?"

I think about this. "No."

"His dad had them scrubbed. Which I guess is a thing you can do when you're a famous Ivy League lawyer. But this is because months after the fire, the cops arrested Leif."

"For what?"

"Turns out he was the one who started it. Leisl claims it was one of those things where he wanted so badly to be a hero that he became the villain. Some twisted savior syndrome. Anyway, instead of going to jail, he was sent off to some treatment place for a year and then they came here."

"That doesn't sound like Leif," I say. "A *savior* syndrome? Are you sure?"

"I don't know what to tell you. People are good at hiding their secrets."

"Hmm." It's not something I can really argue with, but this story sounds pretty far-fetched. *Antihero's* too kind a word for Leif, much less *hero*.

"Weird, huh?" Carlos says.

"Definitely," I mutter under my breath. "Especially considering his sister almost died in a fire last month."

"What was that?"

"Never mind."

"Well, this is the other thing I wanted to show you." Carlos gestures with a flourish as we stop in front of the reflecting pool. It's narrow and long, running the back length of the garden. A beveled headstone set at a slanted angle sits in the very center. It's gray marble, very solemn, and etched with a drawing of a small family of doves.

A mother and three babies.

My heart stutters. "Is this—?"

"Yes." Carlos nods at the words carved into stone:

Honor and shame from no condition rise.
Act well your part: there all honor lies.
  —Alexander Pope

In Loving Memory of Dr. Alexia Trenta-Sousa,
laid to Heavenly Rest with Her Angels
Eva, aged 9, Dan, aged 4, and Roberto, aged 1

14

HANDS SHOVED INTO POCKETS, I walk swiftly from the downtown shuttle stop over to the industrial side of Cabot Cove, which is where Bio-Mar's located. It's after five and already dark, and the air is *freezing*, tiny puffs of white swirling from my lips and nose. I'd be running if it weren't so cold, and my boots clomp on the sidewalk like the horse Leisl said she didn't ride. Oh, and I've already texted her an apology, which she's already accepted. *I'm sorry, too,* she wrote. *I'm just so stressed with schoolwork. Plus, now I'm a wreck with all these sets I have to build. Did you hear what happened at your school? Ugh. I love you, though. XOXO*

The thing is, it's not that I don't believe her about how busy and stressed she is. It's that I don't *understand*. Since the moment I met these three, their sole focus has been on solving tenace, finding the clues, winning this elusive school-wide game. Not for riches or fame or even glory. What they're chasing is what I'm drawn to, as well. Distinction. Mystery. The surety that in a world jam-packed with experts and smartphones and endless content, wonder will always have its place. Will always be a force to be reckoned with.

But now that I'm finally invested, they're struck with newfound complacency.

Or is it *me* they're uninterested in?

My phone dings as another text comes through. With the tiniest flutter of nerves, I pull it out and read the message right away. Only it's not from Leisl. It's a message from *Leif*.

Hey. Sorry about today.

Sis is dealing with stuff. You know how it is . . .

You want to meet up tomorrow?

I can come down to Cabot Cove. Roommate's ride is as good as mine.

I got some stuff that I think will help. You could be on the right track.

He wants to meet with *me*? To my knowledge, Leif's never texted me before. Honestly, I only know it's him because the account is showing up as an email address instead of a phone number. I type back:

Why is this coming from an email account?

How do I know it's you?

Good catch. Sorry about that.

New iPad. I haven't activated the phone service yet. Caveman times, huh.

But here's some verification: In your room you have a photo of yourself as a small child wearing overalls and you are posing with a blue-and-gold furry person.

No judgment.

I can't help but laugh.

That's the Michigan Wolverine to you.

And he's far more refined than your school's whale mascot.

No argument there. Nova scares me.

So how's tomorrow?

I'll drive you home after or wherever it is you're staying with your uncle.

How is it you have such free access to your roommate's car?

I'm starting to think you've buried his body and taken over his life.

Maybe I have.

Seriously, though, Colby hates driving.

His parents got him the car so he can drive himself back to the Holy City for holidays.

He still flies, though.

Holy City?

Charleston. We on for tomorrow?

Sounds good. I'll see you then.

Oddly, this exchange leaves me giddy in a way I don't associate with Leif. But maybe that's really Carlos's doing, since he told me that story about Leif's childhood. The one that cast Leif's more devious tendencies as the product of a troubled soul. A boy longing to be something he's not. I can relate to that. The loneliness and fury that comes with hating yourself. Hating who you can't help but be.

Returning my hands to the warmth of my coat pockets, I round the corner leading to Bio-Mar's front office suite. Immediately I'm greeted by an enormous crowd of vehicles and people and floodlights.

I stop short to gawk in confusion. *It's the news*, I realize after spotting call letters on some of the vans, as well as people setting up portable lighting and camera crews bunching up by the front doors. There's even a drone buzzing overhead.

"Hey, what's going on?" I sidle up to a large group of what appear to be primarily middle-aged lobstermen and women in thick flannels and work boots who have gathered to watch.

One of the men glances over at me, then juts his chin toward the cameras. "News is out here trying to interview this crackpot who thinks she's some kind of ocean expert. Gal looks like she spends more time posting selfies than out on the water making a living."

An older woman with sun-cracked skin wearing a brimmed hat that reads MAINE FIRST leans over to stage-whisper at me, "Looks like she's loving it, too. Always with the attention for these types. You should check it out."

The crowd generously parts to let me get closer, until I'm approaching the front. Then I stand on my tiptoes, straining to peer around the remaining broad shoulders and boom mikes. When I see who they're talking about, my stomach drops like a water balloon.

It's *Aunt Callum*. Sure enough, she's standing up there,

right in front of the big Bio-Mar logo wearing this cute navy suit and kitten heels, which she definitely didn't have on when we left the house this morning. She's also got her hair pulled back, fresh makeup, and I can't help but wince at how young she looks. She's in her late thirties, but the combination of her styling and nerves gives the impression of an overeager high school valedictorian.

This isn't good.

"Could you describe the risks to the public with regard to the red tide?" a male reporter asks.

"Of course." Callum touches her hair, then smiles, flashing white teeth. "You see, the term *red tide* is used to describe the presence of specific algae blooms in our coastal waters. Certain algae produce neurotoxins—potent substances that can cause a range of significant illnesses and symptoms in humans. Now we don't eat the algae directly, but shellfish, our bottom feeders, definitely do. There's real danger in consuming these shellfish until their bodies have a chance to clear the toxins."

"How long can that take?" a different reporter asks.

"A few weeks," Callum says. "But we don't guess. Not when the stakes are so high for everyone involved. Here at Bio-Mar, we've implemented our sophisticated and proprietary round-the-clock monitoring system that measures toxin levels up and down the Maine coastline. Results are transmitted directly to local health departments and informs their decision-making."

"So you didn't personally shut down the coast?"

Callum laughs, a high tinkling sound. "Of course not. That's not within my authority at all."

"Yeah, right," one of the men behind me shouts.

"Monitor this, lady!" someone else roars to a chorus of jeers and laughter.

Callum has to hear the insults, but she doesn't flinch or react. She simply stands there, her hands clasped in front of her, while her lips stay slightly upturned at the edges.

"What can you tell us about your monitoring system?" a reporter asks.

"Well, I can't say too much," she begins. "Our patent's still pending, but I can tell you that after collecting extensive data in both fresh- and saltwater bodies of water, we've built an algorithm that can not only detect the first presence of toxic algae, but also accurately project the life span of a bloom as well as its rate of spread, insertion into the environment, and rate of decay in a given ecosystem.

"This is a widespread issue, and climate change is worsening the situation. Not just on our coasts, where people, particularly children, are at risk of severe gastrointestinal illness and even death from consuming contaminated food—but in lakes, rivers, and ponds throughout the world. Scores of dogs are killed each year after swimming in toxic water, and other life forms, as well."

"Thank you," the reporter says, and Callum holds up a hand.

"That was the last question," she says with a smile. "Thank you all for coming."

I stand very still as the crowd surges with anger and frustration, hurling insults—and in one case a glass bottle—as my aunt turns on her heel and heads inside the building. The reporters and crew are all business. They swiftly pack up their equipment and depart, but the lobstermen and other trappers linger, chanting epithets and darkening threats that chill me. I understand their anger. I really do. Watching this professional young woman who's not from Cabot Cove smugly tout technology that's led to the docking of their boats must feel beyond insulting. As if she knows better. But it's not her fault, and the toxins are real. I *know* they know this.

Yet they hate her anyway.

From the corner of my eye, I spot one of Dane's uncles, an aging man named Garland Pruitt. He's head of the local Lobstermen Association, a real gruff salt-of-the-sea type but a born leader. He's shouting at whoever threw the bottle, then steps back and calls out for everyone to leave.

"Now!" he bellows. "We're not doing this here."

The others grumble their discontent, but obey his instructions, heading for their pickups and SUVs so they can go home or maybe commiserate over beers down at College Lane or Ray's Place, two of the Cove's seediest and most well-traveled bars. Pruitt tips his hat to me as he drives off, and I wave back.

Once the parking lot's emptied out, I gather the courage to enter the Bio-Mar facility where I check in with front reception about meeting up with my aunt. But as I collapse onto the office's fancy leather furniture and wait for her to come get me, my body has this delayed reaction where my breath grows shallow and my chest starts to squeeze my lungs and rib cage, like my body's collapsing in on itself.

I'm fine, I tell myself, everything's fine.

But nothing feels fine. And like Dane said earlier, this day feels seriously cursed. Like a bad omen or dancing on a grave. Glancing outside at the now darkened parking lot, my mind replays the anger and vitriol from earlier. And I can't help but wonder if those displays of barely restrained violence resemble the types of "pushback" poor Dr. Trenta-Sousa faced as she sought to chart Broadmoor's new, forward-looking course. As she tried to make the school a better place.

A safer one, too.

15

"WE'RE HOME," AUNT CALLUM WHISPERS, as I stir awake and sit up in the car to see we've pulled into the driveway of the remote mountain house.

My head's foggy from the ride, from the day, from the strange dream I was having where my uncle told me he regretted sharing his story, that secrets are safer when they're kept. That even if said secrets have grown claws and sprouted fangs, it's better to swallow them whole and keep them inside you than unleashing them onto the universe. But I rub my eyes and peer into the darkness only to see a van parked directly ahead of us.

"Whose is that?" I point. "Is someone here?"

Aunt Callum shakes her head, unbuckles her seat belt. "Looks like your uncle's having guests over."

"Guests?"

She nods.

"That's a thing he does?"

"Nope. Not usually. He only entertains under duress," she says, and I scramble from the passenger side, backpack in hand, and follow her to the front door. Sure enough, as we step inside, we're hit with the thumping bass of a hip-hop beat pouring from the back of the house, where it appears all the lights are on, and I can hear laughter and voices.

Confused, I hang close to Aunt Callum, trailing right behind her as she marches into the kitchen. Safe to say we're both startled to find the place crowded with a dozen or so twenty-somethings who are all drinking beer and eating chips and salsa from a tray on the counter. Uncle Abe's in the middle of it all, a frenzied flurry of activity, alternating between cutting up vegetables for what looks like a salad and mixing margaritas.

"He looks miserable," I tell Aunt Callum, and it's true. My uncle may be the host, but there's a pained expression on his face. He looks rattled by the crowd. The music.

Everything.

"This is unexpected," Aunt Callum shouts at him as she drops her purse on the center island and slides out of her coat, revealing her schoolgirl navy suit. I let my gaze dart around the room.

"You want to turn the grill on?" Uncle Abe shouts back. "Sorry I didn't tell you about this."

"It's fine," she says. "I'm just surprised."

"I had to do something. It's our last full day together. Fall crew's heading out this week."

"It's fine," she says again, but maybe I'm the only one who hears the weariness in her voice. We didn't talk about the television interview on the ride back, but it's got to be weighing on her. It's weighing on *me*, and I had nothing to do with it.

"Can I make you a drink?" Uncle Abe asks his wife, whipping out a pre-salted margarita glass. Callum shakes her head and begs off, pointing upstairs.

"I'll be back," she says, and the instant she's gone, I watch my uncle take the tequila bottle, hold it to his mouth, and tip his head back. As he catches my eye, he sets the bottle down. Reaches for a lime wedge.

"I'll go turn on the grill," I say quickly.

He doesn't answer and I head for the living room slider with a shiver of dread. There's wrongness simmering in the air tonight, and I'm eager to escape. I squeeze out onto the balcony where I find two people huddling beneath a radiant heat lamp. One tall. One short. The tall one's Fritz.

"Hey, kid," he says, and he's got his arm wrapped around the shoulder of a young woman I've never met before. She's curvy with pixieish red hair and she's got the most amazing bird tattoos adorning both of her tanned forearms. "This is Lark Sullivan, my girlfriend. Lark, this is Beatrice. She's Abe's niece and she's visiting for the week."

I hold a finger up, whirl around, and light the ignition for my uncle's gas grill. Then I turn back to the two of them. "Nice to meet you. I love your tattoos. They're so intricate, like illustrations from a book."

"Thanks." She points at Fritz's empty beer. "Need another?"

"Sure."

Lark slips back into the house, leaving us alone with the faint soundtrack of something psychedelic and guitar heavy.

"So this is just an ordinary Monday night for the wardens?" I ask.

Fritz grins and leans against the railing. "Not at all. But it was your uncle's idea."

"That's not what he told Aunt Callum."

"He probably doesn't tell her a lot of things," Fritz says. "Hey, but I wanted to tell you that I dig your writing. Abe turned me on to your column. It's great."

"Really?"

"Absolutely. I love true crime. You gotta look into some of the national park stuff one of these days."

"I've come across that before," I say. "Something about cannibals."

"A lot of it's nonsense. But not all. That's how these things work."

"What things?" I ask.

"Secrets that people up high want to keep hidden. See, if something's truly dangerous, the best way to hide it isn't to try and cover up the truth. That's how truths are found. It's too vulnerable. No, the safest thing is to destroy the notion of truth in the first place. And how do you do that?"

"I have no idea," I say.

Fritz leans forward. "You spread *more* rumors. All kinds. Even outlandish stuff. Now nobody will believe any of it, and anyone who does is instantly discredited."

"So are the stories about abductions in the parks true or not?"

"Some are true. Of course, they are. They just might not be true in the way you think they are. Even when you hear about stuff like colonies of feral humans or a family of bigfoots, don't dismiss it outright. There's probably something in that lore that's functioning as a tool for deeper truths."

"Like what?"

Fritz turns and gazes out at the canyon beneath us. "Did you know that in Colorado people have reported seeing a creature called a slide rock bolter? You ever hear of it?"

I shake my head.

"We don't have them out here, but the bolter's like a giant whale that sits atop the mountains out there, using its strong tail to grasp onto a tree trunk. When it senses humans or another food source beneath it, the bolter releases itself from the tree and slides down the mountain, mouth agape, to devour its prey."

I snort. "A *whale*?"

Fritz nods. "Pretty wild, huh? Wild enough that you'll discount it just based on face value. But where do you think the story came from? What was happening at the time when the first reports of the slide rock bolter were occurring?"

I wrinkle my nose. "In Colorado?"

"That's right."

"I have no idea. Maybe an avalanche? Is that too on the nose?"

"Not really, no. But avalanches—and rockslides—aren't mysteries. There's usually evidence when they occur, unlike the bolter, who leaves no trace." Fritz pauses. "What do you know about the history of coal mine rebellions in Colorado?"

"Very little," I say. "History is not my best subject."

"That's too bad," Fritz says as Lark reappears with a new beer for him and a hard cider for her. She also offers me a bottle of water, which I take gratefully.

"Thanks," I say.

"I was just about to tell her about the Colorado Coalfield War," Fritz says.

"No way." Lark looks at me. "I'm from Leadville. Colorado."

"Leadville sits at ten thousand feet of altitude," Fritz says. "This girl's got strong lungs."

I gape. "Ten thousand feet?"

Lark flexes a bicep. "That's right. Although my lungs aren't actually strong. Deacclimation happens quickly."

"I thought *this* was high altitude." I glance over the side of the balcony railing. "Aren't we at about four thousand feet?"

She shrugs. "Height's relative. It's the change in altitude that gets to people. Not the absolute number. But you want to know why it's so cold at higher altitudes?"

"Why?"

"Less pressure means the air molecules are actually farther apart. So you'll be warmer at sea level where the pressure's higher and the molecules push against you." With the word *push* she playfully bumps her hip against Fritz's.

"You'd better go tell Abe how many burgers you want. Also, you might want to check on him."

"Why?"

Lark mimes drinking heavily.

"Got it." Fritz stands up straight. "Does that mean you'll tell Bea about the Coalfield War? Oh, and show her the logo."

"Done and done," she says.

I put in my burger order, and once he's gone, Lark comes and stands beside me beneath the heat lamp. I tell her I like her nose ring.

"Thanks," she says. "Your hair is really pretty, by the way. So what do you want to know about Colorado?"

"I don't know. Fritz was telling me about the origins of a slide rock bolter and then veered into the coal war thing."

She nods knowingly, sets her cider down, then rolls back her sleeves. "So he's on his whole 'myth is used to hide the truth in plain sight by destroying the meaning of truth in the first place' riff again. Am I right?"

I laugh. "Maybe. Don't think we've gotten that far."

Lark reclaims her drink and holds the bottle up like a game show host showing off a prize. "First, the logo."

It takes a moment for me to see it, but then I do: The cider, somewhat ominously named Harvest Home, is manufactured by Boulder's own Slide Rock Brewing Company and their illustrated logo, placed near the bottom of the label, consists of a tiny slide rock bolter gripping an apple tree.

"That's *adorable*," I say.

"It is." Lark beams. "Okay, and here's the relevant history

lesson. Starting around 1860 or so, coal mining became big business in Colorado. Well, in a lot of places. Coal production was a large part of the nation's industrialization period. The whole so-called Gilded Age, you know?"

I nod, but absolutely don't mention that this is the chapter I haven't read in my textbook for APUSH.

"From early on, the relationship between the mine owners and the workers was contentious. Coal mining was dangerous work—what with explosions, cave-ins, gas leaks, black lung, and twelve-hour days. Plus, the miners lived in tent camps that were run by the mine owners themselves. Company towns, and the workers were often paid in scrip they could only use in those towns. It wasn't quite slavery, but it functioned in a similar way, and around the turn of the century, the miners began to unionize. Who do you think had the power in this scenario?"

"The owners?" I say.

"Individually, yes. But once they unionized, the miners had power, too. Power in numbers, which they applied by engaging in work stoppages. Furious, the owners then pressured Colorado's politicians to declare work stoppages illegal. And when that didn't work, they took matters into their own hands, meaning violence. Eventually the governor sent in the Colorado National Guard, ostensibly to maintain order, but more often than not, the end goal was to force workers back into the mines.

"All this animosity culminated in the 1914 Ludlow Massacre, when the Guard lay siege to a tent city that was occupied by striking miners and their families. On Easter Sunday, the guardsmen swept through, shooting men in the back and torching a tent that was filled with cowering women and children, killing everyone inside." Lark frowns. "That's the real meaning of *law and order*, by the way. It's got nothing to do with right and wrong. If rich folks don't like what you're doing, you can be sure they'll make a law to punish you for it."

"Convictions make convicts." Right then, Fritz staggers out with a platter full of burger patties. "Watch out, ladies. It would appear I'm on grill duty tonight."

"Uncle Abe's not coming?" I try peering back through the sliding door, but there's too much glare.

"He's, uh, busy with the margaritas. As in drinking them." He opens the grill lid and reaches for a spatula. "How's story time going?"

"We're getting there," Lark says.

"Is he okay?" I ask. "My uncle?"

"I don't think he cares at this point," Fritz says.

"You tell her about the bolter," Lark urges. "You're the storyteller."

"Okay." Fritz starts arranging the burgers on the grill grates. "Well, consider this. There are no reports of the slide rock bolter prior to the arrival of Colorado's first coal mining prospects."

I gaze up at him. "You think someone started the rumor to keep them out of Colorado?"

"It's possible. There were existing settlers, native people, who all had reason to resent the intrusion of large-scale mining operations. But what if the mine owners themselves wanted a way to frame disappearing laborers as a cautionary tale? *Behave or the monster will get you.*"

"Psychological warfare," Lark says.

"Then again," Fritz adds, "maybe the miners started it. They could've harnessed the fear of the unknown by spreading gory tales of bloodthirsty monsters as a way to terrorize the guardsmen and run them out of the mountains. Then again, all of these theories could be wrong and right at the same time."

"What do you mean?" I ask.

"I mean, maybe the slide rock bolter story was something people at the time genuinely believed in and retold. While at the same time, others used the monster as a weapon against their enemies. Whatever the origin or intent, the story got away from its tellers and took on a life of its own. Until the truth didn't matter anymore."

"Until it *was* real," I say.

Fritz points the spatula at me and grins triumphantly.

"Exactly!" he exclaims.

16

I WAKE UP TO THE sound of my phone ringing. It takes a moment to acclimate myself, but I feel the warm weight of Lemon sleeping on top of the blankets near my feet and it all comes back. I'm in the basement of my aunt and uncle's mountain home, far from civilization and close to where a girl I never knew met her end.

Eden. She was in my dream. I'm sure of it. Or a part of her was. I was walking toward the lake at night, my feet bare, and my arms shivering. The only light was moonlight, and I stood in the mud and pine needles and watched as her pale body bobbed atop the surface of the lake, bloated and water-logged, only to be snatched away again by the gaping maw of a giant whale.

I work to shake off these gruesome images as my phone continues to ring. Reaching for it, I resist the urge to check my feet for sap and leaves. The dream wasn't real. I know that. But the remnants of my sleeping mind stick to me, stubborn and fickle, all at once.

"Hello?" My voice is a croaky mess.

"Bea, sweetie. It's me. Did I wake you?" It's my father.

"Hi, Daddy. You got my text, huh?" I'd finally sent him a

message about the tarot card thing right before bed. *Not a big deal,* I'd written. *Deputy Williams might call you, but this is all it was. He has a record of everything.*

"That's not what I'm calling about. Look, Bea, I need to tell you something. I wanted you to hear it from me."

I grip the phone. "What's going on?"

"Someone broke into our house last night."

"What?"

"Everything's fine," he repeats. "I've already spoken with the Sheriff's Office who's gone down there and documented the damage. Which is minimal. Looks like it was probably kids goofing off. Deputy Williams says there's been a lot of that recently, petty vandalism and other thefts. He says it's unlikely to be related to the threats you've gotten, although he knows about the tarot card. The package. All of it."

"Is that what you think? That it was just kids?"

"I don't know. I don't like the timing with me being out of town, but it was my office that got trashed. That's the only room they touched. Whomever it was used our porch key—we need a better hiding place for that—and it doesn't appear they took anything. Probably looking for electronics. Maybe some cash."

"Was anything left behind? Like a note? Or more flowers?"

My father hesitates. "There were a couple of messages spray-painted on the walls downstairs. Juvenile stuff. It's not nice, but there's no reason to suspect it's related to . . . you know."

"What kind of messages?"

"Stuff like, 'Watch out' and 'We're coming for you.'"

My chest tightens. I bite back a whimper. "That doesn't sound like goofing off. What if we'd been home?"

"But we *weren't*. And they would've run off if we had been," my dad says soothingly. "People like this are cowards. And you don't need to do a thing; Abe's heading out there right now. He'll handle everything with insurance and cleaning up. I also spoke with Deputy Williams personally, and he'll make sure you're safe, okay? Anything you need, you call him. I wouldn't stay on this trip if I didn't trust the two of them to look after you."

"Okay," I say.

"How's everything else?"

"Fine," I say. "Daddy, I miss you. I wish you were here."

"I miss you, too, love. And look, it's okay to feel scared. It's a violation. But just focus on your school, doing well, and when I'm home, we'll get new locks. Maybe a big dog. With big teeth. What do you think?"

I laugh and run my arm under my suddenly wet nose. "I think Lemon would hate that."

× × ×

I'm running behind schedule by the time I pull myself together. Not only that, but I still have to take my meds, shower, and get dressed, before gathering up my laptop and assignments and heading up to the first floor. There I find Aunt Callum waiting for me in the kitchen while kindly pretending that she's not.

"How're you doing?" she asks before breaking into a sneezing fit.

I hand her a tissue. "Is that because of Lemon?"

She nods, blows her nose.

"I'm sorry."

"Don't be. I just need my allergy meds. Also, your dad told me everything. How disturbing. I already called your school and told them you won't be in today."

My jaw drops. "I'm not that late. I can't miss a whole day!"

She blows her nose again. "I thought I was doing you a favor."

"I need to go in. I really do. Can't I ride with you?"

She must hear the panic in my voice. "Yeah, yeah. It's fine. You can come in with me. But I don't get it. When I was your age, I would've loved having a whole day to watch reality TV with no one around to judge me."

"People judge me whether they're around me or not."

"Funny," she says.

"I don't want be alone," I tell her.

Her expression softens. "I get it. Let me finish this cup of coffee and we'll head out. I'll have you there by ten."

"Thanks, Aunt Callum." I gaze around the sparkling kitchen. "Wow, this place is clean after last night."

"Did you have fun?" she asks.

"I enjoyed talking with Fritz and Lark. They seem like a good couple."

She waves a hand. "Don't know how serious that is. Summer flings are common around here."

"It looked pretty serious. Hasn't been summer for a while."

"Well, she's leaving this week so it'll be long distance from here on out if they want to make it work. Such is a warden's life."

"Lark's a warden?"

"No, but he is. He has to go where he's assigned."

"Hey, was Uncle Abe okay last night?" I ask. "I don't want to be nosy, but he seemed—odd. Like not very happy."

Aunt Callum sighs, then reaches to dump the remaining contents of her coffee mug into the sink. "What else is new?"

17

ONCE WE'RE IN THE CAR, heading down the mountain, Aunt Callum slides back into her usual self. She sings along with the radio, applies a fresh coat of red lipstick, and smiles at the shining sun.

I try and engage her in conversation, something I know she likes to talk about. "Can I ask you a question, Aunt Callum?"

"It's going to rain later," she says. "Gonna be a big storm, too. Coming in overnight. Might even get some hail."

"But it's so nice out. I thought we were supposed to have a heat wave or something."

"I don't make the rules. What was your question?"

"Well, I'm trying to research something scientific."

She looks over at me. "That's a pretty broad topic."

"I know. But Dad suggested I ask you. That it's your area of expertise."

"Go on."

"Do you have any idea how someone who'd drowned in fresh water would end up with salt water in their lungs?"

Her nose wrinkles. "Is this a particular person?"

"Just a hypothetical situation," I say.

148

"Okay." She chews her bottom lip for a moment. "Well, I can think of a few hypotheses that could explain such a finding. But without more context I can't make an informed guess."

"That's fine," I say. "Wild guesses are welcome."

She puffs her cheeks. "First off, if this occurred at a beach resort, it's possible that a person who swam in the ocean might also get in a pool shortly after. If they then drowned in said pool, it's feasible that any salt water inhaled during the ocean swim could still be there. Potentially it could even contribute to their demise, if they'd had a near drowning event while in salt water."

"My dad said the exact same thing. He also mentioned dry drowning."

"Sure. That's a possibility. But if this is based on autopsy findings, our hypotheses can go in other directions. Remember, water's water. What would really be detected is the presence of salt in a person's lung tissue. That doesn't necessarily imply salt water."

"Ah," I say. "Very interesting."

"Right? So maybe this individual swallowed part of a drink wrong. Or inhaled a toxin of some kind. Or smoked something that left a residue. Again, it's difficult to get into specifics with so few details to go on."

"Well, this is super helpful," I say. "I wouldn't have thought of any of this."

She dips her head. "Is this for your column?"

"Not exactly. Do you remember that girl that went

missing from Broadmoor? The one who drowned in Lake Paloma last spring?"

Aunt Callum furrows her brow. "This is about her?"

"Well, the saltwater thing is a rumor I heard up at Broadmoor. From some of the students. But it's probably just gossip or whatever."

"Oh," she says. "I wouldn't know anything about that, but the whole episode was quite traumatic. Your uncle still beats himself up about it."

One of his biggest regrets. "Why is that?"

"He questions his decision-making. But he didn't do anything wrong. In fact, he did more than most people would've. He took her disappearance seriously from the start. Not everyone did."

"Yeah." I feel exhausted suddenly and press my skull into the headrest. Squint out at the blue sky. "By the way, I saw your interview yesterday. I mean, I was there. That was a tough crowd. You handled it well, though."

"Thanks, Bea!" She flips on the Subaru's turn signal, slowing as we approach the intersection that'll lead us onto the coastal highway. "You should stop by the lab today. I'm going to be working on my new top secret project, if you'd like to get a peek."

I cock my head. "Then it wouldn't be top secret."

She laughs. "Everything's worth sharing with a few choice people. I trust you're not a corporate spy."

"Are you working on the algae bloom technology? For monitoring the red tide?"

"Nope. Although that's a pretty sexy project on its own." She gives me a sly smile. "You ever hear of Aquaman?"

"The *superhero*? The one that's part fish?"

"Technically, he's an Atlantean."

"Like Ramtha?" I ask. "Or maybe Ramtha's a Lemurian. I forget."

"Who?"

"Oh, just some ancient spiritual entity from thirty-five thousand years ago that a woman in Washington State claims to channel through the magic of pyramid power. They've got tons of followers, her and Ramtha. Celebrities, even."

"I'm talking about something real," she says.

"Aquaman's real?" I ask.

"Not yet." Her eyes twinkle. "But someday he could be. Or maybe it'll be Aquagirl."

"I don't get it."

"What if I told you there's a chemical compound that makes it so you can breathe underwater without scuba gear?"

"What kind of compound?"

"The kind that turns humans into fish," she says. "It's called the Aquaman crystal. We didn't discover it, but we're currently expanding the research into its utility. It's pretty exciting to say the least."

"But what is it?"

"Oh, just a cobalt-based crystalline capable of compressing and storing immense quantities of oxygen into a very small space. It's also regenerative, so if we can find a way to regulate it with other gases that humans need to breathe, then this crystal will not only allow us to go underwater without tanks, but we'll be able to stay under for much longer periods of time. You won't be able to run out of air."

"Why would we need other gases?" I ask.

"Do you know what's in the air we breathe?"

"Oxygen?"

"Oxygen is what keeps us alive, sure, but the air around us is primarily composed of nitrogen."

"Oh," I say. "I guess you do learn something new every day."

"This is basic science, Bea."

"I think it's interesting," I offer.

"Then that's why you should come tour the marine lab this afternoon. And if you're really interested, I'll take you down to the harbor sometime and show you some of our tech in action."

"You mean go in the water?"

"Not right now, unfortunately, since the coastline's shut down. But if you want to go diving sometime, we could do that. I'm a certified dive master. Water's got to be warmer, though. That won't be for a while."

"Well, I'm hanging out with a friend from Broadmoor today, so I probably can't come by. He's going to give me a ride back, too. But I'd like to see the lab. Maybe tomorrow?"

Aunt Callum lifts an eyebrow. "You're hanging out with a guy?"

I feel my cheeks warm. "Not like *that*. We're working on a project together."

"So he's a project partner now? From a different school? I thought he was a friend."

"He's both," I say. "Sort of."

Her lips twitch. "Uh-huh."

"It's *not* like that," I insist.

"What's his name, this Broadmoor boy? Is he cute?"

"He's fine, I guess. Just not my type." I feel myself blushing harder, which I hate. "His name's Leif. And I'm better friends with his twin sister, but like I said, he and I are working on some research together, so it's just us today. Leisl's been busy with school, I guess. Plus, there's this set design—"

"Did you say *Leif*?" The car swerves suddenly, but Aunt Callum pulls it back onto the road and grips the wheel so tightly her knuckles go white. "Leif who?"

"Schoenholz. Why?"

Her voice lowers. "Does he know you're staying with us? In our house?"

I stare at her. "What are you talking about? I mean, yes, he knows I'm staying with my aunt and uncle while my dad's out of town. I doubt he knows where you live, though."

"Oh, he knows. Trust me."

I feel light-headed. "Why would he know that?"

"Look, I don't know the kid personally . . ." Aunt Callum pauses, clearly weighing her words. "Let's just say I find it strange that you and he are hanging out together and that he's offered to drive you to our house."

"Aunt Callum, what are you talking about?"

"It's a very odd coincidence." Her voice grows louder, more frantic. "Here you are talking about that girl who died and what happened to her, and then in the next sentence mentioning *him*. He was there, you know. When it happened. Your uncle spoke to him *in our house.*"

I'm so confused. Uncle Abe knows Leif? "But a lot of people were there. I was there, and I didn't even know the girl or go to that school."

She shakes her head and slaps the wheel. "No! *He was at the lake when it happened.* When that girl vanished. Leif was part of the hiking group that day, and I happen to know that he was the only one of the students to be taken in for formal questioning. And that decision was based, at least in part, on his initial interview with your uncle. Because it came out later that he'd purposely misled the search team. Like the whole thing was some hoax or a joke to him."

"Who did he mislead?" I ask.

"Your uncle. Everyone."

"What are you saying?"

Aunt Callum turns to meet my gaze. "I'm saying you should be careful."

18

MY BRAIN'S REELING AS I walk into school. Too much is happening right now, and this is on top of our house being vandalized. A part of me wants to rage and scream and find the person responsible. The rest of me wants to crawl into a hole and hide, and not come out until my dad's back home.

But promises are promises, and I told my dad that in his absence, I'd focus on doing well in school and making him proud. So after signing in at the front office, I use my tardy pass to rush through the halls to get to the last half of algebra.

Fortunately, I'm caught up with my assignments in this class. Unfortunately, from the moment I sit down, I can't follow a word Mr. Sheridan's saying. He keeps writing equations on the whiteboard and moving variables around to solve for x, but all I can see is a different set of variables.

Like the story Carlos told about Leif, the young arsonist, committing a crime and saving a girl's life solely as a ploy for attention.

Like the revelation my uncle interviewed said arsonist after a different girl went missing and now my aunt claims he may have intentionally misled the authorities about the hiking group's whereabouts that day.

Like the fact that, in addition to the harassing notes and weird items I've received, there's been a series of break-ins and thefts around town. And not only has Leif been emailing me on his brand-new iPad, but he saw where we keep our spare key under the plant on our front porch.

Like the fact that the first package I received had a South Carolina postmark. And Leif's roommate hails from Charleston.

The Holy City.

The bell rings and I pack up and step out into the crowd, making my way toward the cafeteria with my head still in a daze. I don't know what to do or what any of this means, but meeting up with Leif later no longer feels like a wise thing to do.

"Hey!" Someone taps me on the shoulder as I get into the lunch line.

I turn around and see that it's Ivan, from history class.

"Where were you this morning?" he asks. "You missed a test."

"Someone broke into my house last night."

"While you were there?"

"No. My dad's traveling. I'm staying with family."

"What'd they take?"

"I don't know. Not a lot apparently. Just trashed some stuff."

"That sucks. My grandpa says crime's everywhere now. No place is safe. Not like it used to be."

"I'm pretty sure there's less crime now than when your grandpa was a kid."

Ivan shrugs. "Who can tell?"

"There are public records!"

We reach the food area, and both Ivan and I select grilled cheese sandwiches and apple slices. The dessert, however, is some sort of burnt pudding concoction with a glossy skin on top. I know better than to take that. Fool me once and all.

"Give me yours," Ivan insists.

I hand it over.

"Hey, so I talked with my grandpa about what you asked," he tells me.

"You did?" We walk together to the nearest table.

"Yeah, but my mom won't let you talk with him, unfortunately. She says it's bad for him to get agitated, which is true because the last time his home health aide came by and changed his meds, he locked himself in the bathroom and couldn't get out again. We had to call the fire department to take the door off its hinges."

I nod as we sit down. "That's okay. I wouldn't want to upset him."

"I did find out some stuff, though," Ivan says. "I asked him about that woman who died, the one you wrote about, and if he knew anyone who would've targeted her or her husband. He said it wasn't a matter of who but who wouldn't. The list was that long."

"What list?" I ask. "Whose list was it?"

Ivan pulls his phone out and starts scrolling through something. "I wrote everything he said down. He has a tendency to ramble. Anyway, he didn't say anything more about the list, but he did say, 'You need to tell that girl that she's wrong, but that she's also right about the Honor Guard. Honor isn't a character trait or a description of an action. It's a gift.'"

"A gift?"

"I don't know what that means. He did say no one liked the woman because 'she was too radical and thought she was an expert on other people's lives.' Also, he used some words to describe her that I will not be repeating." Ivan sets his phone down. "Is this helpful?"

I think for a moment. "Definitely. Thanks, Ivan."

✕ ✕ ✕

After lunch, I go outside and fire off messages to two people. The first is Deputy Williams:

> Hey. You probably heard what happened at my house.

> I have some thoughts about who might've done it but want to be careful.

> I also have some questions about Eden . . . where you were first directed to look for her and by whom.

> Call me when you can.

The next to Leif:

> Sorry. Today won't work.

> Some family stuff is happening.

> Let's reschedule soon?

Shivering in what's becoming an increasingly windy day—looks like Aunt Callum was right about the storm—I remain outside, waiting for a response. Waiting for something.

I'm still waiting by the time the bell rings.

I turn and head back inside.

19

Evie finds me after school, bounding up to me fully dressed in her volleyball clothes, including kneepads. I know she's got practice and a match tomorrow that will determine the team's ranking in the state tourney, so I'm surprised she's taken the time to seek me out. Lucky for her I'm not doing anything but checking my phone again. Still no replies, but I also don't spot Leif anywhere, so I assume at least one person got my text.

"I heard what *happened*!" she exclaims. "Are you okay?"

"Aren't you cold?" I can't stop staring at her bare legs.

"This is insane!" She practically tackles me, wrapping me in a bear hug. "I couldn't believe it when the cops came by our house this morning and talked to me for the second time in one week. Mom says I'm going to end up on a watch list. Or maybe I'll be a jailhouse snitch. I bet I'd be good at that."

"You're planning on going to jail?"

Evie throws her head back and laughs like I've just told the funniest joke.

"It's nothing," I tell her. "Just a run-of-the-mill break-in. It's surreal knowing someone was in our house, but Dad says the Sheriff's Office is looking into it. Guess there's been other incidents of vandalism lately. We're not the only ones."

Evie's eyes go wide. "Are you sure? That tarot card was weird."

"Maybe they're not connected."

"You can't really think that," she says.

"I don't know what to think."

She reaches to squeeze my shoulder. "I gotta go, but call me if you need anything. I mean, these next few days are busy, but we'll keep an eye on the house."

I smile. "Thanks."

When she's gone, I pull out my phone and dial the Sheriff's Office, the nonemergency line, and ask for Deputy Williams by name.

"He's not here," the woman who answers tells me. "What is this in reference to?"

My heart pounds. *What indeed?*

"Do you know where he is?" I ask.

"I can't discuss our deputies' whereabouts over the phone."

"Do you know when he'll be back?" My voice goes up an octave, mimicking my desperation. "He's helping me with something. A harassment situation. It's important."

"I don't know," she says, then lowers her voice. "Look, I heard he might be taking a day or two off so if this is an emergency, you should probably dial 911 and ask for assistance."

I think quickly. "Is there anyone else I could speak to about the Eden Vicente situation?"

"Eden Vicente?" the woman pauses. "Do you have new information about her that we should know?"

"Maybe."

"And this is in regard to harassment you've been receiving?"

"Kind of?"

"Well, the Vicente case isn't under our jurisdiction. You'd have to contact state police for that."

"Okay, fine." I hang up because this is getting me nowhere.

Next, because I crave purpose, I set out walking across town, heading north, toward the far end of the cove. Set back from the coastline, the streets run narrow and are lined with residential homes. Cutting through the foothills, I spy the lighthouse, which sits even farther north, outside of Cabot Cove city limits, atop a long fingerlike jetty where riptides are common, a risk that's warned of with tons of signs and pictures.

Luckily no one's out on the water today, since the waves look rough, the rattling white-capped precursor to the evening's forecasted storm. It's eerie how quiet the coast gets with everything shut down. I'm so accustomed to a seascape filled with boats and trappers dotting the rocks that their absence feels dystopian.

Like the end of the world.

I follow the road downward until I reach my destination: a picturesque Victorian cottage with white shutters and a lush cottage garden that's been trimmed back in preparation for the cold. After entering by way of a white picket gate, I approach the front door where I knock sharply. A wreath of lavender and seagrass hangs as a greeting, and as I wait, I inhale the sweet scent of dried herbs and ocean spray. After a moment the door opens, and a tall woman in corduroy pants and a thick cable-knit sweater waves me in. Gives me a tight hug.

"She's in the library," she tells me.

"Thanks, Gina." I squeeze past her and make my way toward the back of the house, where the library, with its high coved ceilings and walls of books, is nestled.

"Aunt Jess," I say when I get there, standing in the door-frame. Behind me a radiator hisses and clangs, filling the room with warmth.

My great-grand-aunt—and renowned mystery author—Jessica Fletcher looks up her from her writing desk, pulls off her glasses, and smiles warmly, her blue eyes crinkling in the process. "Bea. It's so wonderful to see you."

"Is this a good time?" I ask. "I don't want to bother you."

"Of course." She waves me in. "I'm actually doing a little research this afternoon. Maybe you'd like to help?"

"For a new book?"

She nods and sets her pen down, curling both hands together and watching closely as I sit in the wooden chair across from her. With her sharp humor and deep well of patience, Aunt Jess is one of the smartest people I know.

"Have you ever heard a rumor about a dead celebrity being alive?" she asks once I'm settled.

"Like Elvis?" I say. "Or Tupac?"

She nods approvingly. "That's right."

"What about these rumors?"

"Well . . . why *them*? Why not other celebrities?"

I ponder the question. "I don't know. I don't think I've given it much thought, but I suppose such theories must be linked to something unique in that person's life or something about who their fans are. Fandoms can be intense. Or maybe it has something to do with the way they died."

"What else?" Aunt Jess urges. "There's got to be more to it. For instance, why Elvis and not Jimi Hendrix? Why Tupac and not Biggie? Why JFK Jr. and not Beau Biden?"

I grin. "Tupac and *Biggie*? Not a topic I'd expect you to be interested in."

"Well, why not?" She raises her chin. "Two unsolved murders. An artistic rivalry between the two. Plus, tons of theories but no real answers. I'd say it's *exactly* the type of thing I'm interested in."

"Fair enough," I concede. "And to your question about rumors and faked deaths, I have no idea. Maybe it comes down to timing? Something else that's in the news at the same time that makes people skeptical. Although someone was just explaining to me last night how secrets are best hidden in the open."

"Say more about that."

"He meant that rather than burying a secret—which would be obvious if it were found—the better hiding tactic is to flood the space the secret already lives in with an ocean of outlandish rumors. Most levelheaded people would reject any semi-related story to avoid being associated with conspiracists."

Aunt Jess nods and stirs her tea. "It's an interesting idea. Diluting the truth with lies."

"Don't know if it fits for Elvis," I say. "I think he's just dead."

"Can I get you something to drink?"

"No, thank you. I'm good."

"Am I right in assuming you're here to do some research of your own?" she asks.

"Is it that obvious?"

"Only because I read that column of yours. I figured you'd have questions about the Sousa family. That poor woman and her children."

"Were you surprised when it happened?"

Aunt Jess looks startled. "Of course. Not just *that* it happened, but a crime as heinous as that one—there's no way to be cynical about something like that. I was as horrified as the next person."

"Was I wrong to write about it?" I ask.

"Absolutely not," she says. "But as someone who's written plenty about humanity's darker impulses, I know that not all readers appreciate looking into that sort of abyss. Because crimes like this don't come with easy answers and they can't be placed neatly on shelves marked with REVENGE or GREED. They're more complex and complexity scares people. If one person's capable of something like this, aren't we all? People don't like to think about that."

"That's an understatement," I say.

"How's Abe doing?" she asks. "It was Abe, right? That's who you spoke with?"

"Yes," I say.

"You know he was unwell for a good while after it happened. Your grandparents both struggled to help him. And your father, well, he was away at school, but he didn't know how to relate. Abe's done so much since then, but to read your column and realize he's been holding on to other information? All this time? It's . . . concerning."

"Dad's always concerned when it comes to his brother," I say. "And I don't know how Uncle Abe's doing. I can't tell. He's not very . . ."

"Very what?"

"Available," I say.

"Hmm."

"Have *you* heard of the Honor Guard?" I ask. "The one he mentioned?"

"No. Never."

"Well, Ivan Sussman's grandfather knows about it. And he said something strange. He told Ivan that honor isn't a character trait or an action; it's a gift."

"A gift?" she echoes.

I nod. "He also said his grandpa hated my column because I'd 'gotten it all wrong.' That it wasn't a question of who would've targeted Dr. Trenta-Sousa for being too radical, but who wouldn't."

Aunt Jess sits back in her chair. "*Eli* said this?"

"Apparently." I catch her pensive expression. "Do you know what he means?"

"Not at all. Eli's health has been deteriorating for years now, so I'm not sure how seriously to take him. But that line about honor does make me think of something. Do you remember that tenace game you told me about?"

I lean forward. "Of course."

"Well, it's making me wonder if Abe misheard what Daniel Sousa said. That it wasn't an Honor *Guard* he was afraid of, but an honor *card*."

"Like a greeting card?"

Aunt Jess shakes her head. "I told you that tenace is a bridge term, right? It's a trap you set for your opponent. Well, an honor card is what you can use to thwart that trap. They're the high-value cards. Ace through ten. You see, bridge is a game of balance. Every move has a countermove. That's what makes it a near perfect game. One that relies almost entirely on skill."

"As opposed to what?" I ask.

"Luck."

20

I'M EXHAUSTED BY THE TIME I leave Aunt Jess's place, but without a ride home, I've got no choice but to meet up with Aunt Callum at Bio-Mar and listen to her brag about all her new research studies. I opt to take the bus this time. It's too cold outside and my legs are tired.

I text Aunt Callum when I get off, and she's kind enough to be waiting outside for me at the loading dock for Lab C, which sits all the way at the back end of the industrial park.

"I'm so glad you made it." She hustles me inside, through an airlock door and metal detector. "I can't wait to show you around. Forget the stuffy offices. *This* is where the real magic happens."

I step into shocking brightness. There are no soft corporate colors or carpeting or even mood music. The research lab is a mostly windowless warehouse space that's been painted white and is lit by powerful overhead lighting. Walking through the maze of work areas and following directions to stay within the marked "mobility pathways," I realize I have been here before, with my dad. Not recently, though, and it's evident the company's grown exponentially. My recollection is of rows and rows of powerful computers and sleek refrigerated shelving where my father was growing cultures. Now the place hums with human energy as well as machine, and everywhere I look, people are collaborating and working intensely on an array of different projects.

"What's that?" I point to what appears to be a room filled with bubbling tanks of different-colored liquids interconnected by an assortment of tubing and heat sources.

"What does it look like?" Aunt Callum asks.

"A distillery?"

Aunt Callum laughs. "Not a bad guess. They're attempting to isolate certain compounds through a process that bears a passing resemblance to distillation."

"Is this the Aquaman thing?"

"Nope. It's a process meant to help with the by-products of desalination."

Something pops into my head. "Do you make weather here?"

"What do you mean?"

"I have a friend who's taking all these advanced science classes. He told me there was a lab at Bio-Mar where you make weather."

"Oh. Well, yes, there's a small team focused on atmospheric science and modeling. They're funded through the university, but their facility's capable of re-creating atmospheric events. On a very small scale. Not anything extreme. It's not that specialized, but that's likely what your friend was talking about."

"So students in the advanced program choose what research area they're interested in learning about at Bio-Mar?"

"Not just Bio-Mar. There are other partner institutions across the state, but we do offer shadowing opportunities to high school and college students from all over. Including your school. This isn't just rich-kid stuff. Or dude stuff. You can apply if you want to."

"Not sure I've got the grades for that," I say.

"You never know." With a little bounce in her step, Aunt Callum hops forward and beckons for me to follow her through an airlock door and into a more sterile space, walled off from the rest of the facility. "Okay, this is what I wanted to show you. It's my baby. I've put a lot of resources into her."

I take a cautious step forward. "What am I looking at?"

"Look up."

So I do. I crane my neck back and see that hanging from metal brackets about twelve feet over our head is what appears to be a sleek black-and-yellow submarine-type vehicle, with a wide rounded glass front and propellors in the rear. I circle the whole thing, trying to discern its purpose.

"What *is* it?" I ask.

"I call her *Elysium*," Aunt Callum says. "And she's a submersible. When the water warms next spring, I plan on doing data collection from inside her hull. I'll be able to get to depths I never could by diving and finally work on my theory regarding the relationship between oceanic circulation and atmospheric radiation."

"How deep?" I ask.

"She's designed to go to five thousand meters, but I'm not planning on going that far down."

"It looks terrifying. But even snorkeling scares me."

"No way," she says. "When you're underwater, it's like the opposite of being claustrophobic. You're free, unbound from gravity, from all the limits of land. I'll take you. I promise. Couple lessons in the pool and you'll be down to sixty, eighty feet in no time. You'll see a part of Maine you didn't know existed. A whole world beneath ours. Snorkeling can't take you there."

"I don't know," I say. "I just read a whole journal article about occupational diving accidents. And these were professionals! They all died."

"You read an article about this?"

I nod. "It was a safety review. But these people were trained. One got stuck trying to clear a dam. Another got trapped in a sluice gate. The third was performing routine maintenance on a lock system in New York."

"Oh," she nods knowingly. "You mean Delta P."

"What's Delta P?"

"It's a real hazard for occupational diving. Not so much for the type of stuff I do. There's a horrifying video of it in action that makes the rounds online every now and then." I must still look confused because she keeps talking. "It's not diving that kills them. It's the danger of being caught between two separate bodies of water that are not equalized. They're trapped by the water pressure differential. Otherwise known as Delta P. It's extremely powerful."

"Water pressure differential?"

Aunt Callum gives a weary sigh. "Have we not taken physics?"

"Next year," I say.

"Okay, so imagine you have two beakers that are connected by a tube near the base of each. If you fill one with water, what happens?"

"The water goes into the empty one," I say. "Through the tube."

"How much water?"

"All of it?"

"No."

I try and picture what she's described. "Until the beakers are both even?"

"Correct. That's equalization of the water pressure. Because of gravity, the weight of the water in the full beaker is pushing downward. Since there's a tube, the pressure from the water weight will push it through the tube because there's nothing on the other side pushing back. Eventually they will equalize when the pressure coming from each beaker is the same."

"That's not very complicated," I say.

"No, it's not. But now imagine there's a clog in the tube and the tube is actually a huge drainage tunnel connecting a giant lake to an empty reservoir. What do you think would happen if a diver went down there to clear out the clog? Where would all the hundreds of thousands of gallons of water in the lake be trying to go?"

"Into the tunnel." My eyes go wide. "Oh! I get it. They're trapped by all that water trying to equalize. The change in pressure."

"Bingo." Aunt Callum nods approvingly. "You can't escape something like that if it gets you. It's physically impossible."

"Is that how someone could get trapped in a pool with a missing drain cover?" I ask. "I read about that, too."

"It's similar. Drain entrapments are a significant hazard in hot tubs and swimming pools. But in that case, the force is made even stronger by the suction action in the filtering system. That's on top of the water pressure. Children have literally been sucked against a missing drain cover or an unsafe one, and multiple people can't pull them free while the filter's going. It's horrific."

"What a nightmare."

"Indeed."

"One more," I say. "What about a resort diving situation where people get the wrong mix of gas in their tank? And it makes people disoriented or pass out? How would that happen?"

She frowns. "That's not the same thing at all. Unless you're talking about people succumbing to nitrogen narcosis. That can be brought on by deep water diving. Nitrogen has risks. Oxygen does, too."

"Okay, that makes sense."

"But if they got the wrong mix, it was probably due to negligence or just a mix-up, not anything worse."

"What would be worse?" I ask.

Aunt Callum laughs. "There's always murder."

21

IT'S LATE, ALMOST EIGHT O'CLOCK by the time we return to the house on Fire Mountain, and Uncle Abe is nowhere to be found. There are no lights on, his truck is gone, and the place is just empty.

"Did he ever come back from my house?" My mind, traitorous as always, fills with grisly images of him crashing in a ditch or driving off the side of a mountain, and no one knowing where he is.

Aunt Callum appears unworried. She's very calmly walking around the first floor, turning on lights, flicking on the heater. "He definitely came back. I talked with him this afternoon. He said he had."

"But how do you *know*?" My voice rises an octave brewing with urgency.

"Here's our proof." Aunt Callum points at the counter where a fruit bowl has been newly filled with oranges and grapefruits. "I asked him to stop by the store and he did."

"Okay," I say.

"There's also that." Aunt Callum nods at two empty beer bottles sitting by the sink. "Those are new, so he's definitely been here."

"With someone else?" I ask.

"Let's hope so. He's probably out with the junior wardens, making preparations for the storm."

I nod. This makes sense. The wind's already howling through the woods.

"Are you okay?" Aunt Callum asks. "You seem . . . tense."

"Just tired," I say.

"Why don't you go rest? I'll make something to eat and bring it down to you. Nothing special, though."

"Thank you." But before I turn to go: "Aunt Callum, is my uncle okay?"

She cocks her head. "What do you mean?"

"It's just that I was talking with Aunt Jess today about everything he went through. With Daniel Sousa . . ."

"Does this have to do with your column?" she asks. "I still haven't read it."

"You don't know about the Sousa murders? About what happened to him when he was in high school?"

"I'm sure Abe's mentioned it."

"Well, Aunt Jess made it sound like he's carried a lot of guilt for not intervening before people were killed. It kind of matches up with what you said about him feeling bad after the Eden Vicente thing, so I was worried that after talking with me, he might be . . ."

"Triggered?" she offers.

"Unhappy," I finish.

"Oh." She pauses. "I appreciate your concern. Your uncle

has been distracted recently. Working later than usual. Not coming home at night. But I don't think it's about his past, and I don't think you're the one who needs to worry about him. I'll do that. Okay?"

I don't know what this means, but Aunt Callum's tone indicates the topic is closed to further discussion. So I thank her and tell her I'm going to do some studying.

"I'll bring dinner when it's ready," she calls out.

Lemon greets me upon my arrival downstairs, mewling with feline gusto and what I interpret as deep resentment. She's hungry, obviously, and also appears to be shedding, which is likely a stress response. I lean down to put food in her bowl and then scratch her behind her soft ears.

"I know how you feel," I tell her as she mewls more. As I straighten up, I glance out the bedroom window just as a sudden wind gust grips the house, shaking it hard so that it feels like a high-speed train's roaring past.

The downside to living on a mountain.

I plug my dead phone in to charge and sit down with my laptop and the tenace articles. With all the science stuff from the lab floating fresh through my mind, I figure I ought to take advantage of trying to put the pieces together. It's the dive tank mix-up story that I need to look into more, now that Aunt Callum has explained the phenomenon of Delta P to me. The tourist gas mix deaths stand out as the anomaly of the four articles. There's no element of pressure change that caused their accident.

Or is there?

I'm scrolling through articles on nitrogen narcosis, which Aunt Callum had mentioned, as well as other underwater dangers. It sounds terrifying—divers essentially becoming intoxicated by the narcotic effects of the gas. *Raptures of the deep* it's called, although it's not always deadly. Clicking through links, I make my way to a scuba-diving forum where all manners of diving accidents are discussed. Being left behind by dive boats, propeller injuries, people suffering heart attacks underwater, or getting the bends. There's even a whole section on that awful dive boat fire out in California where thirty-four people perished. It must really be beautiful down there for so many people to be willing to risk their lives to swim in the ocean's depths.

Sufficiently charged, my phone eventually turns on and as it reconnects to the Wi-Fi, it dings with an incoming notification. I reach for it, anticipating a text message from either Leif or Deputy Williams. Or maybe my dad. Instead it's a voice mail. I hit play.

"Beatrice," a familiar male voice says. "It's Dr. Wingate. Please call me as soon as you get this."

× × ×

"Dr. Wingate," I say when he picks up. "It's me."

"Bea," I hear the warmth in my old therapist's voice and already I miss him so much. It's hard enough to have professional relationships end, but even though I understand the boundaries and ethics, he's meant more to me than just being a doctor. In some ways, he's meant everything.

"How are you?" I ask softly.

"Things are good," he tells me. "We're spending a lot of time in the country on the weekends, but during the week, we're both still in town. Working. Doing our thing. Leah's starting on a new book."

"That's cool."

"How are you?"

"I'm okay. Mostly. I'm still waiting to get in to see Dr. Miura. But I appreciate the referral. She seems nice."

"You still have refills?"

"I think so. I'll have my dad check."

"Good, good."

There's an odd pause, so I jump right in.

"You left me a message?"

"I did." He clears his throat. "Bea, what are you getting involved in?"

"What do you mean?" I ask.

"I think you know."

"Is that what you're calling me about? The Daniel Sousa thing?" I bite my lip. "Are you going to scold me, too, for having the audacity to ask questions that have yet to be answered?"

"No, of course not. But I am worried you're digging up memories you don't understand. I want you to be safe."

"Why wouldn't I be safe?"

"*She* wasn't."

I know who he's talking about. "You think I'm like her? I'm some kind of uppity woman who needs to be put in her place?"

"Just the opposite. I know you're smart and passionate and brilliant in much the same way that Dr. Trenta-Sousa was. But I think some people see you in a different light. Like you, Dr. Trenta-Sousa was a woman who'd found her voice and could be perceived as different and certainly not from here. These are qualities that threaten a certain kind of person. It's strange to think about it now, but even when your aunt Jessica first started writing, there were plenty of people in Cabot Cove who didn't like the stories she was telling. Or the fact she felt she had a right to tell them. She got a lot of flack. Harassment. Threats. It was ugly."

"Aunt Jess didn't give up, though."

"I'm not telling you to give up. But she was a grown woman. You're a teenager. I have a responsibility to keep you safe."

"I'm not your patient anymore."

"That doesn't matter."

"But I'm not *doing* anything!" I cry. "Someone told me that story, a true story, and I retold it. And I asked my readers if they knew anything about a group who might target people they don't like. The only answer I got was from a friend's grandfather, who said something about how a lot of people would've wanted to target Dr. Trenta-Sousa. That she was a troublemaker. A problem in need of a solution."

"Doesn't that worry you?" Dr. Wingate asks.

"What do you mean?"

"Have you noticed anything in your life recently that would make *you* feel targeted? Marked for harassment?

Maybe someone who doesn't like what you're doing with your column."

For a moment I don't answer.

I can't.

"Beatrice?"

"How did you know?" I whisper.

"I don't *know* anything," he says. "But I have some suspicions about what's going on and I've had them for a while. Your most recent column—and the person you spoke with—has only reinforced these suspicions."

"But the things—what's been happening to me—it started *before* I wrote that column. It started right after the whole HOA stuff."

"What things?" he asks.

"A package sent to me that contained a photo of my mother's grave, along with a bunch of dead calla lilies—those were her favorite—and a note that read 'YOU'RE NEXT.' Then a prowler left a tarot card by our back property line. It was a card representing death. It didn't seem like a big deal, but then last night someone broke into our house, only we weren't there at the time. My father's out of town and I'm staying with my uncle out at Fire Mountain."

"You're at Abraham's?"

"Yes."

Dr. Wingate pauses. "Is he still married to that marine biologist?"

"Callum? Yeah. *She's* going to be targeted next if she's

not careful." I explain to him how angry the lobstermen and trappers were when she was interviewed about the red tide.

He listens carefully. "Well, I'm not saying there isn't a potential safety issue there, but I don't think she has to worry about what we're talking about. Not yet at least."

"What are we talking about?" I ask.

"Not class resentment or labor tension, that's for sure. There's a myth in our society that it's the poor and working class who perpetuate bigotry and inequity. But they rarely have the power to do so on a systemic level. They've been scapegoated into poverty just like other groups have. But you know who does have that power? I know you do because you already wrote about it. Who was it who first indicated displeasure at Dr. Trenta-Sousa's hiring?"

I think back, racking my brain. "Rich alumni? And Broadmoor parents? Maybe board members?"

"That's right. People with means and a desire to maintain the status quo."

"The people you're talking about—are they related to tenace?"

"Why would you ask that?"

"My aunt Jess, she says it's possible Daniel Sousa was talking about an honor *card*, not an HONOR *GUARD*. It's a bridge term, apparently. It's a card that can thwart a trap known as tenace."

"I'm very familiar with tenace, Beatrice. But believe me when I tell you that whatever's going on isn't a game. Both of these ideas may have their origins at Broadmoor, but tenace, the game I know, is a force for truth. There may be trickery involved and strategy, but at its core it's about discovery. It's about awe and chasing the kind of mysteries that remind us to always keep looking. That there's always meaning in the journey. But remember Newton's third law: Every action has an equal and opposite reaction."

"I don't get it," I tell him.

"Think about it this way," he says. "What if what Daniel Sousa did—and he did do it—isn't the point in all this? What if that one heinous act is actually a symptom of a larger illness? One that infects all of us in some way or another."

"How?"

Dr. Wingate sighs. "If a man murders his family in cold blood and we arrest him and put him away in prison for the rest of his life, is the world any safer?"

I falter. "Maybe? I guess."

"Okay. Maybe. We've now stopped him from being able to hurt more people in the future, which is something. But what would it take to stop such a crime from occurring in the first place? And how does locking him up stop the next murder from happening?"

"I have no idea," I say.

"But you *do*, Beatrice. The answer is right in front of you."

"It is?"

"Yes," he says. "And now you need to figure out who's standing in the way of you being able to see it."

TRUEMAINE.COM

Home Page for the State of Maine . . . and Murder . . .

"The Princess with a Thousand Enemies"

Consider this a continuation from my last column, the one where I wrote about Daniel Sousa, the man who murdered his wife and three young children. That column evoked a strong reaction from readers who felt my wanting to explore the details leading up to Sousa's murders meant I was open to excusing Daniel for his actions. Given this misunderstanding, I wanted to pose the following question:

What's the difference between a victim and a victimizer?

In some ways, the answer's easy, right? Daniel Sousa is a murderer. This undeniably makes him a victimizer. His wife and children, his victims.

But here's another example: For the past few weeks, I've been receiving threatening notes and messages in the mail and at my home. Most recently, my house was vandalized, broken into, and someone left a message spray-painted on the wall that read: "We're coming for you." Now, I don't think I deserve this kind of treatment, so I feel as if

I'm the victimized one in this scenario. So who's the victimizer? Well, the jury's still out on that, but if you've got any info, let me know.

Then there's this: Imagine a group of people who attended Broadmoor Academy in its heyday, back when matriculation there meant something, when Broadmoor was still a feeder to the Ivies and hadn't yet slipped in the rankings to hover around the dreaded "third-tier boarding school" designation. From what I can tell, this slip happened in the mid-nineties and the school's recovered since, but that means the group of graduates I'm talking about must be in their fifties or older, by now. We also know Broadmoor was established as a boys' school, only going coed in 1978, so this group likely skews male. There's also a good chance they come from wealthy families. Old-money types.

Now imagine how this group might've reacted during those turbulent nineties to the presence of a new dean on campus. And not just any dean, but the publicly educated daughter of immigrants who was very explicit in her desire to extend the opportunity of a Broadmoor education to a broader, more diverse student body.

What if the perceived threat the dean's presence evoked spurred this group to put out a call in the surrounding community of Cabot Cove, asking who was willing to do what they could to get rid of her? And whether through payment or persuasion, what if, among our ranks, they found the right person for the job? What would that make Dr. Trenta-Sousa?

And what would it make us?

—Bea

22

I awake hours later with a start. There's a loud noise some-where. Dazed and groggy, I struggle to lift my head and I'm unclear what's going on. Or even where I am. Familiarity seeps in slowly—drip, drip, drip—but I soon realize that I'm slumped over a desk in my uncle's basement with my lap-top in front of me. A line of drool's crusted across my cheek, there's a tray of barely touched food by my left elbow, and I blink quickly, still working to orient myself because I don't *remember* falling asleep.

Vision blurred, doubling, I squint at the clock and con-centrate hard. It's almost midnight. Around me the house moans and shudders as sharp, bullet-like patters strike glass in a sudden machine-gun burst. I rush to the nearest window on wobbly, sleep-weak legs and peer out. The wind must've woken me, but it's too black outside to see the storm. Its fury's audible, though. I listen with bated breath as the falling rain builds to a deafening crescendo, as if the clouds themselves have come crashing down to earth.

I remember.

My *column*.

I stagger back to the desk, shoving aside the food tray

that Aunt Callum must've brought down for me. My fingers fly across the keyboard as I navigate to my TrueMaine account to check and see that, no, it wasn't a fever dream. I actually did it. I actually published the whole thing, including my claims of possibly being targeted by a long-standing secretive group of Broadmoor bigwigs who conspire to set sociopathic minions after women they don't approve of. My hands are trembling, but I'm able to check the page stats and I can see there've been thirteen views so far. Only, unlike my last column, there are zero comments.

This doesn't feel like a good thing.

After shutting the laptop, I sneak a guilty look at the food tray, which consists of a bowl of uneaten pasta and a half-empty glass of milk I don't remember drinking. Guilt or not, it still kind of warms my heart that my aunt cared enough to bring this to me. And since I'm awake, I might as well clean up and not leave the dishes for her to find in the morning.

I grab the tray and lumber my way up from the basement. The staircase is steep, and with my hands full, I can't use the banister to assist me. I'm winded by the time I reach the top, and I can barely catch my breath as I nudge the door open with my socked foot.

Everything's dark and silent. I walk down the long hallway, passing the laundry room where the dryer's thumping softly and the air's filled with the scent of fabric sheets. The room's lit by a night-light, and glancing in, I spot a pair of filthy hiking boots positioned by the washing machine on a mud-splattered rug. Relief washes over me. Uncle Abe's made it home.

But where *was* he?

My head starts to spin as I approach the kitchen, an odd merry-go-round sensation that threatens to send me crashing into a wall. With my elbow, I'm able to flip on the countertop light, set down the dishes I'm carrying, then lean against the sink to keep from collapsing.

The spinning subsides, but my limbs tingle and my ears roar with the whooshing race of my pulse. Maybe this is the altitude or something to do with the storm. I've never felt so weirdly incapacitated, just all at once. With a groan, I reach for an upper cabinet and grab a glass that I fill with water from the sink and chug. Then I chug another. This helps to clear my head, and I'm able to rinse the dishes from the tray after scraping the food into the compost bin. I also pour the rest of the milk down the drain then place everything into the dishwasher. Once it's closed, I grab for a dish towel and wipe down the counter.

A thundering crashing sound from outside startles me. With a squeak, I drop the towel and hurry to the living room slider, flipping on the outside light. The rain's falling in sheets now, but I can't see where the noise came from. I keep looking, but it must've been a tree coming down or a boulder knocking loose, something huge pinballing its way down the canyon with a roar. My mind envisions this house doing the same, sinking, sliding down the hillside, and I scurry back to the kitchen, bending to grab the towel off the floor.

"Ouch!" Something stabs me and as I straighten up and hold my hand under the light, I see *blood*.

Twisting the sink faucet on, I shove my wounded hand under the stream of water as more red spatters out. Something's in my hand, and a flurry of poking and squeezing dislodges the object from the soft skin of my palm. It clatters into the stainless-steel bowl. Pinching it carefully, I hold it under the recessed countertop lighting. It's a piece of brown glass. A jagged shard of it.

Something's on it, too. Part of a label and although I can't be sure, I swear it's from the back half of the slide rock bolter logo. Just the bolter's whale tail twisted around an apple tree.

My whole body's shaking. I reach for the overhead light, turning it on and illuminating the entire room. A quick sweep of the floor reveals more shards of glass scattered across the tiles to the right of the sink. There's not a lot—maybe four or five large pieces and a smattering of smaller ones. It looks as if someone had tried to clean up a smashed bottle but had been sloppy about it.

I think back to the two empty bottles Aunt Callum had pointed out when we arrived home. Although I hadn't inspected them, I did notice they were different brands, different types of bottles. My assumption was that my uncle had had a drink with someone else. Someone he'd invited over. I'd originally assumed Fritz, but if the other party had had cider, did that mean *Lark* had been here?

Alone?

Suddenly there's more banging from outside. It's a different sound, though, a persistent slam—*slam, slam, slam*—that's close to the house. I return to the slider and press my face to the plate glass door.

The storm's whipping up wilder than ever, but I spot the problem immediately. It's the lounge furniture. The chairs have been stacked up and chained to the porch, but there's a separate iron and glass table that's flipped onto its side and is now partially dangling through the balcony railing. The wind keeps grabbing at it, lifting it a few inches before it slams back down again.

I pull open the sliding door and step barefoot into the maelstrom. The gales are hurricane-force madness and I'm soaked immediately, but I lunge across the balcony and pull at the wedged table, gripping it from the top. The storm's greedy, pulling hard and refusing to let go. Finally, with a furious yank, I pop the table back through the balcony railing and hold it victoriously to my chest.

"Get out! Get the hell out of here right now!" a man's voice bellows. "I won't let you do this!"

I freeze and stare up, straight into the dumping heavens. Through it all, I spot the domed shape of the glass observatory directly above. It's lit up like a star or a spaceship, perched atop its mountain home, but I can't step far enough back to see what's going on inside the dome. To see who's up there. It must be Uncle Abe shouting.

But at who?

The answer comes a few seconds later when Aunt Callum bursts down the stairs and into the living room. She's dressed in a robe and her hair's down and wild, and as she crosses the room she stares out at the open slider and catches my eye.

"What're you doing?" she shouts frantically. "Why aren't you asleep?"

I scamper inside, pulling the door shut behind me and dropping the end table on the rug in a shuddering heap. My heart's in my throat and I see that there's water's everywhere.

"The table was banging around in the wind." I gasp. "What's happening upstairs? I heard—I heard someone yelling in the observatory."

Aunt Callum's eyes are wide, frightened. "You're bleeding."

I look down to see that she's right. Blood's dripping down my hand again, onto the floor. "I'm so sorry. I cut it. There was glass. I'll get—"

"No." She reaches for my arm as she glances up at the ceiling. "Leave it. Let's get you changed into something warm and dry."

"What's going on?" I ask. "Where's Uncle Abe? Is he okay?"

"He's been drinking. Something upset him. He's not in a good place."

"Was it something he read?" I ask.

She tugs on my hand. "It's got nothing to do with us. But he needs to be alone right now. Okay? Let's go downstairs. You won't mind sharing with me, will you? If I stay with you tonight?"

"Of course not," I say as we hurry down the hallway to the basement staircase together. Once we're in the in-law unit, I rush to the bathroom to bandage my hand and change into dry clothes, and when I come out, Aunt Callum's turned up the heat and buried herself on the couch under a pile of blankets.

"Are you okay?" I whisper.

She smiles and holds up a bottle of what look like prescription sleeping pills. "Want one?"

"I just want to know that you're safe."

"I'm fine, love. Everything's going to be fine. Your uncle just—he has these moods. I don't know what's setting him off tonight, but it's been other things on other nights. He's not—"

"He's not what?"

"Happy," she whispers before sneezing into her arm. Then she sneezes again.

"Was he reading something earlier?" I whisper. "Something online?"

"Go to bed, Bea," she says groggily. "We'll talk in the morning."

23

BEFORE LONG, AUNT CALLUM'S SNORING away on the couch, and after grabbing my computer and charger, I retire to the bedroom, because she's right. I do need to lie down and rest, and things will undoubtedly be less confusing in the morning.

Only I *can't*.

Not with this niggle of dread worming its way through me, whispering: *You wrote that post to be provocative. To get attention. To flush out something evil.*

Have you?

But this can't be the whole story, I tell myself. It just can't. Yes, my introverted and morose uncle has been acting out of character for the past few days: confessing decades-old secrets, throwing parties while looking miserable, and drinking a lot. And yes, there's a possibility he might've been meeting up with Lark, the young attractive girlfriend of his trusted junior warden. I'm not naïve enough to think he's not capable of making bad decisions, but it's just so *reckless*. Although hasn't Uncle Abe always been a restless soul? It's the portrait my father's always painted—someone who's physically unable of staying in one place for any extended period of time. Instead he chases tragedy to assuage his guilt. His sense of failure.

But guilt over *what*? He hasn't done anything wrong.

That I know of.

I roll over and grab my laptop from where it's charging on the floor and navigate my way to the TrueMaine site once again to see if there are any updated metrics or if anyone's left a comment.

Before I can do that, the lights go out.

It takes a second to realize what's happened. The reading lamp by the bed flickers out along with the bright hum of the heating system. My laptop still works, but no web pages are loading, and when I get up to flip the switch to the overhead light, nothing happens. I flip it again and realize the storm's knocked out the power.

I stay calm. There's a backup generator and I wait for it to switch over. Only nothing happens. I grab for my phone but there's no cell service, either. Still, it makes for a decent flashlight, and I scramble around looking for socks and boots and a heavy jacket because I know the transfer box for the generator is in the garage. I've seen it and I can make the switch manually.

Leaving the bedroom, phone light in hand, I dart back up the stairs. The only interior entrance to the garage is through a door in the front entryway, across from Thoreau Hall, the room with all the dead animals. On the way, I duck into the laundry room, rifling in the cabinets for a real flashlight, a waterproof one with a handle. After testing that it works, I put my phone in my pocket and turn to go.

Something catches my eye.

Or it's the opposite, really. Because the work boots from earlier; they're gone.

I'm staring directly at the muddy spot on the rug where they were situated just thirty minutes earlier.

But now there's nothing.

Uncle Abe came and got them, I tell myself. He's probably doing the same thing I am—finding a way to turn on the power.

Stepping out of the laundry room, I use the flashlight to cut through darkness as I continue toward the front of the house. The storm's still raging, but I swear I hear what sounds like footsteps just ahead of me. They're barely audible over the howling wind.

"Uncle Abe?" I call out softly. "Is that you?"

There's no answer. The train whistle roar and whine of the storm's wrath grows louder, more frenzied. I swiftly cross through the living room and enter the front hall.

A blast of cold air hits me and it's not hard to see why—the front door to the house is standing wide open.

I gape at the sight. The door opens outward and it's been blown back against the exterior and continues to bang in the wind. The entryway's near flooded and I rush outside to pull the door closed, feeling like Dorothy doing her best to beat the oncoming twister.

Backing inside, teeth bared with the effort, I spot something, far in the distance—what appears to be a bobbing light and the silhouetted shape of someone walking away. Then they're gone, swallowed up by the night.

After pulling the door shut, I slide through the narrow passage that leads down a half flight of stairs and into the attached garage that's built partially into the hillside. It's a dusty space, crowded with old machinery and tons of boxes. The rain is near deafening in here, pounding on the uninsulated walls, and my face is a magnet for cobwebs. They coat my eyebrows and make it difficult for me to see, even with the flashlight.

I start searching for the transfer switch that will allow the generator to power on. I know it's in here. Two years ago, when Aunt Callum and Uncle Abe first moved in, my dad and I came out to help them with the house. A lot of upgrades were needed to make it a welcoming space for a newlywed couple, which included adding a satellite dish, upgraded plumbing, and a backup generator for the winter.

I watched my dad install the generator along the back side of the house, and I remember asking how it would know when the power had gone out. Dad said it had a sensor but assured me that if it failed, anyone could come into the garage, find the transfer box, and flip over the power source directly.

Crawling on top of a perilously wobbly shop vac, I peer around and scan the wall with the light, until finally, I find what I'm looking for—both the fuse and transfer box.

Shoving cardboard boxes and plastic bins and possibly an old table saw out of my way, I forge a path forward, finally reaching the transfer box. While gripping the flashlight under my chin, I pop it open and switch over the power to various zones of the house. One by one.

Only nothing happens.

Confused, I reset the zones, but still nothing happens. I lift the flashlight to inspect the regular fuse box. Everything looks fine, but then I spot the issue. Yes, there are wires coming out of the fuse box. And yes, there are wires going into the transfer. But they're no longer connected.

They've been cut.

× × ×

Aunt Callum doesn't wake up when I try and rouse her, to tell her about the power and that someone might've been in the house. I shake her again and I don't recognize the bottle of pills she's taken, but they're clearly effective because she's out cold.

I also can't tell her Uncle Abe's not in the house any longer. That maybe he's chasing the person who cut the power. Or that maybe he's the one who did it. I've already searched everywhere for him, the whole house, every room, including his observatory, which was a mess of beer bottles and papers strewn all over.

But he's gone.

With growing desperation, I consider my options. Staying here, I've got no way to communicate with the outside world. I can't drive and I don't dare try in this storm.

But staying here, trying to wait out the night in a house someone's actively sabotaged, feels wrong. *Something's* happening and although my mind's simmering with worst-case possibilities, one thing is clear.

I need help.

After scrawling a brief note for Aunt Callum: *Power's out; generator won't start. Gone to the warden's village.* I zip my jacket, pull the hood over my head, grab the flashlight, and head into the storm.

24

I RUN AS FAST AS I can, my boots slapping, slipping in the mud. The wind's eased up, but the rain continues to fall in huge, blinding sheets.

It's only a half mile or so to get to the village, but going through the woods means dodging fallen trees, rushing water. I'm also gasping for air within minutes, still strangely weak and winded. The altitude remains the most likely possibility, but I'm starting to wonder if something was in the milk I drank earlier. It would explain how I fell asleep so fast. Maybe, like Aunt Callum, I'm not meant to be awake tonight. Maybe someone wants us out of the way. Fighting fatigue and despair, I rally on until at last I reach the paved fire trail that dips down, leading me straight into the warden's village.

The power's out here, too. There's usually a streetlamp leading into the village, illuminating the sleeping gas station and general store, but tonight everything's dark. I'm braced for disappointment; I know a lot of the crew moved out yesterday, so it's like a mirage when I spot the row of single-story cabins and see a handful of trucks parked out in front.

I run to the first cabin that looks occupied and pound on the door.

"Hey!" I yell out. "Open up! I need help!"

My voice is devoured by the storm, but I keep pounding. Then I shine the flashlight through the front window, and after what feels like forever, I hear footsteps.

The door slowly opens, and it's Lark standing there, wearing thermal pajamas and looking very confused.

"Beatrice?" she says. "What's going on?"

"The power's out," I tell her.

"You're covered in *mud*."

"I ran here."

"From Abe's?"

"Something's wrong," I gasp. "I can't find him, my aunt's passed out, and someone sabotaged the generator back at the house."

"Come inside." She pulls me in. "Hold on. I've got some camping lanterns around and a few candles. I didn't know about the power. I was sleeping."

"Where's Fritz?" I ask.

"His cabin's two doors down." Lark's rummaging around in a closet, but returns to the small living area. She sets two kerosene lanterns on the table and lights them, twisting the knob until they glow. They're so bright, in fact, that I turn off my flashlight. Might as well save the battery.

"You okay?" she asks. "I can make you some hot chocolate. I've got a gas stove."

"I need to find Fritz. I need to speak with him."

"Right! Let me get him. Sit tight, okay?" Lark pulls on her own jacket and shoes and heads out into the night.

Alone and shivering, I look around. These rustic wood cabins consist of a main room and kitchen, two small bedrooms with bunk beds and one shared bathroom and shower. They're furnished with institutional couches and coffee tables and other bare-bones supplies, but I'm too wet to sit anywhere. I do, however, slide out of my wet coat and hang it on a row of hooks by the front door. My hands are shaking, and I hold them close to the lanterns' heat.

Lark returns soaking wet and with her teeth chattering. "It's wild out there! But he's coming. He's trying to get the generator to the village going. I think it's hooked up to just lights and heat, but it'll be enough."

I try peering out the window. "Okay."

"Sit down." She gestures at the couch. "It's fine. I don't mind that you're wet. Put a blanket on yourself."

"Thanks," I say. "Is someone else here?"

Lark looks at me. "Like who?"

"Like a roommate."

"Oh. No. I have this whole place to myself. On account of being the only girl around. Lucky me, huh?"

"My aunt says you're not a warden."

"She's right. I'm a researcher. I've got a grant through the state, which is why I can stay here. Your uncle had to approve it, but he's cool."

"Yeah, he is," I say. Then: "How well do you know him?"

"Pretty well, I guess. Like I said, he's cool."

"Has he seemed weird to you at all lately?"

"Weird how?"

"I don't know. I just get the feeling he's stressed about something. He and Callum had a fight earlier and she wanted to stay in my room. She said he'd been drinking."

Lark shrugs. "Marriage is hard. It's probably not for everyone. Between them, my parents have ruined five."

"But you like Fritz."

"That's not the same as marrying him."

I frown. "Why's he taking so long?"

"He's coming," she says. "He'll be here soon."

"Maybe he needs help."

"I doubt it."

"Where're you moving to after here?" I ask.

She grins. "Vail. Ski season. Might be back next year, though, if I can get another research position."

I jump to my feet. "I'd really like to help Fritz. Can you just tell me where he is?"

"Of course," Lark says. "The generator for the whole village is located past the general store. On the side with the office. He was headed down there."

"Thank you."

"I can go with you," she offers. "I just need to get dressed in something warmer."

"No, it's fine." I grab my jacket from the hook and slide it on, but as I push my arms through, I happen to look down and spot something: a pair of brown work boots. They're identical to the ones I saw in the laundry room earlier, all wet and mud-stained. I pretend to lean down to tie my own boots so that I can get a better look. Obviously these could just be a different pair of the same brand. But also they're huge—way bigger than Lark's feet—and then I notice red stains dotting the toe frame, little spatters, as well as more pooling on the vinyl floor.

I straighten up, reach for the door. "Thanks a lot, Lark."

"No problem," she calls out.

Back outside. My whole body's trembling.

Was that *blood*?

I take off, panic propelling me in the direction of the general store. Only I don't see Fritz anywhere. Plus, the power's still not on. Frustrated, I search everywhere until, finally, I spot two lights coming toward me. Thank *God*. It's a vehicle, what appears to be an SUV, moving slowly with its wipers and high beams on, almost as if it's looking for someone. Rushing into the road, I wave my arms frantically.

The SUV inches closer before rolling to a stop and flashing its headlights. I rush to the driver's side door. Knock on the window.

"Fritz!" I call out. "It's me, Bea."

The window rolls down, revealing the driver. I lift my flashlight to his face. And gasp. Because it's not Fritz.

It's *Leif*.

25

"WHAT ARE *YOU* DOING HERE?" I ask. "Where's Fritz?"

"Who's Fritz?" he asks. "I'm looking for your uncle."

"Did you try the house?"

"Yes," he says. "Why don't you get in? It's freezing."

"But where are you going?"

"Get in, already!"

Against my better judgment, I run around to the other side and crawl into the SUV's passenger seat. Turns out it's a fancy late-model Volvo with heated seats and soft tan leather. Once inside, my body melts in appreciation of the warmth, the comfort. The rest of me, however, remains on high alert.

I look over at Leif who's looking back at me, his expression as infuriatingly aloof as ever, with his dimpled chin raised and shaggy blond hair tucked into the collar of his expensive-looking raincoat. On closer inspection I spot shadows under his eyes, sunken half-moons I've never noticed before. To me they suggest he's either seriously sleep-deprived or he's lost a significant amount of weight in the past few days.

"Leif," I say, straining to meet his jittery gaze. "Why are you looking for my uncle?"

He reaches to pull his seat-belt strap across his chest and buckles it before indicating that I should do the same.

"*Leif,*" I repeat sternly.

He sighs, a long exhalation of weariness. "What?"

"Tell me what you're doing here. It's the middle of the night."

"I told you I was looking for your uncle. Same as you, right? You're looking for him because he's not at his house during a violent storm and that's scary because the power's out and he's not acting the way he usually does. Like maybe he's been drinking too much and keeping to himself and not really telling anyone anything. How am I doing so far? Do I have this right?"

My hand reaches for the door handle. "How can you know all that?"

"I'm here to help you. Don't you think you should be a little more grateful?" Leif whips his head to look at me, teeth bared and his tone dripping with malice.

I glare back. "What were you doing at his house?"

"What do you think?"

"I don't know."

Leif releases the emergency brake and nudges the Volvo forward with a lurch. "Maybe I don't, either."

"I don't want to play games."

He shudders, a whole full-body motion, but ignores my inquiries and focuses on navigating the vehicle back through the village and farther into the preserve, easing his way down the rain-soaked pavement. The storm's quieted, but damage is everywhere.

"Leif," I say. "How do you know my uncle?"

"Asking the same thing over and over isn't going to get you the answers you want."

"What should I be asking?" I ask.

Leif shrugs and keeps driving, blowing past the turnoff to Lake Paloma, and also the one that leads to the deserted campground. He continues farther, finally turning down a steep semi-paved road labeled PRIVATE: DO NOT ENTER.

We're swiftly devoured by trees, by isolation. I haven't been this way before and I twist my neck to look over my shoulder, watching the road vanish behind us. Then I face forward again, sneaking glances at Leif who's hunched over the steering wheel, hands gripping tightly as we bounce and jolt over endless potholes, the road we're on leading us down, down, down.

"Nothing's out here," I say.

"Big-Brain Bea." Leif rides the brakes but pushes the Volvo farther as the slope steepens. In the darkness and slick weather, the angle gives the sensation of weightlessness, as if we've crossed over some critical tipping point and are hurtling to our end. Finally, with a sharp dip and bounce, we hit bottom and level out, tires churning and gnawing their way through dirt and gravel as the paved section ends.

"It's the lake." I realize. The murky surface of Lake Paloma fills the view from the windshield, swirling and lapping in the uneasy weather. We've arrived at the north end, at the spot where the lake is dammed and overflow spills down the mountainside in the form of Paloma Falls. The road directly in front of us is flooded so Leif rolls the SUV into the high brush where he parks and sets the emergency brake.

"Come on." He unbuckles his seat belt, opens the driver's side door.

I stare after him as he slides into the wind-whipped night. "Where are you going?"

"Don't make me say it again." He closes the door and hikes up the hillside in an effort to skirt around the pool of standing water that was once the road. I hesitate, loath to leave the Volvo's warmth. Loath to follow a boy I don't trust.

But I have to.

With a snarl, I unbuckle my belt, leap from the vehicle, and hurry after him, slipping and sliding my way up the hill and over piles of wet leaves.

"Can I tell you a story?" Leif asks when I finally catch up. His tone's softer now, near melancholy. Our shoulders practically touch, that's how close I have to be to hear him. "You've probably heard some version of it already, a kinder, gentler one. But I'd rather you hear my version."

"I thought we were going to find my uncle," I say.

"We are. But it'll take a while to get there."

"Okay," I say wearily, as we clamber back down toward the trail. Safe from the puddle, we walk side by side in a mist of light rain while mud slops and squelches beneath our shoes. "Yes, yes, tell me your story."

26

"I was twelve when the feed shop in our hometown burned down," Leif begins. "It was late morning, and I watched the whole thing happen because I was skipping class that day. I hated school and being forced to sit in a room at a desk made me feel like I was going to explode."

"Why?" I ask.

"It's how I've always been. It's hard to describe, though. What it's like to have so *much* inside of you that sitting still feels like punishment. But a personal one. Almost like a trap. And what does a trapped animal do?"

"I don't know."

"It fights," he says. "But for a while I had other ways of dealing with it. See, when Leisl and I were little, *I* was the funny one. I could make people laugh, while she would sob and sob when Mom would drop us off for the day. Later she learned to read and draw and stay in her own little world, while I kept upping the ante on my schtick. Soon I was doing pratfalls in the school plays and making fart noises whenever a teacher dropped something. Just to get that laugh. It was invigorating, learning how to control others when the rest of me felt so out of control.

"But it wasn't always laughs. Even at our fancy private school. There was a lot of focus on *intervening* with my bad habits and helping me explore my alternatives before it was too late. When I was in grade school it felt as if the adults around me could see my whole future, and I was destined to fail. They were probably right; by the time I was ten, I'd been suspended more than six times and each one broke my heart because I didn't know what I'd done wrong. Or I knew what I'd done. But not why it was wrong. Anyway, one day in fourth grade my art teacher told me I couldn't finish a watercolor that I was making for Mother's Day because I'd already wasted too much paper. It didn't matter that it finally looked good, and I'd gotten the shape of the flowers just right. No, she said, what mattered was that prior to this painting I'd used too many sheets of paper and that meant I couldn't have this one. She grabbed it from me so I told her she was a terrible teacher and that the only thing she'd ever taught me was how to lie and steal to get my way. Then she tore up the painting and threw it in the trash, and I couldn't help myself. I threw the glass of water I'd been using to clean my brush at her, and it hit her in the chest. Didn't hurt her. Just splashed some and broke on the floor, but I was expelled and had to go to behavioral therapy to 'deal with my anger issues.' Only I didn't learn to deal with anything on account of who my parents are."

"So what happened?"

"I stayed home for a year with private tutors while I did more therapy. Leisl stayed at the school, and everyone knew what happened, but if anyone asked, our mom would tell people I was gifted and that the lack of rigor was why I'd left. Leisl hated that because it implied I was smarter. Anyway, that school ended at fifth grade so we were together again in middle school, at a new place, a real prep school that prides itself on feeding into the best boarding schools in the region. It's advanced everything, which was fine. I'm not dumb, despite what anyone tells you."

"I don't think you're dumb," I say. "I've never thought that."

"But you've never liked me."

"I don't know you."

We walk in silence for a moment. "Did you grow up coming out to this lake?" he finally asks, gesturing at the dark water. We've almost reached the cement dam, and the roar of the waterfall's grown louder.

"Not really. My uncle's only lived out here a few years."

"With his wife?"

I nod. "They moved into the house after they were married. My dad was the one who introduced them, believe it or not. They're kind of an unlikely couple. In some ways, she's got more in common with my dad. They're both scientists. They're both focused on making the world a better place or whatever. For a while, I worried my dad was interested in her. Not that that's bad. But I'm glad he wasn't."

Leif scowls. "That's right. I forgot your mom died."

I wasn't aware he knew. "It's been almost five years."

"What was that like? Losing her?"

"For me . . . very, very sad. And isolating. At first there's this protective thing, not wanting to see other kids with their moms or being reminded of what you don't have and people pitying you. But when that's over, you're more alone than ever. Now the hardest thing is knowing what was lost. There's no wondering who my mom would've been or what she would've done if her dreams hadn't been cut short. She *had* the life she wanted. She would've given anything to watch me grow up and to grow old with my dad."

"How's he taken it?"

"He was sad, at first. And angry. Now I think he's lonely, but he won't say it."

"Do you want him to date or get married again?"

"I want him to be happy."

"I hate death," Leif says. "I don't ever want to die."

"Finish your story," I tell him.

"You're sure you want to hear it?"

"I just said I did."

"Fine. I was twelve when the feed store in my hometown burned down," he repeats. "The fire started in the back of the store, where the fertilizer and everything was kept, so the place went up fast. Early in the day, there weren't a lot of customers, but I saw people running out, pointing and shouting. Flames spilled from the windows and thick smoke poured from gaps in the wood siding. It was so hot. I wasn't close, but even from the parking lot it felt like the heat might reach me, might devour me whole.

"Then I saw this woman who was screaming her daughter's name. *Ellie! Ellie!* I heard her wailing to a man that Ellie was inside, that she'd run back in to save the big tub of chicks they had in there. Well, I knew where that was, the chick tub. It was by the cat and dog food, kind of in the middle of the store, and so I took off running, heading around to the front of the building and sprinting inside. The flames were still concentrated near the back, but the smoke was everywhere and the instant I got inside, I dropped to the ground and army crawled to where I knew the chicks were kept. And there she was—this little girl sitting with a lapful of dead chicks. I didn't hesitate. I pulled her with me, dragging her through the store. It took forever. I thought we would never get out, and I was coughing so hard I nearly puked. But I kept going, dragging her, just barely making it to safety before I passed out. Later, when I woke up in the hospital, everyone told me I was a hero. That Ellie would've died without me."

We've reached the dam and stand side by side, looking down at the moonlit waterfall. It's usually calm, but with the storm and the rain, the water's shooting out, a plunging spray that drops nearly forty feet into a churning pond that becomes a river and a creek and eventually stretches to the ocean. An almost inconceivable journey. From this vantage point, at least.

"Why'd you get arrested?" I ask Leif.

He twists his head to look at me, his gaze sharp, almost probing. "You know why."

"I do?"

"Of course. Just like you know other things. Like the fact that I was on the hiking trip that day, which is how I know your uncle. And about—"

"About what?"

The smile he gives is a sick one. "Me and Eden."

27

I SWALLOW HARD. "YOU AND *Eden*?"

Leif smirks. "Stop playing coy. She's the reason you're here, isn't she?"

"I thought we were here to find my uncle."

"That's not what I'm talking about. I'm talking about all your digging around and your writing. The questions you go around asking and the way you won't let things go—even when you should. *That's* what's brought you here. I can see it. Because you're just as obsessive as I am."

"You lied to him, didn't you?" I say. "You lied to my uncle about where Eden had been, and you sent him searching in the wrong place."

Leif cocks his head. "Why would you think that?"

"Because none of the stories from the day she went missing add up. Plus, my aunt said *you* were the cause of my uncle's guilt. That you're the reason he hates himself for not saving Eden, even though he did nothing wrong. Even though he was never in a position to save her."

"I didn't lie about anything," Leif snaps. "I told him the truth on that very first day. He brought me to his house and

asked me what I knew, and I told him. Right from the start. Whatever he did next and what he chose to believe is on him."

"What did you tell him?" I ask.

"That I brought her out here."

My eyes widen. "*Here?* Out to the dam?"

"That's right. And later the group walked out this way. I told him that, too."

"That doesn't make sense. Deputy Williams told me there was a photo taken of Eden hiking out from the south end of the lake. And then she was found in the water. That's why he's never felt comfortable calling Eden's death an accident. The timeline and the evidence don't add up."

"Who told you that?" he asks.

"The sheriff's deputy from Cabot Cove. You know him." I sigh. "He's the one whose older brother went to Broadmoor on a scholarship. Chrissy Lambert's boyfriend. He was part of Eden's search party."

"Okay."

"So how did you end up out here if there's a photo proving otherwise?"

"I'm happy to show you," he says. "We're out here anyway, and I can take you the same way that Eden came that day. If that's what you want."

"I do."

He brushes his wet hair out of his eyes. "Fine. We'll have to cross over the dam, though. If you want to see everything."

Cross the dam? I squint out at the narrow walkway

spanning the cement structure. There are metal railings on each side, but everything's wet and slippery and the water's running so high, it's practically flowing over the top.

Leif clocks my hesitation. "Scared?"

"Should I be?"

"Do you know what it's like to be a hero?" he asks.

"Not at all," I say.

"Oh, come on. That's not true. You just had that write-up in the paper a few weeks ago after you exposed the Seacrest HOA. I read the whole thing. You're the newest Fletcher sleuth, and not only are you clever, but you saved a bunch of kids whose parents wanted to torture them. Sounded pretty heroic to me."

Was that really just weeks ago?

"I wasn't looking for glory," I insist. "I was looking for Jackson. He was the hero. He's the one who saved the others. He saved himself, too. He just didn't want people to know what he'd done."

"So *you* got the attention. What was that like?"

"Not good," I tell him. "I don't like being in the spotlight, but it felt important to have the truth out there. To try and offer as much transparency as I possibly could. That's kind of the whole point of journalism. To help inform people and to also shine a light where maybe other people have been hiding their secrets. But having my name attached to it all has meant . . ."

"It's meant what?"

"It's invited some unwanted attention," I say.

"From who?"

"I don't know."

"Do you think I did it?" Leif asks. "Do you think I killed her?"

"I don't know what to think."

"I'm going to ask you again. Do you want to cross over the dam? Do you want to see where Eden went?"

I don't want to do it, of course. The thought terrifies me. But Leif's also right about my obsessive nature. About why I'm here.

"Let's go," I say.

× × ×

I regret my bravado almost immediately. My short stature and overthinking tendencies haven't gifted me with any extra grace or coordination when it comes to physical challenges. Just the opposite, actually. Standing at the dam's edge, I can't stop looking down at the drop below with its foaming spray and churning depths.

Still, what choice do I have?

With gritted teeth, I go for it, slinging both arms over the railing and doing my best to hold tight. Wet metal's about as easy to grip as a wet fish, and my movements are halting, shaky, as I reset my balance with every step, every slip that threatens to send me flying. Leif's out in front of me, already edging over the center of the dam, at the point where the water's the highest and lapping at his feet. I watch, terrified, as a wild gust of wind suddenly roars through, grabbing his coat, his legs, and causing him to sway.

"Hold on!" I cry out, my voice rising in fear as I watch

him freeze, regain composure, then continue the crossing, his boots stepping evenly and without hesitation.

Fixing my gaze on the back of Leif's jacket, I force my own feet to keep moving, progressing forward by means of an awkward shuffle. I don't get how he's able to move with such ease, even in peril, and I'm also not sure if it's a quality to admire or avoid.

Leif reaches the end, hopping onto the ground with a triumphant bounce before turning to watch me with an amused smirk. A surge of anger pulses through me. I'd like to punch that smirk off his face. He's not even trying to offer encouragement. He's just watching, like my fear is entertainment to be consumed.

My rage emboldens me and I push for the end, jumping down to the ground on my own and ignoring Leif's outstretched hand.

"Let's go," I growl. "This is stupid, being here with you. I should never have come. I should've kept looking for Fritz."

"Who's Fritz?"

"A junior warden. He works for my uncle. His girlfriend said he was back in the village, but I didn't see him. And there were bloody boots in her cabin."

"You saw blood?"

"I think so. It was hard to tell."

"Let's keep walking," he says, gesturing to the lake trail. "We're already here."

"Fine."

"Do you want to know how I got arrested?"

"Only if there's a point to it. Which I doubt."

"There *is* a point," he insists. "I promise. You see, I was twelve when the feed store in my hometown burned, and *I* wasn't used to being the hero. But I'd saved little Ellie, and her family was endlessly grateful. My picture was in the paper. I was awarded a medal from the mayor. Everyone was so *proud* of me. Even that art teacher, the one I told you about. She came up to me at the medal ceremony and apologized. As if what she'd done hadn't been wrong until she decided I was a person worthy of caring about.

"But none of that mattered. Sure, it felt good to be told I was a good person, but it didn't feel good to have to live up to that image. And that feeling I had in school? Like a trapped animal whose body was going to explode? I started feeling like that all the time, even when I was alone.

"The only good thing in my life was Ellie's sister Amanda, who was in my grade. Because of what happened, we became friends and eventually more, although we were still kids and figuring what *more* meant. For us, it mostly involved late-night phone calls and messages. But Amanda never made me feel like I was rotting from the inside out. No, she made me feel like I could still grow and be someone different from who I was but not the kind of different adults were trying to turn me into. Being with her was like a waking dream, and it lasted maybe all of three months. Still, it was enough to let me think that even though I wasn't a hero, I *could* be. I could be anything if a girl like Amanda believed in me." Leif pauses. "But you know what happened next, don't you? You have to know."

"Does it have to do with the feed store fire and why you were already there watching it burn?" I ask.

He grins sickly. "I knew you were smart. And yeah, it took them a while to do all the forensic analysis of how the fire started and where, which was complicated by the fact that the building's air-conditioning unit wasn't up to code—multiple extension cords had been used—but they finally got there. They finally figured it out."

"How'd you do it?" I ask.

"You ever hear of an electrical match?"

I shake my head.

"It's a way of lighting matches from a distance. You can rig them up to wiring and light them using a portable power pack. I'd been working on building a remote model where I could set off the matches from even farther away. Like from the parking lot of a feed store. I guess the investigators found the device but didn't understand what it was at first because it wasn't a bomb. But someone finally recognized the low-volt power pack as being identical to the one they'd seen their kid use as part of a middle school science fair project. And you want to know who that kid's partner had been?"

"You," I say.

He nods. "Even then they got it wrong. They thought I'd started the fire in order to rescue Ellie. That's a thing people do, I guess. Manufacture ways to be a hero. Don't really get it, but I didn't deny it, either. I couldn't tell them the truth—that

I just wanted to burn the place down. Didn't matter, though. Amanda never forgave me."

"You still went in. You didn't want to be a hero and you went in."

"That's not the moral triumph you think it is, I'm afraid." He shivers. "But that's it. That's the whole story. Now you know who I am, and why people like your uncle or that deputy you know just might think my past has something to do with what happened last spring. Or why they think I might've lied or had something to do with Eden's disappearance."

"So what did happen with her?" I ask.

Leif abruptly turns off the trail, ambling down toward the water's edge. "I don't *know*. She was with us until she wasn't. I know it sounds impossible and that's what nobody gets—how no one noticed she was missing. But it's not that far-fetched. First off, the teachers didn't care. Ms. Diamond's this avid bird-watcher, and she was busy taking photographs for some online community she's in. And I don't know how Mr. Jameson got roped into coming. He's the tennis coach and spent the whole time trying to recruit Jerry Reinhardt and Marley Higgins. No one paid any attention to the rest of us. Which was fine and normal, but the news acted like we were kindergarteners who should've been walking in line holding hands or whatever. It was just a hike on a public trail."

"Why'd you go?" I ask.

"You already know why. I've told you."

"You have?"

The look Leif gives me is a pained one.

"Wait," I say. "You had *feelings* for Eden? I thought she was dating Carlos. That's what Leisl told me. Him, too. He's pretty devastated."

"Devastated?" He snorts. "Did either of them tell you *I* was dating her first?"

I shake my head.

"That's what I thought. But Eden was Leisl's roommate. Of course, I met her before anyone else. And, Bea, she was special. For the first time since Amanda, here was a girl who brought out the best in me. She was beautiful, yes, in this ethereal sort of way, but she was also witty and wise and talented. If Amanda was a dream, Eden was a dream within a dream. Until . . ."

"Until she found out what you'd done," I clasp a hand over my mouth, "Oh god. That's awful."

"Her response was exactly what you'd think. She was confused and upset. Worst of all, she pitied me. I hated that." A snarl edges into his voice. "She bought into the same story everyone else had. That I was such a sick and needy boy that I'd staged a fire in order to play hero to a little girl."

"But who told her?" I ask.

"You tell me. But one minute Eden was mine and the next she's with Carlos. My best friend."

"You think *he* told her?"

Leif shrugs. "Nah, not really. It's not his style."

"Leisl?" I ask.

"Uh-uh. That's the thing about my sister. She's brutally honest. It's her best quality. If she was going to tell Eden anything like that, she would've let me know. Leisl doesn't go behind my back. For instance, did she ever tell you any of this?"

"No," I say.

"Voilà." He does a flourish with his hands like a magician revealing a trick. "In the end it doesn't matter who told Eden. What matters is that she knew."

"But what happened?" I ask. "What happened when you came out here with her?"

"I wanted to talk to her that day. I wanted to tell her how sorry I was and that I still thought about her, and also, that what she'd heard about me wasn't the whole truth. That I'm not needy. I'm just really—"

"You're what?" I ask.

"Irredeemable," he says.

28

"LEIF . . ." HIS RESPONSE NEARLY TAKES my breath away. "Why on *earth* would you tell her that?"

He turns around and starts walking again, following the lake's perimeter trail. "Because it's true. I swear I wasn't trying to win her back or make her feel guilty or get her to dump Carlos. I didn't want any of that and I told her so. It was just important to me that she know the truth. Even if it was worse than what she thought."

"What did she say?"

"Mmm." Leif shakes his head. "That's not something I'm going to get into. But she wasn't impressed with my confession and perhaps was a little weirded out by it."

"Okay."

"I wasn't angry with her. That's not what this is about. It was about me finding my own truth, defining it for myself. But I know how it looks. An ex with a history of violence taking a girl into the woods, alone. Only for her to end up missing and dead."

"Were you the last person to see her?" I ask.

"No way. It's not possible."

"Why not?"

"Because *I* last saw her by the dam. We hiked out on the trail that's just up ahead."

"No, you didn't," I say. "You walked out the way you came in. By the beach trail."

Leif frowns. "No, see, that's wrong. We were supposed to go that way and we started to, but then some lady we ran into—she had all these tattoos—she told Ms. Diamond about some rare bird she saw nesting out by the dam. A rusty something. So then we had to come all the way out here and cross the dam, and at that point, it was easier to walk out from the north side. It takes you around the mountain ridge, which was steep, but then it connects back to the Skyline-to-the-Sea Trail."

"Does law enforcement know this?" I ask.

"Of course. I told them. Only they acted like I was lying when they were trying to pin Eden's disappearance on me."

"They knew about the feedstore fire?"

He nods. "But I know I wasn't the last to see her because I last saw her by the dam. I was trying to distance myself since I'd already been humiliated, and so I put earbuds in and kind of tuned out. But we took the long way around the waterfall, hiking down to the pond, crossing the suspension bridge, then hiking back up. Eden slipped and cut her leg on a rock, and I helped her get back to the lake path. She was shaken up by that and her asthma was getting bad. I remember that. She was woozy and kind of flushed and she was struggling to breathe. I made sure she had her inhaler and gave her my water bottle, but then I took off ahead of the group, which is why I didn't notice anything. I was actively trying not to notice her. But I couldn't have been the last one to see her because of where they found her. All the way back by the beach. She wouldn't have gone back past the waterfall on her own. Not after falling the first time. So something happened to her, but I don't know what."

"Why don't people know this?" I ask. "This is a completely different story."

Leif stares at me. "What makes you think people don't know it?"

"I was part of the search party. We were told that the route taken in and out was the one by the beach. There were marked maps handed out."

He shrugs. "Like I said, your uncle was the first person I spoke to. No one realized Eden was missing until we were back at Broadmoor. Ms. Diamond and Mr. Jameson started panicking and first they wanted to head back on the trail we'd just come in on. Then they thought she might've kept going on the trail and headed into town. But I had a bad feeling. I borrowed Colby's car and came out here on my own. I had this image that she'd be waiting for us by the lake with no cell service. Only she wasn't. So I set out in search of the head ranger."

"Uncle Abe."

"Exactly. He let me come inside his house and he asked me what happened. I explained everything. Later, I'm sure he must've heard from Broadmoor and everyone else involved, but I was the one who told him she was missing."

"And he took you seriously?"

"Very. But after that first day, things changed. I was treated like a suspect. Like *I'd* done something wrong."

"You really believe someone killed her," I say. "Are you saying you think someone in law enforcement had something to do with it? And *that's* why the story changed?"

"I don't know," he admits. "But yes, I think someone killed her. Only . . ."

"Only what?"

"Not everyone feels that way."

"Like who?"

"You know."

"Carlos and Leisl?"

"See, you *are* smart," Leif says. "Big detective brain."

"Wait a second." Spotting the silhouette of a crumbling boat dock bobbing in the lake, I stop walking abruptly. "Where are we?"

Leif lifts his flashlight and shines it on the bushes above, illuminating the overgrown cabin with the wide screen porch and fenced yard.

I turn to stare at Leif. "What are we doing here? What do you know about this place?"

"Nothing, really. Wait, what do *you* know about it?"

I jab a finger at the cabin. "*This* is the place that wouldn't let us search their property. I was with Deputy Williams. He was *furious* when we weren't allowed to enter. The cabin's a rental but apparently permission had been granted then revoked without warning. He wanted to get a warrant to get in there. He was going to, but then the dive team found her."

"Interesting," Leif says.

"Did you see anyone when you were here?"

"No. But it's not like we were trying to invite anyone out to play. We were just walking by."

"Want to know something weird?" I ask.

"What?"

"Deputy Williams *still* hasn't been able to figure out who was in the cabin at the time and who put up the signs telling us to keep out."

"And you believe him?" Leif asks.

"I do." I quickly explain what Uncle Abe told me about the probate court and how a judge handed over maintenance and renting duties to some remote management company. "He's still looking into it. Deputy Williams. But I haven't heard from him in a few days. Which is . . . not great."

"Uh-huh," Leif says. "Well, you want to know something even stranger?"

"Sure."

Once again, he points the flashlight at the cabin, and this time I notice something I hadn't seen before; in an upstairs window, there's a light on inside, casting a soft yellow glow into the night.

"What's that?" I ask.

"That," Leif says, "is your uncle."

29

"UNCLE ABE?" I CRY OUT, my breath heavy and labored from scrambling up the cabin's rickety staircase, running down the hall, peering into rooms.

I find him in the very last bedroom—there's no furniture, the walls are lined with wood paneling, the floor's covered in shag carpet, and my uncle is sitting cross-legged and alone in the very center of the room wearing his heavy Department of Inland Fisheries and Wildlife jacket. He's also surrounded by empty beer bottles and a few flickering candles. I can only see the top of his head, his thick dark hair, because he's holding a notebook on his lap and he's writing, his hand moving fast, a scrawling swoop of cursive lettering.

Uncle Abe doesn't stop or look up as Leif and I come crashing in, although he has to hear us. There's no other sound but the soft pattering of light rain falling on the roof, from the trees.

I stand, frozen, watching him.

"Uncle Abe?" I say again as Leif pokes me in the shoulder. I glance up and see he's got a finger pressed to his lips. Then, very slowly, he gestures at something in the room, just beyond where my uncle's sitting. I'm too short to see what it is, and I shake my head. Leif frowns, then mouths a word I do recognize.

Gun.

Oh god. No, no, no.

I take a tentative step into the room. Then another. Sure enough, his service revolver is just lying there on the floor, not far from my uncle's crossed knee.

"Uncle Abe," I say softly. "It's me, Bea. I'm with my friend Leif. We've been looking all over for you. We've been worried. The storm knocked out the power."

"You shouldn't be here," he says. "I didn't want you to come. I didn't want you to be a part of this."

"A part of what?"

"Finding answers."

"About Eden?"

Uncle Abe suddenly looks up, his face blanching at the sight of Leif. "What's *he* doing here?"

"He's helping me."

My uncle lets out a barking laugh. "Him? Oh no. I don't think so. He's made this whole mess worse from the start. Tells me to look one place and makes me look bad. Like he thought it was a joke. A girl *died*."

"He doesn't think that," I say. "He cared about her. It's why he's here. Why we're both here."

"Did he tell you that? If so, then he's as bad at lying as I am."

"You aren't bad," I insist.

Uncle Abe gives me a withering look. "I know how you

feel about me, love, and I wish I could live up to being the uncle you deserve. I've wished that for a long time, but wishes aren't real. Only action is. And I've failed you. I've failed everyone because I've never had the courage to do the right thing at the right time. Shouting about the devil once you've opened the door and let him walk inside is no virtue. So trust me when I tell you I'm not a good person. I haven't been for a long, long time. Maybe ever."

I look helplessly back at Leif.

"Mr. Fletcher," Leif says. "I'm here tonight because of you. Because I'm as lost as you are. I've seen you out here for the past six months searching for the same truth that I'm looking for. Trying to find an answer for a tragedy and maybe righting some of the wrongs in my life. But also, this isn't just about Eden. I think you know that as well as I do."

"It's not?" I ask.

"No." Leif walks over to my uncle and kneels beside him, blocking the candlelight and the gun so all I see is their silhouettes, the way they blur together. "Look, sir, I read Bea's column about Daniel Sousa, and I know what happened to you. Not what she wrote, but I know what *really* happened. I recognized it the minute I read it. The patterns. The pressure. The deep, deep shame. *That's* why I'm here, why I came all this way in a storm to find you. Because I need your help, and you're the only person who can possibly understand what I mean. Who can help me figure out how to face what I've done. Because I don't always know that I can."

"What are you saying?" Uncle Abe asks.

"That *I'm* part of it, too! That thing we're never supposed to talk about. That thing that lives inside us and eats away at anything good or beautiful or wondrous in our lives. I'm part of it, and I hate myself for it. I can't live with it. But I don't deserve to die." Leif's voice cracks as he collapses into my uncle's arms, chest heaving with sobs.

Reaching to comfort and soothe a boy he barely knows and certainly doesn't trust, my uncle glances over at me, catching my gaze for just an instant with an expression that reads as both remorseful and relieved.

"What's he a part of?" I whisper. "What's he talking about?"

"The Honor Guard," Uncle Abe whispers back.

× × ×

An eternity passes while I say nothing. I'm near invisible in that room as these two, bonded by shame and secrets, flood the space with a raw intensity that's difficult to witness. My uncle's kind, and with the wisdom of age and experience, he calms Leif with assurances that he's no longer alone in his despair, and that the truth matters.

That it's everything.

They go on like this and I can't parse every word or detail passing between them. I don't need to, either. This moment isn't for me, an outsider. It's for them, for their hushed confessions and shared involvement in what sounds less like an organized secret society than a whisper network powered by male rage and resentment. One that harnessed that rage in the form of harassment, derision, and intimidation aimed at women in positions of power, under the guise of preserving tradition and protecting civility. One that licked its moral wounds by touting noble ends, if never noble means.

The Honor Guard.

"For me it started with one of the guys I worked with at Broadmoor," my uncle tells Leif. "Garrett Sullivan. He was older, this stuck-up kid from Colorado who actually attended Broadmoor. When he told me what he wanted us to do, our four-person work crew of high schoolers, he made it sound like a game but also an uprising. We'd band together, he told us, like a guard determined to protect all who were power-less. It was play stuff, silly, until he somehow convinced us to rebel against authority by getting one over on Daniel Sousa, our crummy, strict, rule-obsessed boor of a boss. Oh, and Garrett had another friend, Henri, who was just as eager, but they didn't tell us about Alexia until later.

"We started with small stuff, and it felt like a joke at first. An in-joke only we understood. We'd pretend to say things to Sousa that we would later deny, and we'd back each other up on this. Then we'd move furniture around the dorms when he wasn't looking and act innocent when he got confused. Garrett was also doing stuff on his own, though. Sicker stuff, like sending Sousa photos of his wife and pretending she was unfaithful. Or playing recordings of their conversations over hidden speakers. And look, I don't think anyone—not even Garrett or whoever put him up to it—ever thought Sousa would do what he did. They just wanted his wife gone and thought that if her marriage imploded then that would do the trick. No way would the school want an adulterous single mother of three in such a public position. But Garrett had a nasty streak in him; he just had this way of exploiting people's weakness. We didn't need to torture Sousa as much as we did, but Garrett had a plan and we followed it, and then a complete and a total nightmare ensued. And look, the fact we didn't know what Sousa was capable of doesn't matter. If you choose to harass somebody, you don't get to claim innocence when they snap."

Leif listens, still emotional, still distraught. "But did anyone threaten you? Did they say they'd come after you? Or make your life miserable?"

"They didn't have to," Uncle Abe says. "After the murders, Garrett made it plenty clear that he, 'didn't remember doing anything.' But he'd kept a record of all the things the rest of us had done. In private, he told me I was the one who scared him the most. He said I was a real sadist—not unlike Sousa—because the quiet ones aren't ever to be trusted. This screwed with me for a long time because no one *had* threatened me. I'd joined in on the harassment because everyone else was doing it and because Sousa had talked down to me. It felt good at first. But later, I started to wonder if it *had* all been my fault. That maybe I'd just imagined Garrett and the others joining in, and that I'd been the real villain all along. I even started worrying that maybe I'd flown to California and killed them myself. How could I know I hadn't? How could I know anything? The murders were so unbearable, so gruesome, that I sort of lost touch with my own reality for a while.

"Eventually, I wrote a letter to Sousa's lawyer, trying to explain what I could and how a group called the Honor Guard had targeted Sousa. I wasn't in a good place and it wasn't a very coherent message. My point wasn't in trying to take blame off him so much as I wanted to also put blame on a group I hardly understood at the time. A group whose complicity I'd contributed to. It didn't do any good, obviously, and so I focused on moving forward and trying to put more kindness in the world than the bad I already had. Which is why Eden's death has meant so much to me. It's like a second chance to do the right thing. Because I know something happened to her. Something connected to my past. But I haven't been able to figure out what."

"How do you know that?" Leif asks. "How do you know there's a connection?"

Uncle Abe gives a long sigh. "Because the state trooper who took over the investigation on the day Eden went missing was Garrett Sullivan."

30

LEIF PULLS HIMSELF UP TO sitting, red-rimmed eyes glittering with intensity. "You think *he* killed her?"

My uncle shakes his head. "I don't have evidence of that. What I do know is that the official story doesn't add up. It hasn't since he took over the investigation. First, there was the thing with the trail and where we were searching, although I thought that was your fault. That you'd lied to me about the route you'd taken to purposely misdirect me."

"I thought *you* were the one who switched the stories," Leif says.

"No. I told Sullivan everything you told me. Then the staties released a completely different narrative. I was embarrassed, but since it was their case, I assumed they'd gotten new information from the rest of the hiking group. Plus, there was no reason for me to question the official account. You weren't the most trustworthy. Or so I'd heard."

"What else made you suspicious?" I ask.

"Well, there was the thing about the occupants of this house not letting law enforcement search the property, even though I'd personally called and spoken with the management company, and they'd agreed. So I tried getting Sullivan to tell me who'd revoked permission and under whose authority, but he just mocked me. Said he'd heard I was a head case who couldn't handle pressure and implied *I* might've hurt Eden. None of it sat right with me, and since then, this house has felt central to whatever happened. And now, thanks to Leif, I know Eden actually *did* come by here."

I'm confused. "But none of the other students or teachers contradicted the story in the papers? Why wasn't that clarified?"

"We were told not to talk to anyone," Leif says. "We weren't allowed to join the search, and after that first day, the lawyers Broadmoor hired warned us to keep our mouths shut. Me, especially, since they hinted that my 'past issues' could point the finger at me, although I did give a statement to the state police. But I didn't care about that. I already didn't trust anyone involved, that's for sure. So I've been looking into this on my own ever since."

"But the Honor Guard stopped you?" I ask.

Leif furrows his brow. "No. Nobody did anything to me."

"Someone told Eden about your arrest."

"Sure. But I don't know who that was."

"Hold on." An idea comes to me, and I turn to my uncle. "Where did you say Sullivan was from originally?"

"Colorado," he says. "He was a big ski bum."

"Does he have a sister?"

"I don't know. Why?"

"Because there's another Sullivan out here. And we *know* her. In fact, I just saw her tonight and she was acting kind of weird."

My uncle tilts his head. "Who are you talking about?"

"Lark," I say.

✕ ✕ ✕

Leif's able to get my uncle's truck keys from him and convince him that he's the one who should be driving the pickup that's in the cabin's driveway. The gun, however, is a different story. It's state issued, yes, but with the drinking, with his state of mind . . .

"I wasn't planning on doing anything with it," Abe says. "All these years, I could have. But I never did."

"Then why bring it?" I ask.

"I have enemies," he says.

"That's not a good enough answer."

"I know," he says. "And I appreciate the concern. It's absolutely something we can talk about at a later date, but I'm not letting either of you have it. That would not be responsible."

"Then lock it up," Leif says. "In the glove compartment. It's also not responsible for someone who's been drinking to have a loaded firearm."

"Fine," my uncle agrees and together we walk out of the cabin. Dawn is on the horizon. The storm's cleared out but the air's still breezy, an icy whip and snap, and the sky's dotted with thick clouds and a pink-rimmed haze.

"Power's back," Leif says.

238

31

Lark's gone.

We arrive at the warden's village to find the power restored and her cabin cleared out. It's surreal, walking into her living room in the morning, with the lights on, after my strange encounter with her in the middle of the night. The first thing I look for are those boots. The ones possibly covered in blood spatter.

They're gone, too.

Did I really see them?

"Hey, Leif," I call out. "Was anyone around when you drove up last night?"

There's no answer.

I turn around and see the door to the cabin standing wide open. Peering out in the morning haze, I spot him and Uncle Abe approaching Fritz's cabin, two doors down.

Ducking back inside Lark's, I go through every room. There are only four, technically—two narrow bedrooms with bunk beds, a bathroom, and the living room and kitchen combo. The bedrooms are cramped, like bunks on a boat or a cabin at summer camp. Everything's dark wood and built into the wall, including shelf units and drawers. With a groan, I haul myself up the wooden ladder to the top bunk that Lark was using. I know it's hers because the sheets are still stretched across the thin mattress. Flopping onto the bed from the ladder, I think I feel a foam topper under there, but it's far from comfortable.

A narrow window lets light spill in, and I dig around in the shelves for anything that might've been left behind when Lark rushed off. There's mostly trash, like food wrappers and empty water bottles. But reaching into the back of one of the built-in cubbies near the head of the bunk bed, my hand closes around a small hardbound book. I pull it out.

Turns out it's one of those narrow graph-ruled Moleskines, and wrapped around it is a scarlet red bow. Perplexed, I slide the bow off and shove it into my coat pocket. I'll show it to Leif later. To see what he thinks.

Then I flip through the notebook. It's definitely Lark's and it contains page after page of tightly scribbled words in handwriting so small, I'm unable to decipher most of it. Maybe it's related to the research she's working on, but there are so many acronyms and archaic symbols in her notes that it feels like she's using deliberate shorthand.

What I am able to interpret, however, are the charming doodles she's drawn around the edges in colored pencil. Living out here, Lark has clearly been enchanted by the wildlife. I spot illustration after illustration of bushy-tailed squirrels chasing one another, swooping dragonflies, and delicate marsh birds with striking plumage. The art's reminiscent of her tattoos, which she must've designed herself. Later, I spot a drawing of what I assume is a slide rock bolter—a big fish-tailed creature lashed to a tree on a mountaintop with its gaping mouth wide open. Beneath the creature, far below, are tiny stick people swimming and fishing by a wind-churned lake, seemingly unaware of the danger lurking above.

Toward the center of the book, Lark's scribbles transform into what look like mathematical equations, although some have numbers and others appear to be Greek letters and chemical symbols, so they represent formulas of some kind. I've gleaned that much from chemistry.

But formulas for *what?*

The notations I recognize are N_2, O_2, and He. I stare at the pages and the first thing that comes to mind is the Aquaman crystal.

But further on in the notebook are more doodles, new ones, what appear to be sea creatures and not from the mountains. I spot crabs, lobsters, shellfish, even a tiny pink prawn. And finally, a hasty drawing of something I've seen before.

Very recently.

My jaw drops.

It can't be.

"Bea!" a voice calls out. "Where are you?"

"Coming!" I shove the book into my pocket and scramble back down the ladder to find Leif and Uncle Abe waiting for me by the open front door.

"What were you doing?" Leif asks.

"Just looking around," I say quickly.

He scowls. "You look weird."

"Did you find Fritz?" I ask.

"No luck," my uncle says. "We should go back to our house. We'll have phones. Internet."

"When did Lark first move here?" I ask.

Uncle Abe pauses. "Over the summer, I believe. She had a six-month grant."

"Do you know where she was before that?"

"No idea."

"And how well do you know Fritz?"

He frowns. "Very. We've worked together for two years as the only permanent staff at this post."

"What're you thinking?" Leif asks me.

"A couple things. First off, something's still not adding up about the whole trail route discrepancy. We know someone changed the story regarding the path the hiking group took after Leif was interviewed that first day. But when did that happen? When did the new story come out?"

"Sunday," Leif says. "I remember seeing it on the news that afternoon."

Uncle Abe nods. "That's right. Initially we were searching at the swimming area, where the group had lunch, but I tried to get a search going by the dam Sunday morning. That's when the staties called it off, said we were in the wrong place."

"Then how is it that I'd already heard that the group had 'hiked out the way they came in' story on Saturday night?" I ask.

"You couldn't have," Uncle Abe says. "I didn't know that then. No one did."

I shake my head. "I swear I saw that somewhere, and I first heard about Eden online. On the TrueMaine forums. But I need my computer. I wrote all of this down when it was happening. I can check there."

"Then let's get back to your uncle's house," Leif urges.

I turn to Uncle Abe. "The wires to the generator were cut last night. I couldn't switch it on."

"Really?" His face is awash with confusion. "I tested it yesterday afternoon. What did Callum say?"

"She was asleep. She didn't say anything."

"Does she know you left?"

"I left a note. She was sleeping downstairs with me before that, though. She said . . ."

"She said what?"

"That you were angry about something."

"Me?"

I nod. "She mentioned you'd had a fight. That's why she was downstairs with me. She thought you should be alone."

"Callum said that?" Uncle Abe rubs his chin. "What would we be fighting about?"

"Did you happen to have Lark over yesterday? For a drink maybe?"

"Lark?" My uncle looks more confused than ever. "No. Absolutely not."

"But you *were* drinking," Leif points out.

"Okay. Sure. But I was in my study, alone. Callum came up eventually, around dinnertime, but she'd been working in her own office. I heard her on the phone."

"I also saw broken glass in the kitchen," I say. "It looked like it was from a beer bottle."

"Let's go back and find Callum," Uncle Abe says. "I'm sure this is all a misunderstanding. I don't know why she'd say any of this. It's true I left the house as the storm was starting, but there was no fight. And no one else was there but you. And Callum said you were sleeping."

We spill out of the cabin and head for the truck.

"Did he lock the gun in the glove compartment?" I whisper to Leif, as we hang back, a few steps behind my uncle.

"Don't think so," he whispers back.

32

THE MAIN ROAD'S BLOCKED BY a downed tree, which means Leif has to turn my uncle's pickup around, head back into the park entrance, and take the unpaved trail through the woods. The obstacle adds a good ten minutes onto the drive, but we finally pull up in front of the mountainside home.

"Someone's here." Leif nods at a Jeep parked behind Aunt Callum's Subaru. It's got a Cabot Cove Sheriff's Office insignia on the side. Beside me, Uncle Abe tenses, and before Leif's even turned off the ignition, he's leaping out the truck. Racing for the front door.

Leif and I follow after. Something feels wrong.

Really wrong.

Uncle Abe's shouting. "Cal! Cal, where are you?"

"Is that your friend?" Leif points to the sheriff's vehicle as we rush past it.

"Don't know," I say. "I don't know why he'd be out here."

Inside, we find the house lit up, the heater running, and Leif and I trail behind Uncle Abe as he barrels from room to room, shouting and desperate to find his wife. In the living room, he stops short at the sight of the wrought iron and glass patio table lying on its side.

"I did that," I say hastily. "It was banging around in the wind last night. I came upstairs and brought it inside. That's when I ran into Callum."

"What time was that?" Uncle Abe asks.

"Midnight, maybe? You were still upstairs by that point."

He cocks his head. "No, I wasn't."

"But I heard you. You were shouting. And your boots were here."

"My boots?" He looks down. "What about them?"

"I saw them by the dryer last night. They were all muddy and wet. Later, when the power went out, they were gone and so were you."

"Those weren't mine," Uncle Abe says. "Maybe they were Fritz's?"

"Maybe. They were the same kind as yours. Later I saw similar boots at Lark's place. But those, uh, looked like they had blood on them."

His jaw tightens. "I'm going upstairs."

"I'll check in the basement," I say.

"What should I do?" Leif asks.

"You want to look outside? Maybe she's out there."

"Whatever. Sure."

"Meet me back here in ten minutes," I tell him.

"Got it."

✕ ✕ ✕

I hurry down the basement steps, hoping to find Aunt Callum still curled on the couch and dead to the world from her sleeping pills. But she's not. Thankfully, Lemon's still in the bedroom, crying to be let out. I pour her food into her bowl, refresh her water, then grab my laptop.

Once the screen wakes up, I go into my documents folder and pull up my drafts for TrueMaine articles. I officially started working for them over the summer, but I was thinking about pitching my column last spring and started taking notes on local crime events as a way of immersing myself in Cabot Cove's most interesting stories.

Here it is. The file titled "Missing Child Lake Paloma," since that was all I knew at the time. I open it and there, right at the top of the page, I'd typed:

Day 1: Saturday, April 29

Facts: Teenage hiker (female?) went missing today out at Lake Paloma.

Was part of hiking group from Broadmoor Academy

Walked in on Skyline-to-the-Sea Trail and ate lunch at the south end beach.

Walked out same way. No one noticed girl missing until group was back at school.

Possibilities: Separated and lost from group; injured and separated from group; abducted by stranger; abducted by someone known to her; hiking group killed her; she ran away on her own and doesn't want to be found (this is Aunt Callum's theory).

An idea hits me. I pull my phone out to scroll through my photos, but before I can do that, I see a ton of different text messages have come through now that the Wi-Fi is reconnected. From my dad, from Leisl and Carlos. And Deputy Williams.

Is that his Jeep outside?

His messages are the most recent, so I open them and read all the way through. Stunned by what I find, I read through them again and I also look at an attached image that he's sent. His last message, sent early this morning after not hearing from me, reads:

Hang tight. I'm coming out there. Don't tell anyone about this.

I text back: *Power just came back on. Where are you?*

Then I send him a photo from my phone's photo roll. It's a picture of Lark from the party the other night. She's standing with Fritz and you can make out the bird tattoos adorning each of her forearms. A horned lark and wide-eyed raven.

Do you know who this is? I ask. *The girl.*

No answer.

My mind's spinning. I return to my laptop and start researching more. A narrative is starting to come together, but the answers aren't what I expected, and I don't have any proof. Not without Deputy Williams, and if he's here, then something might've happened to him.

Something bad.

A sharp knock on the basement's external door startles me. But it's Leif. I see him waving at me through the window. I rush to the door and pull him inside.

"Did you see anything?" I ask.

"Nothing," he says. "Well, lots of trees are down. It's a big mess."

"Oh."

"Why're you shaking?" he asks.

"I can trust you, can't I?" I reach to hold his hand, and he's right. I am shaking.

"Why are you asking me that?"

"I need to know if I can trust you. Not with, like, my life, but can I trust you to have Eden's best interest in mind?"

He pauses, then cups both his hands around mine. "Of course."

"I'm going to ask you a question," I tell him. "And I need you to be honest with me."

"Okay."

"Carlos once told me that he and Eden were part of some accelerated STEM program that lets students shadow real scientists and engineers out in the field. In fact, I think it's a program Dr. Trenta-Sousa set up years ago before STEM was considered a real thing and not just a lowly trade skill."

Leif nods. "Yeah. They were both in it. Eden's dad was big in biotech or something. Carlos is just a nerd about weather. Which is why he forgot to take an art class."

"Did Eden ever do an internship at Bio-Mar?"

"Don't know. She was really into marine biology, though. I know she wanted to swim with dolphins and save sea otters. She liked animals. She wanted to be a dive master one day."

I blink. "Diving? As in scuba diving?"

"Yeah. She'd actually gone out that day. Before the hike."

"In the ocean? With who?"

"No clue. But it was a real early morning thing. Like, at sunrise. It was probably with a local club or something. I guess they wanted to get out ahead of the trappers."

"Did she say how deep they went?"

"No. Why?"

"The tenace clue," I tell him. "Those articles were all about the dangers of diving and pressure differentials. I read a ton about all the ways things can go sideways."

"You think something happened to her underwater?" he asks.

"Not exactly." My brain churns and spits, trying to put the pieces together. "But what if—what if someone knew she was going for a hike at altitude that day and then deliberately made plans for her to go diving beforehand? Going in planes, climbing mountains, any extreme change in elevation can be a risk factor for developing decompression sickness. This mountain isn't that tall, but we also don't know how deep she went, and the risk of illness would increase with other post-dive factors, like heavy exertion, dehydration—or a history of lung problems."

"Like asthma?"

"Exactly."

Leif frowns. "You're talking about the bends? That's the sickness?"

"Sort of. But rather than occurring right when someone

ascends too quickly in the water, it can also happen later, over a period of time. For Eden it would've happened as she climbed in elevation and got worn out. The diving—as well as the gas mix—would've left tiny nitrogen bubbles in her blood, and these bubbles would've expanded with the change in altitude, with her fatigue. They can cause joint pain, organ damage, decrease lung functioning, even impact the central nervous system. In its worst form, the bubbles can cause embolisms."

"You really think this happened to her? That it was intentional?"

"You said yourself Eden was getting woozy and confused when you started climbing out again. That she needed her inhaler."

"Couldn't it just be a terrible accident?"

"I think that was the point," I say. "To make it look like an accident. But there's too much evidence suggesting the opposite. Too many things that don't make sense otherwise."

"Like what?" he asks.

"Have you seen this woman before?" I hold up the one photo I have of Lark, the one I sent Deputy Williams.

Leif examines it closely. "Something about her looks familiar. Where would I have seen her?"

"Her name's Lark Sullivan. She's the woman we were just looking for at the warden's village and potentially Garrett Sullivan's little sister." I pull out the Moleskine journal, along with the red ribbon. "I found this book in her cabin, right by her bed, with this wrapped around it."

Leif reaches for the ribbon. "Tenace. We've solved the clue."

"Then that means the answer is in here, right? In this notebook? The answer to what happened to Eden?"

He nods.

I flip through the pages. "Look, you can see here that Lark knows science. She has notes on different chemical compounds and formulas that I think have to do with the gas mix in the scuba tanks, which she may have tampered with. Plus, she clearly loves animals. She's got doodles and illustrations all throughout this book. But specifically, there's this one."

I point as Lcif's mouth falls open. He gasps. "*That's* the bird we were looking for! The rare one. The rusty blackbird. I remember that name. Kind of looks like a grackle, though."

"The coloring's different," I say.

"Yeah, well, as we were leaving a woman stopped Ms. Diamond and told her she'd seen one nesting by the waterfall. That's why we turned around and went out there."

"Was it Lark? Was she the woman?"

"I can't say for sure. But yeah, it's possible. I think I recognize her tattoos."

"Leif, what if you were purposely directed to go that way? Because it's the steeper trail, with increased exertion and altitude, there would've been a higher likelihood of inducing decompression sickness. And also, it took you past the cabin."

"But who would do that?" he asks. "Who would want Eden dead?"

Which is when my aunt Callum steps out from behind the staircase and comes toward us.

She grins. "Why, me, of course."

33

"You killed Eden!" The words leave my mouth before I'm able to think better of it.

Before I register that my aunt is holding a shotgun by her side.

"*I* didn't do anything," she says mockingly, before tucking her black hair behind her ear. Her eyes, darting back and forth, are bloodshot and swollen. "That was the beauty of it all. All I did was take a girl I'd been mentoring scuba diving—something she'd begged me to do—on the morning before she was going on a school-sanctioned hike with the mean boy who'd broken her heart. That's you, right?"

Leif glares at her but says nothing.

Aunt Callum looks him up and down, then shrugs. "Personally, I don't see what all the fuss is about. Prep school boys with good hair are a dime a dozen around here. Give me a guy with some edge to him. Although, you've got your secrets, don't you?"

"Why would you hurt her?" I ask. "She looked up to you."

"Stop saying that!" she snaps. "I just said I didn't do anything. There was no guarantee she'd fall sick. Or if she did, where it would happen. But sometimes every piece falls into place just perfectly. Some call that a miracle. But I'm a scientist. I understand the nature of probability. The importance of control."

"Where's Fritz?" I ask. "And Lark?"

"Who knows?" Aunt Callum says before sneezing. "I hate your cat, by the way."

"You *have* to know where she is," I insist. "She's your accomplice. She's the one who kept the police from searching the property back when Eden first went missing."

Leif stares at me. "What are you talking about?"

"Deputy Williams sent me the rental agreement this morning. L. Sullivan was the contact listed, but she"—I point at my aunt—"was the cosigner. The contract said that the rental was to be used for research purposes regarding algae levels at the lake."

Aunt Callum sneers at me. "God, you're so whiny. You know everything would've been fine if you'd just stayed asleep last night. You couldn't even eat your food like a normal person."

"You drugged me, didn't you?"

"'You drugged me, didn't you,'" she mocks. "I did what I had to in order to protect my vision. You've got no idea what it takes to run R&D at a company like Bio-Mar. As a *woman*. Everybody's always coming after you, putting pressure on you, waiting to see you fall. You have to take risks. You have to get the job done."

"Why would Eden want to see you fall?" Leif asks.

"Enough." She lifts the shotgun. "You two need to get upstairs. All the way. We're heading to the observatory."

I hesitate, wondering if there's a way to signal to Uncle Abe, but Aunt Callum reads my mind.

"Lark's already taken care of my husband. Don't get any ideas. Now move."

× × ×

Leif goes first, followed by me, then Aunt Callum, who's pointing the shotgun right at my back.

"Hey, pretty boy," she calls out. "Any wrong move up there and you'll be responsible for another girl's death."

"I didn't kill anyone!" he retorts.

"Sure you did. Eden wouldn't have been on the hike if not for you. From the moment I met her, she told me all about you. How in love you two were. That is, until she found out you started that fire."

"*You* told her?"

"Not me. I told you I didn't do anything. But someone was looking out for her. Trying to protect her."

"You're sick," Leif snarls. "You didn't look out for her. You killed an innocent girl. A sweet, smart, brilliant, innocent girl."

"She wasn't innocent, pretty boy. Now keep walking."

We march all the way up to the second floor and then are forced to crawl, one by one, up the metal ladder leading to the observatory—the geodesic dome at the top of the house.

The dome is filled with light, with views in every direction and the storm-wracked sky above. Crawling up after Leif, I emerge onto a gray-carpeted floor that's lined with books and papers in one corner, a large telescope in another.

And directly in front of me, my uncle Abe is seated on a faded leather ottoman, held at gunpoint by Lark.

"Are you okay?" he asks us.

I nod. "Have you seen Fritz?"

He shakes his head.

Lark frowns at the sight of me and Leif. "What are they doing here? This isn't what we talked about."

"They know," Aunt Callum says. "They know everything."

"How?"

"Some deputy found out about the cabin. They know you were there."

They don't know about the sheriff's vehicle outside, I realize.

Oh, please, please, please.

Please help us.

Lark looks furious. "How? Garrett took care of all the records. There was no way to trace this to me. He promised."

"He's *your* brother," Aunt Callum says. "You vouched for him. It's not my fault he's bad at his job."

I try and catch my uncle's eye. "They killed her. They killed Eden."

His face goes white. "You're sure?"

I nod.

"But why?"

"You want to know why, sweetheart?" Callum saunters over, puts the barrel of the gun by her husband's chin. "That little witch was stealing from me. After all I did to mentor her. I invited her into my laboratory, where I trusted her with some

257

of our most important work. And then she had the nerve to try and steal the work we'd done on the red-tide modeling. It was all on her phone. She'd copied the algorithm, our research results that went back years, and she was going to send it to her father. He heads Eco-Solutions out of Kentucky. I should've known he sent her to me for a reason. Maybe he was the one who told her about you." She points at Leif. "Although that turned out to be a helpful piece of information."

"What're you *talking* about?" he asks.

"Knowing your secret let us put the right pressure on you to keep your dumb mouth shut. Like when you tried reaching out to Deputy Williams last month? We've been watching you. Lark made sure you knew that was a bad move."

"How did she do that?" I ask. "And when did you reach out to Deputy Williams?"

"She means the fire," Leif says under his breath. "At the library."

Faintly, beneath my aunt's legs, I spot movement coming up the ladder to the observatory. My own legs start to shake, but I hide my fear with offense.

"You're wrong, you know," I tell Aunt Callum, trying to come up with something, anything to distract her. "Eden wasn't the one spying on you or plotting to steal your work. You were tricked, but not by her."

"Don't go down your detective route," she sneers. "You're not as smart as you think you are."

"But I can prove it. In my back pocket, I have a journal that I found in Lark's cabin."

Lark's head swivels in my direction.

I keep going. I need to get the words out. "It was by her mattress. She and her brother are the ones who've been stealing from you. You can see for yourself. She's got your plans for the Aquaman crystal in there. All the details are written down alongside the formula you're using to eliminate neurotoxins from the shellfish. That's your real use for the crystal, isn't it? Not swimming underwater."

My aunt turns on me. "What did you say?"

"It's in my jacket pocket. Take a look if you don't believe me." I raise my hands. "There's even a blueprint of your precious *Elysium*. Lark's behind all of it. I swear. She handpicked Eden for you out of all the Broadmoor students who were interested in Bio-Mar. Probably had her brother doing background checks on Eden's dad. And on Leif here. Gathering info that she could use to bond you to Eden before making you feel betrayed by her. Lark knew which of your buttons to push and she used them to propel you right into killing that girl, giving her all the power in the world over you."

Aunt Callum meets my gaze, scanning for earnestness, which I assume she finds. Leaning forward, she reaches her hand into the side pocket of my jacket, fingers grasping for the small journal.

She's pulling at it when the gun goes off.

I scream, falling to the floor. Two more shots are fired and someone lands on top of me. I'm vaguely aware of Deputy Williams rushing into the dome and my uncle raising his own gun. There's more screaming and snarling and bodies crashing together. I whimper, terrified, unable to move, and all I can think is *I'm sorry, Daddy* because this isn't what he wanted for me, and I shouldn't have gotten involved in something I don't understand. And more than anything, my one hope when I die is to be with my mother again.

"Move!" a voice shouts in my ear. "Hurry! Go!"

I lunge forward, diving for the railing that leads back down the ladder and out of the observatory. I tumble through the opening, slipping headfirst before being able to grab at the ladder, catching myself and banging hard against the rungs. My hip and shoulder explode in pain, and I drop the rest of the way, crumpling to the floor. Leif comes down after me, his leg twisting and cracking as he falls. He grabs for me, pulling me by the arm and dragging us down the hallway. I push open the first door we encounter, and we crawl our way in, slamming the door behind us. Leif shoves a nightstand under the knob as a lamp goes crashing. We're in the master bedroom, I realize.

"Come on," I shout because there's a balcony. I slide open the door leading out to it, Leif hobbles over, and we clamber out into sunshine, falling back against the railing and turning our faces upward to get a look at the observatory.

"What happened?" I gasp. "What just happened?"

"Lark shot your aunt," Leif says between breaths. "Then that cop you know, he tried to shoot her, but she shot back."

"And my uncle?"

"I don't know."

Another burst of gunfire explodes above us, followed by

a shower of breaking glass. Leif and I watch as a woman's body falls from the third floor, cartwheeling out over the canyon before dropping

down

down

down.

I look away before my aunt hits the ground, but the sound is sickening.

"It's okay." Leif wraps his arms around me, holds me to him. "It's over now. It's really over."

34

Two days later, I show up in the Critical Care waiting area of the Portland Medical Center with my dad in tow. He's still in a state of shock. I guess I am, too.

There's a flurry of handshakes and greetings as we're introduced to Leisl and Leif's parents, the Schoenholzes. They came up immediately to be by Leif's side when they heard he was injured, and now that he's been transferred here ahead of the surgery he'll need to fix his leg, we've been invited to see him. Just briefly. Turns out his leg's not only broken in two places, but there's significant ligament damage as well. His recovery will be a long one.

My eyes fill with tears and I want to apologize, to tell Leif's parents how sorry I am that he was hurt saving me. How sorry I am about everything. That my aunt was a killer and that she and her accomplice came so very close to killing Leif. The details are still coming out, but from what little we know it seems Lark Sullivan was never who she appeared to be. After forging a degree from Scripps, she was hired on as a research assistant at Bio-Mar last year, and her initial duties included meeting with high school students who were interested in exploring scientific career paths. This is where

Lark first met Eden. It's also where she met my aunt, and by all accounts they were fast friends, connecting over the isolation of being women in biotech.

A lot remains unknown about their interactions, but I hypothesize that Lark, who'd come with bad intentions, seeded ideas about corporate espionage into my aunt's head, fears of other companies wanting to take her down or humiliate her professionally. Offering my aunt emotional support when no one else did, Lark fostered a sense of dependence, of unshakeable trust. But somewhere along the way, my aunt must've begun to suspect she was being taken advantage of. So to deflect attention from her own treachery, Lark set out to frame Eden, and goaded my aunt into concocting a plan to kill Eden by inducing decompression sickness. Lark used paranoia and outrage as weapons, just like her brother Garrett did with the Sousas.

And like Garrett's threats to implicate my uncle, Lark held their secret over my aunt's head. She moved into the warden's village and hooked up with Fritz in order to be close to Callum, while at the same time her Maine State Police brother was using his position to obscure the truth about Eden Vicente's disappearance. Including any connection to the fact that it was Lark who'd intercepted a woozy Eden as she passed by the rented cabin that day.

I imagine poor Eden would've been so relieved to see her, eager to ask for her help. And maybe Lark had been kind and seemingly concerned, inviting her in, sitting her down, and then waited for her to die. Worse, though, is the newly floated idea that she'd put a debilitated Eden in an unheated salt-water hot tub at the back of the rental property, drowning her and storing her body until she could dump it in the lake. That would explain the panic about the search party. The traces of salt in her lungs. But none of this has been confirmed yet. The FBI's now taken over the investigation, and I hope for Eden's family's sake that they're able to get real answers this time.

And now I *am* crying in the waiting room, racked with guilt and sorrow and grief for a girl I didn't know, an aunt I thought I did, and for all the ruined lives that have been left in the wake of this disaster. Anyway, someone must've told Mrs. Schoenholz nice things about me because she pulls me close and whispers, "Thank you, my love. Thank you for bringing him back off that mountain. He's the one I worry about. He's too sensitive for this world and that's a hard thing for a mother to know."

× × ×

Stepping into the hospital room, I barely get a glimpse of Leif before the memories come flooding back. Our panicked scramble from the observatory. The gunshots. Leif shouting for me to save myself.

Carlos turns around. He's the first to notice my presence.

"Hey, look who it is." His handsome face lights up and he uses his shoulder to nudge Leisl. "It's our danger girl. *God,* we were so worried about you."

The words are barely out of his mouth before Leisl's launched herself into my arms, driving me back and bear-hugging me and sort of laughing and crying all at once.

"Why didn't you call me?" she whimpers. "Why didn't you tell us what was going on?"

"I'm sorry," I say.

"I expect that sort of thing from *him*. But not you."

"I'm sorry," I say again as Carlos crosses the room to reach me. He kisses my cheek and the hug he offers is firm and quick and reassuring in a way I didn't know I needed.

"Leisl, let her go," he says. "The girl needs air."

"No, she doesn't." Leisl grips me harder, squeezing my rib cage so tight I can hardly breathe. But the thing is, I don't want her to let me go.

Not ever.

It's from over her shoulder that I finally get a good look at Leif. He's lying on the bed, all glassy-eyed and zoned out on pain meds, with his leg elevated and wrapped in a temporary cast. But he's looking back at me, his lips twisted in the faintest hint of a smile. He's so thin, I realize. A boy waiting to be broken. Why hadn't I seen it before?

But there's something else in Leif's eyes, something I definitely haven't seen until now, at this very moment. It's a kind of radiance. Not joy or anything like that. It's more like, he's alive.

Living, really.

Heart soaring, I lift my fingers and wave to him. Then I watch as his eyes flutter shut and he drifts off to sleep.

35

SIX WEEKS HAVE PASSED SINCE the night of the storm. The investigation's still ongoing but there's been a steady march toward closure. First of all, Aunt Callum's family had her remains transported back to Arizona so they could bury her in the ground against her express wishes to be cremated. They also didn't personally come and get her. Her body was transported alone in the bottom of a plane, which only proved true her earlier lament that her family had no interest in leaving their lives to find a space in hers. Although I'm sure there were other reasons, too.

Fritz has not been found, and while I long to hold out hope that he learned who Lark really was and fled her cruelty to hide out in a national park somewhere, it doesn't feel realistic. The bloody boots were also never found, and it breaks my heart to think he died trying to stop my aunt and Lark from whatever it was they were planning that night. To kill my uncle. To kill Leif. Or me.

Speaking of my uncle, well—he's not been doing a lot of that lately. Speaking, that is. This is much to my father's consternation, who's convinced his brother's teetering on the edge of a breakdown. Only I'm not so sure. He hasn't run off or gone underground or sought escape like a skittering prey animal. He's grieving his wife, yes, and coming to grips with what she did, but the times when I've seen him, he's mostly been focused on his work. On rebuilding. What more could anyone do?

And then there's Leif. They say bonds are formed during the adrenaline rush of survival. Maybe that's meant to be a specific reference to times of war and life on the battlefield. The way in which those moments likely shape who you are, not only by what you've lived through, but by the fact that there are so few people who understand what it means to not die.

Well, we may not have gone to war together, but there is a bond between us now. One that's hard to explain to anyone outside of it. Especially Leisl and Carlos who seem to intuit a change but don't know what to make of it. I guess I don't, either.

But it's there.

Exhibit A would be Leif dropping by my house today, on a Monday afternoon in January. His leg's still healing; he recently moved from a hard cast to a full leg brace and can drive and hobble in out of the cold on his own. I'm slightly terrified he'll slip on ice, but he doesn't, and once inside he greets me and my father and reminds us to hide our spare key somewhere other than under the plant on our front porch.

It's already dark out, these dreary winter days, and my dad brings us hot chocolate to sip by the wood-burning stove. It's not the first time Leif's asked to come visit since returning from winter break, but today, I get the feeling there's something more to it. Something he wants to say.

"Your leg doing okay?" I ask.

"Not exactly," he says with a grimace. "The bottom bone's still bent and it's been reset twice already."

"What happens next?"

"More surgery."

"I'm sorry."

"I'll live."

"How are Leisl and Carlos?" I ask. "We've been texting but haven't gotten together lately. How's the play coming? I really want to see it."

"They want to see you, too," Leif says. "Especially my sister."

My cheeks warm. "Yeah?"

"She's a good person. You should spend more time with her. If that's a thing you like doing. You're a good person, too, Bea."

"Thank you."

"They still have a lot of questions, though."

"I don't blame them," I say.

"How's your uncle?" Leif asks.

I smile faintly. "You'd know better than me. I hear you've been out to see him a few times."

Leif shrugs, sips his drink. "Turns out we have a lot in common."

There's the bonding thing again. "What do you do when you're out there?"

"Mostly he puts me to work. Even with my busted leg he has me organizing files, reviewing checklists for various projects. Which I like. It keeps my mind off other things. His, too, he says."

"Fritz is still gone, though."

"Yeah. Your uncle's pretty broken up about that."

"It sucks. Fritz was a good guy. A good person. Did you know he once told me that the best place to hide a secret was out in the open? That if you hid something, it just meant people would know when they'd found it."

"Do you think he's hiding?"

"I want to." I look at Leif. "Do you think I could ask you something? Would that be all right?"

He nods. "Absolutely. I owe you that . . . and more."

"Why?"

"What's your question?"

"Is the Honor Guard real?" I ask.

"Yes," he says slowly. "It's real. At least I think it is. But I don't know in what way. I don't get the sense that it's organized or has any sense of formality to it. More like, it's real the way an urban legend or a campfire story is real. It exists because we believe in it. And beliefs guide our behavior more than most of us want to admit."

I frown. "But the name's so close to what Aunt Jess said. And honor cards are used to defend against tenace. That makes me think it is more organized. That's it's a group of people who don't like their mysteries being dug up. Newton's third law or whatever."

Leif shrugs. "Anything's possible. For all I know *tenace* was established to counter the Honor Guard, not the other way around. Human cruelty and exploitation aren't new. But the game—harnessing the cumulative drive and ambition of an entire student body as a means of rooting out buried secrets, or even not-buried ones, and righting wrongs from the past—well, now, that *is* novel. That's innovation."

"True," I acknowledge and I'm thinking of how Lark's notebook was somehow left for me to find. I still don't know who left it there or why. "I wish we knew more about the game. How it started, how it works."

"Wouldn't that take the magic away?" Leif counters. "It'd be like asking your parents if Santa's real."

"Don't tell me you believed in Santa."

"You'd be surprised."

I wrinkle my nose. "So much for not having a conspiratorial mind."

Leif smiles.

"What else do you and my uncle talk about?" I ask impulsively. "He's so quiet with me. My dad kind of smothers him. Grandpa Grady does, too. They mean well, but it's hard to get a read on what he's thinking or feeling."

"We really don't talk a lot. But if you want to know what we're feeling, it's shame, mostly. I mean, and that's a hard thing to talk about with anybody. But since that's where it started for both of us, there's sort of a peace to being with someone who understands that."

"Shame about what?" I ask.

"Who we are. Our character. We're both people who believed strongly in our ability to be independent thinkers and not be swayed by social norms. Yet those qualities were what made us the perfect targets. We let ourselves be persuaded into inflicting harm onto others out of—cowardice? Out of a fear of being judged. What's more shameful than that?"

I nod slowly, absorbing these thoughts, their implications. "But you've both been willing to admit what you did. That matters. That makes you different."

"No one owes us forgiveness," Leif says. "The fact is, we *weren't* different when it mattered. Now we have to live with that."

"You know you still haven't told me how it happened to you. What you were coerced into doing and who you harassed."

Leif's whole body stiffens. "You don't know?"

"No!"

"It was you," he says.

I stare at him, unable to answer. I'm not even sure I've heard him correctly.

Leif leans forward. "It happened right after we first met. You were looking for your friend Jackson and I was trying to find Eden's killer. Then the library caught fire and I started getting these messages on my phone saying you couldn't be trusted. That you weren't researching a cold case; you wanted to write an exposé on me, on what I'd done back in Connecticut. They said the only way to stop you was to do

271

what they told me to. Send that package. Leave that tarot card. Break into your house. I also broke into your school and ruined that theater stuff to keep Leisl busy."

I blink quickly, thinking back. "But I didn't know anything about you. And I wouldn't write about you, even if I had known. I'd never do something like that."

"I know," he says. "I could tell when we were together that night, the night of the storm. You'd clearly never heard the whole story, not all of it, and that was when I knew I'd hurt you for no reason other than fear. Maybe anger, too. But I'm so sorry, Bea. There's no way I can make up for what I've done, but I am so, so sorry."

36

Later, after he's gone, I go up to my room and sit at my desk. The snow's falling harder now, piling up thick on the ground, the bushes, the branches of the trees. Even under the cloak of night, the winter landscape evokes a deep sense of nostalgia. Of longing for what once was.

Leif's confession has also stirred up a confusing mix of emotions inside me, and on top of that, I've got homework to do, papers to write, and I've been meaning to check in with Deputy Williams. Not for anything official, but just to talk. He's pretty sick of me thanking him for saving my life, but maybe, like the bonding guilt both Leif and my uncle carry, this is the kind of gratitude that sticks with you. It's transformative. Or it should be.

That's up for to me to decide.

So many thoughts are buzzing through me right now that I feel electric. Like instead of being a normal girl with free will and agency, I'm a lightning rod for all confusion and confused intentions. There are so many things that I want to say and know and understand and I can't, and I hate that. More than anything. But then I catch a glimpse of the item

Leif left with me. The one he'd pressed into my hand before leaving. I'd tossed it onto the bed as I came into the room.

An unopened red envelope.

I'm curious, of course. How could I not be? I've always opened doors and chased down mysteries and pursued wonder with all of my heart. It's *in* me.

But for now, for a moment, the chase can wait.

So with a deep breath, I flip open my laptop, pull up the TrueMaine site, and start to type.

TRUEMAINE.COM
Home Page for the State of Maine . . . and Murder . . .

"Paradise Lost"

In 1963, Yale philosophy professor Fredric Fitch upended a long-running debate by questioning the concept of "knowability." That is, the belief that everything in the universe is potentially knowable, given ample supply of rigor and research and curiosity.

Fitch argued such a claim was illogical. That there's no way to prove the unknown is knowable without it first being known. Hence, the paradox.

In a sense, this can be seen as an argument of semantics—no, we don't know everything, but we *believe* we could. But this is also the *point* of the paradox. Our beliefs aren't logical, and any system built without proof lies closer to faith than reason.

This is something I've thought a lot about lately in relation to how I write about true crime. Writing has often felt like a way for me to get closer to understanding the unknowable. Only now, after finally learning the terrible truth about Eden Vicente—how she died and who killed her and why—I'm suddenly gripped by another paradox.

What good is the truth if she's dead?

Now I'm not saying Eden's death is meaningless or that we shouldn't punish her killers' accomplices. What I am saying is that it can't stop there. And I wonder if that's the problem with a lot of true crime storytelling. That there's both a belief in knowability, along with a deep willingness to forget what's already known.

Imagine you live in a town where members of your community have colluded to murder a teenage girl. Or harass a woman they don't like. Or play tricks on a man until he no longer trusts his own mind. You can and should point to everyone individually and demand accountability for their actions. But then what? If we know where the problem lies, aren't we obligated to do more? Shouldn't we, collectively, take responsibility for this place we call home and work to fix the underlying problem?

Because the alternative is ignoring that sexist comment. That small act of spite. The demeaning put-down or act of outright violence. It's excusing the moments of entitlement and resentment and bold-faced hostility, and it's also excusing ourselves for not being brave enough to take action. Because these small things add up until one day the whole system fails. Which, too often, is the moment that true crime swoops in to gawk and linger and reassure us that no one saw this coming.

That nothing could've been done.

But inaction doesn't have be Eden's legacy. She shouldn't be defined by the brutality of her last moments but by the love she inspired during her short time on this earth. What's known can have meaning. *That's* the power of knowability. It's a choice we can make. Goodwill and good wishes have never been enough, and a community tragedy deserves a community response. One that honors the truth and builds on it. Eden deserves that and more.

So in her name and memory, let's work to make Cabot Cove a safer place for our most vulnerable citizens. And while we're at it, let's nurture our collective sense of grace and promise to care for one another in a way that seeks to lift us all and guide our better angels.

Until next time,

—Bea

TO BE CONTINUED . . .

ACKNOWLEDGMENTS

Many thanks to all who've helped bring these books into the world. Thank you especially to Michael Bourret, Jenne Abramowitz, Cassy Price, Katt Phatt, Rachel Feld, Mary Kate Garmire, Michael Moccio, Susan Weber, and everyone at Scholastic and NBCUniversal. I am so grateful for your insight and creativity and care. Thank you also to my wonderful family. I love you with all of my heart. And finally, thank you to the late Dame Angela Lansbury, for everything.

FIND OUT HOW IT ALL
BEGAN IN

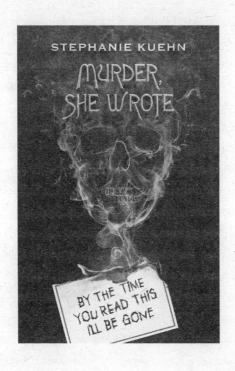

TRUEMAINE.COM

Home Page for the State of Maine . . . and Murder . . .

"Death, Disrupted"

I was twelve when I first heard about the Lambert murder. It was the day the Sussman triplets became b'nei mitzvahs. The celebratory afterparty was held at the Ocean View Country Club in my hometown of Cabot Cove, Maine, where it was—and still is—the biggest social event I'd ever attended. Wrapped in a lace shawl and a yellow silk dress my mother had once owned, I can remember huddling outside behind the banquet hall with a dozen or so other kids. There, a scruffy waiter on a smoke break regaled us with the story of a dead girl.

Thirty years or so earlier, he told us, his uncle had worked for the club's groundskeeping crew. This uncle arrived early one morning to repair a faulty sprinkler valve only to discover a dead body on the golf course. A gruesome sight—the victim was a teenage girl, and she'd been strangled, left for dead, her limbs twisted beneath her like a felled deer resting atop the lush emerald green grass.

"Who was she?" my friend Jackson had asked, because that was the most important part of the story to him. This girl, this long-ago dead girl, she was someone, a real person, and to Jackson, her humanity would always come before the lurid details surrounding her death.

Chrissy Lambert, the waiter replied. That was the girl's name. She was seventeen, a rare beauty, and not only was she someone, she turned out to be *somebody*—the daughter of the late George Mitchell Lambert III,

Cabot Cove's very wealthy and much beloved mayor at the time. This fact, above all else, ensured that the town's full resources were poured into finding her killer.

Only no one ever has.

So now this is where I come in, and perhaps you do, too. To this day, Chrissy's case still haunts me, and as a resident of Cabot Cove, my goal is to finally track down her killer. To be sure, in the years since her death, far better sleuths than me have attempted to do the same. They've chased down every lead, followed every clue, only to come up empty.

But thanks to both modern technology and the power of the TrueMaine family, I believe we can achieve what they couldn't by pooling our efforts and working toward a common goal. Only we'll do it methodically—this is New England, after all—and true disruption requires discipline. Think proof of work, not propaganda.

In upcoming columns, I'll highlight what's currently known about the crime, who the early suspects were, and how Cabot Cove reacted in the aftermath. Meanwhile, hit me up in the comments if you have any information about Chrissy Lambert's death or the circumstances surrounding it. We're all safer when we work together.

Until then, be watchful, my friends! Killers walk among us. Statistically, at least one of them knows your name . . .

Yours truly,

—the Downeast Girl

1

"HEY," I SAY WHEN JACKSON finally answers the phone. Like me, he's stayed in tonight, opting out of attending our school's homecoming game and related festivities. There're good reasons for this, but we're definitely in the minority with our choice. A recent social media check featured post after post of our highly identifiable classmates engaging in acts of pregame debauchery before packing the bleachers to cheer on the hometown Cabot Cove Devils in their annual matchup with the South Harbor Seals.

On the other end of the line, Jackson Glanville yawns. Loudly. Clearly, I've woken him. Or at least that's what he wants me to think.

"Don't play coy, Bea," he says. "This is the fifth time you've called. I assume there's some sort of emergency unfolding."

"I wouldn't have to call so many times if you actually answered your phone. Or responded to my texts."

"Texting's not secure. We've talked about this."

"So now you think the feds are reading your messages?"

"When did I ever mention the feds?" He lowers his voice. "They could, though, you know. Us Glanvilles aren't to be trusted."

I laugh because this is what Jackson wants me to do. To pretend I don't hear the current of fear and paranoia running through his voice. To pretend I don't know how much he's suffering.

"Don't worry," he says brusquely. "I'm not going all conspiracy theory on you. The only people I'm worried might be spying on me are of the homegrown variety."

"Well, I'm relieved to hear it."

"So why *are* you calling?"

I bend to double knot the laces of my Caribou boots. "Maybe I just like the sound of your dulcet voice."

"How flattering," he says. "Hey, I read your latest column, by the way. The one you just posted."

So he *wasn't* asleep when I called. I knew it. "What'd you think?"

"Did you have to mention me by name?"

"I said good things!"

"Yeah, well, my dad might not see it that way. He'll probably ground me for being in the presence of nicotine over three years ago. You know how he is. 'If you were truly committed to God's path in your heart, then your body would follow . . .'"

"I'm sorry," I say quickly. "I won't do it again."

"Nah. Don't worry about it." Jackson forces a shot of bravado into his voice. "I'm just being my usual dramatic self."

"You're not dramatic."

"How's that whole thing going?" he asks. "Writing for that true crime site?"

"Well, I'm averaging about three readers a post, but also

they're not paying me. Kind of hard to tell who's coming out on top there."

"They're really having you lean into the cryptocurrency lingo, huh? The disrupting Downeast Girl. Plus all that 'proof of work' stuff?"

I laugh. "My theory is that both owners are heavily invested in Bitcoin. But it's not such a bad metaphor, is it? Cyber detectives as the modern-day crypto miners. It's all decentralized work being generated by anonymous internet users. I think it fits."

"Did you just say *modern-day crypto miners*?"

My cheeks warm. "You know what I mean."

Jackson pauses, and the thing is, I've known him so long that I can picture him perfectly. Right now, he's up in his room with the door locked, and I'm positive he's shirt-less. Given the option, Jackson's always shirtless, which is beyond annoying, although he looks great and he knows it. He's probably pacing, too, long legs carrying him back and forth in front of the wide bay window that spans the length of his bedroom. Plus, I'd bet anything Jackson's staring out at the ocean, watching the dark waves churn beneath him as he ponders—not for the first time—what it would feel like to sink. To lose himself in those watery depths.

And look, morbid as that is, I *get* it. Despite our friendship—or maybe because of it—it's been years since I've personally stepped foot inside the Glanvilles' sprawling showcase waterfront home. But suffice to say there's a reason for that.

It's also the reason I'm calling.

"Jax," I say softly.

"It's an analogy, by the way. Not a metaphor."

"What?"

"The crypto mining thing."

"Oh." A quick glance at the clock tells me it's past time to get to the point. "So do you think you can meet up tonight? Are you able to get out?"

"Where?" he asks. "When?"

"At the Hollow. Thirty minutes."

Jax groans. "I *hate* that place."

"I know you do."

"Those Broadmoor kids make me want to puke."

I sigh. Jackson rarely has anything nice to say about the local boarding school or its two hundred or so snobby inhabitants. "Well, tonight those Broadmoor kids are going to be your alibi."

"Hold on." His voice tightens. "Do you mean—"

"Yes," I say as my heart starts to pound. My palms start to sweat. Is this really happening?

Are we really going to do this?

"I'll be there," he tells me, then hangs up.

I grab my stuff and go.

✕ ✕ ✕

Outside in the darkness, frigid air nips my cheeks, stings my eyes. I gird myself by zipping my fleece coat and cinching the hood as tight as it will go as I make my way into town on foot. There's a saying in Maine that the farther north you go, the more resilient Mother Nature makes you. This is meant to explain our hardiness, our rugged core of self-reliance, but if you ask me, "natural selection" works just as well.

It's a twenty-minute walk under good conditions. But it's Friday night and football means people are out and ready to let loose. Not just high schoolers, either. Cars, SUVs, even a few semis whiz dangerously close as I follow the narrow shoulder of the coastal highway. I've seen enough roadkill out here over the years that I don't dare risk crossing to the ocean side. Not after nightfall. But trust me, that's where the better view is. Even by moonlight you can see over the cliffs and down to the craggy beaches, swirling mist, and pounding surf below.

More cars race by, some honking, and a few passengers even take the time to roll down their windows to yell, wave, pound the paint, and make other—less generous—gestures at me. I can't understand what they're saying, and it seems early still for the game to have ended. But the general spirit of their efforts tells me that somehow, some way, our side's emerged victorious.

This isn't a total surprise. Cabot Cove High's football team is notoriously terrible—as in, our school should cut their funding and spend the money on stuff that actually has a positive impact on students, like, you know, teacher salaries and the girls' volleyball team. But our rival school, South Harbor, has had a serious run of bad luck this year. Okay, luck's an understatement, because what really happened is that two of their players were killed in a car accident back in July. A third came down with Lyme disease during preseason, and now their star quarterback abruptly withdrew from their school just *last weekend*. Rumor has it he's got a drug problem and failed a test, but I've also heard it was an overdose. Regardless, it's not exactly a miracle that we beat them this year, and I'm not sure that it's even worth celebrating. Feels a little like cheering for a win after the other team's bus breaks down.

"Go *Devillllls!*" I duck right as a beer can flung from the open window of a pickup comes flying at me. Missing my head by inches, the can ricochets off the asphalt, and I watch as it spins, sparks, then skids into the grass. Whirling around, I'm ready to confront whoever's responsible, but the truck's long gone. Screeching tires leave the air charred and smoke-filled as the pickup's red taillights swerve across the center line then back again before fading into the fog.

Heart pounding, fists clenched tight, I continue my march onward while allowing my mind to indulge in a series of gruesome revenge fantasies that I'll never have the courage to act on. It's times like these when I lament not having my license yet. There're still six whole *months* until I can take the test, which is practically an eternity in high school years. Everyone in my grade is driving already, and this includes Bobby Miller, who's riding a D average these days and spends most of his time doing donuts in the marina parking lot. But that's what I get for having the audacity to skip third grade.

No good deed goes unpunished, and in the eyes of the law—not to mention my dad's insurance policy—raw intelligence holds no bearing on personal liberty.

Well, there are greater injustices in this world, which is why I'm meeting up with Jackson tonight. He and I have been friends since grade school. It's been more off than on over the last couple of years—until recently, that is. But Jackson's troubles run deep. They always have, though you wouldn't know it to look at him. At school, he represents that most perfect of clichés: He's seemingly got it all. From his reluctant rock star good looks to a starting spot on our school's all-state basketball team. Not to mention he's, like, a genius. His academic ranking's top of the class, and for the past two years he's been a part of this statewide accelerated science program you have to be invited to apply for. He's already got his college sights set on the Ivy League. Maybe MIT or Caltech, if they're lucky.

But if appearances can be deceiving, then Jackson Glanville could make a liar out of just about anyone. His bright-eyed ambition and endless accomplishments don't stem from drive or passion or even God-given talent. No, his striving is the very twisted consequence of having been raised by a pair of sadists who equate fear with morality and obedience with virtue. I used to think this was a religious thing—Jackson's dad is an ex-military officer turned Episcopalian deacon. But there's nothing spiritual about the way the Glanvilles treat their son—like he's fundamentally rotten to the core and their job is to prevent him from spoiling the rest of the world. I've had to talk Jackson off more than a few ledges over the course of our friendship. Some of them literal. Anyway, he's recently been offered a lifeline—one I've helped to arrange—and my goal tonight is to ensure he takes it.

My muscles tense as I approach downtown Cabot Cove. There's so much *life* out tonight. Sparkling confetti from the earlier parade litters the street; red, white, and blue ribbons snap from light poles; and the whole atmosphere swirls with postgame revelry. It's infectious, even catching up with the tourists spilling out of the overpriced seafood restaurants and brew pubs running along Main Street. Live music blaring from the speakers at Neptune's Palace adds to the chaos, plus my phone won't stop buzzing. I pull it from my pocket and see messages from Evie, Dane, Roo, everyone—they're all heading to Rock's Head Beach for a bonfire. *Where are you?* they ask. *Game got called at halftime. Too many injured Seals. Arf arf arf. Get out here already.*

Well, this explains the early celebration, and the invitations are tempting. I'm a sworn introvert, but even I can get behind an evening on the beach with people I like, one that ends with salt in my hair and sand in my shoes. They're good people, too, the kind who don't mind my awkwardness or my inability to get out of my head. Only none of them are Jackson, and I won't let myself be distracted. I can't. Not tonight. So rather than respond, I switch off notifications, slide in my earbuds, and hit play on the podcast I've been listening to. It's different than what I usually go for. Rather than a deep-dive true crime story, this is an audio drama—a fictional one. It's about a murder that takes place on a ship and it's told Rashomon-style with its cast of characters rotating to share their version of events as the listener tries to solve the crime along with them.

Like I said, fiction isn't my usual preference, but this came recommended by a family member whose taste I trust without question. "It's the writing," she told me, gripping my arm with an eagerness that felt electric. "You have to listen all the way through. Then listen to it again to figure out how they pulled it off. It's genius. These writers, whoever they are, know precisely what matters in a mystery."

"What's that?" I asked, because I've always assumed that what matters most in a mystery is whether or not the case gets solved.

But she disagreed, emphatically. "The solution's the least important part."

"Really?"

"Yes, really." Her blue eyes twinkled as she pressed her lips into the most inscrutable of smiles. "You see, I've always believed mysteries aren't about uncovering what's hidden so much as shining a light on what you've always known, deep down, to be true."

Yeah, well, I'm not sure what I think about that. As someone who dreams of becoming an investigative reporter someday, true crime doesn't interest me because it somehow manages to represent the totality of human experience or whatever. Honestly, I kind of like when it does the opposite by refusing to hand out easy answers or offer pat platitudes about tragedy. I also like when it asks us to confront the most slippery parts of ourselves. The parts that so rarely end up in fiction because they're the hardest to own and easiest to look away from.

This is the tone I aspire to with my cold case column for TrueMaine, which is the newly launched brainchild of two Portland tech bros aiming to fill the gap between Nextdoor and Netflix. Regardless, this fictional podcast is just what I need at the moment—something that can hold my attention without demanding more. And it's not like good writing and storytelling don't have their place in crime reporting. Story's always what draws me in, and if nothing else, this show's been darkly entertaining so far.

Murder or no murder, there are a lot of ways to be trapped in this world, and I know I'd hate to be stuck on a ship with a group of strangers. Even more, I'd hate having my survival hinge on learning how to depend on said strangers.

What could be worse than that?

ABOUT THE AUTHOR

Stephanie Kuehn is a clinical psychologist and an award-winning author of six novels for teens, including *Charm & Strange*, which won the ALA's 2014 William C. Morris Award for best debut young adult novel. *Booklist* has praised her work as "Intelligent, compulsively readable literary fiction with a dark twist." As a lifelong *Murder, She Wrote* fan, Stephanie recently introduced the series to her own teenagers, who now share her love of mystery and all things Cabot Cove.